The door slammed behind them

Devin sighed. "I have the funny feeling we've made our last foray into Eli's lab."

"It won't be easy," Nick said, "but I think something can be arranged."

"Oh?" She arched her eyebrows. "Now I suppose you're going to tell me you've dabbled in breaking and entering?"

Nick smiled. "It has you worried, doesn't it?"

"What?"

"The things I know and how I know them."

She turned to stare at him. "What are you saying, Nick?"

"I'm not saying anything."

His sly response did not amuse her. "Why do I get the feeling this is a game you've played before?"

He laughed. "I told you I was a fast learner."

"Sure you are." Devin didn't believe his innocent routine for an instant. Her curiosity was growing by the hour. But the mere fact that he could bend the truth so easily made it an itch she couldn't scratch.

ABOUT THE AUTHOR

Linda Stevens loves mixing intrigue and romance, never knowing what might turn up around the next corner as the book develops. The author's story ideas come from many sources, particularly newspaper and magazine articles, but most of them start with the simple question: What if? Linda Stevens lives and works in Colorado Springs, Colorado.

Books by Linda Stevens

HARLEQUIN INTRIGUE
130—SHADOWPLAY
156—ONE STEP AHEAD

Perilous Pastime

Linda Stevens

Harlequin Books

TORONTO • NEW YORK • LONDON
AMSTERDAM • PARIS • SYDNEY • HAMBURG
STOCKHOLM • ATHENS • TOKYO • MILAN
MADRID • WARSAW • BUDAPEST • AUCKLAND

Harlequin Intrigue edition published November 1992

ISBN 0-373-22201-7

PERILOUS PASTIME

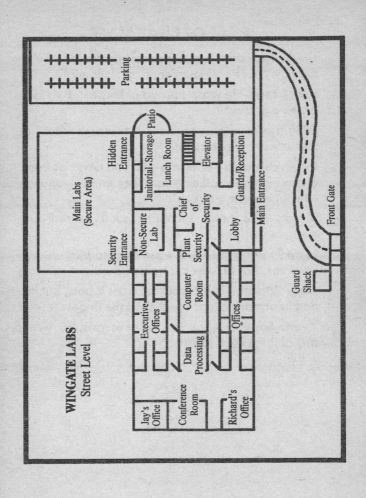

WINGATE LABS
Street Level

CAST OF CHARACTERS

Devin Prescott—Her music mastery couldn't help her now, but her improvisational skills might.

Nick Lang—He wasn't proud of his past, but it was proving useful.

Eli Wingate—Years of scientific research would be lost unless he was found.

Richard and Jay Wingate—Eli had never gotten along with his brothers—had they finally gotten him out of their way?

Myrtle—The faithful secretary usually knew Eli's every move.

Lucinda Wingate—She wasn't one to play favorites, but Eli was her golden child.

Jerry Wilson—This accountant was a pest, but he had information that could point the finger.

Yvette Soomes—She was full of secrets, but would any of them lead to Eli?

Chapter One

Devin Prescott crouched in the darkness of her bedroom. The nightstand she was hiding behind gave her little cover, but it was the best she could do at the moment, just as the red baseball bat she held slung over her shoulder was the only weapon at hand. Its solid weight was reassuring.

Someone was in her apartment.

She didn't know if the intruder had made a noise, or if some kind of instinct had awakened her, but all the proof she needed was on the wall to her left, in the form of an alarm system monitor. The glowing orange dot wasn't on, a sure sign it had been disarmed. *Disarmed*. Devin drew in a shaky breath.

It was quiet in the apartment. Too quiet. All she could hear was the soft whisper of the air conditioning. To her anxious ears it sounded like someone breathing. How long would it take for the police to respond to her call? Would it be soon enough?

She peered into the darkness. Before her, pitch-black voids marked the two open doorways of her bedroom. One door led into a windowless bathroom, the other to the living room, where not even a tiny slice of light seeped through the drapes she always kept tightly drawn against the hot Phoenix sun. But morning was still far away. Evidently, so were the police.

Indecision filled her. Should she stay hidden and wait for help to arrive? Run? Confront the intruder? The last choice was definitely the least appealing to her. Though a concert violinist by profession, Devin hardly fit the fragile, fine-boned stereotype. But she wasn't foolhardy, either. Nevertheless, sitting there like a tin duck in a shooting gallery wasn't her style. She had to do something!

Baseball bat in tow, Devin began crawling quietly on her hands and knees toward the bathroom. From its far door she'd have a clear view into the living room and kitchen.

She had to hitch up her nightgown to make the going easier, and the cold linoleum of the bathroom floor on her bare knees made her shiver. Devin crawled over to the tub, its porcelain finish smooth and cool beneath her touch as she used the edge to push herself into a standing position. With the baseball bat clutched at the ready in both hands, she carefully peeked around the edge of the opaque shower curtain. The tub was empty.

Changing directions, she headed for the doorway that led to the living room. It would be dawn in about an hour, so some light did outline the drapes covering the picture windows with a soft gray halo, but it was too dim to see much by. Her furniture looked like nothing more than dark, odd-shaped blobs.

Her narrow kitchen was off the living room. There, the predawn light filtered through the sheer-curtained window over the sink, giving slightly better illumination. It, too, appeared empty. On her left stood the bedroom, still dark and quiet. Nothing moved as Devin continued to look around.

Suddenly the dim light around her changed colors, a flashing red and blue that seemed to bounce off the bedroom walls. It was at once frightening and reassuring. At long last, the police had arrived. Devin stayed put until she heard a loud knock on her front door, accompanied by a comforting if strident voice.

"This is the police!"

Baseball bat in hand, Devin ran straight to the door and yanked it open wide. Two officers in dark blue uniforms were poised to each side, their weapons drawn. One was a young man; the other, slightly older, was female and had the definite air of authority.

"You called about an intruder in your apartment?"

Devin nodded. She was trembling with a jumble of mixed emotions now—receding anxiety, fear and relief. It helped to see two more uniformed officers arrive right behind the pair positioned on her front porch.

The woman gently but firmly pulled Devin outside. "Stay with me while we check the place out," she ordered brusquely. "Where's the light switch for this room?"

Fingers trembling, Devin reached back inside and twisted the dimmer switch by the front door, blinking as the overhead lights in the living room reached full brightness.

The officers moved cautiously into the apartment, their guns held in that way Devin had seen in countless movies and television shows. While an older, gray-haired man stayed in a central location, the other two slowly worked their way through the different rooms, lights coming on in the bedroom, bathroom and kitchen a short time later. They came back into the living room at the same time and joined the third. All of them reholstered their weapons.

"Clear," the youngest announced.

His partner nodded. "Same here."

The three conferred quietly for a moment, then the older man shrugged and turned to look at Devin, who was still standing near the front door with the fourth officer.

"There are no signs of a forced entry," the gray-haired man informed her. "In fact, the back door was still chained. Does anyone else have a key to this place?"

"Yes, but no one who would do something like this to me." Devin still had a tight grip on her trusty baseball bat. "I know someone was in here when I called you."

"Well, there's no one here now, Miss..."

"Prescott, Devin Prescott. And I'm telling you someone was here, inside my apartment!" She thumped the bat on the concrete porch for emphasis and glared at the man. "I can prove it! Whoever it was managed to circumvent my alarm system."

Devin knew she could be quite intimidating when her temper was on the rise. She leveled her pale blue eyes on the officer, her auburn hair tangled around her shoulders. Gently, the policewoman beside her removed the baseball bat from her grasp and guided Devin back into the living room.

"No one is calling you a liar, Ms. Prescott," she said in a soothing tone. "Why don't you have a seat on the sofa while we take a look. Where's the main alarm unit?"

"On the wall by the kitchen." Devin pointed it out. "And there's another unit in my bedroom."

The gray-haired officer spoke. "We'll check 'em out."

After Devin was seated on the sofa, the policewoman looked at her, notebook in hand. "Now, Ms. Prescott. Are you sure the alarm system was set?"

"It's always set. It was designed that way for people who are absentminded, or very busy like my uncle. He built and installed it for me."

"I see." She wrote something in her notebook. "Why don't you put on a robe or something and we'll go through the apartment step-by-step, see if anything's missing. But try to touch as little as possible, please."

Devin went into her bedroom and grabbed a robe from her closet, then took a good look around, accompanied by the female officer. Her best violin was still in its case, undisturbed. As far as Devin could tell, nothing had even been touched, let alone stolen. The policewoman wrote the fact down, as well as the answers to more basic questions she would need for her report. She then closed her notebook and joined the others. Devin stood in the living room, fidgeting nervously.

What was going on? This was supposed to be her summer break, a time for relaxation, quiet practice and contemplation of the next concert. Her much-needed vacation was starting out all wrong.

"I think I've found something," one of the officers standing near the kitchen door announced.

Devin hung back. Now that the police were there, her mind was clearing enough to think about the situation. Her uncle had told her that not even a complete power loss could shut down the system once set, and it was always on. She could override it, of course. That simply took punching a few buttons in the correct sequence, with permutations far too complex to arrive at by chance.

She moved closer to the police officers and glanced at the alarm display. Another light right next to the orange one indicated if the system had been overridden. It hadn't. What had happened, she realized, was that the alarm had been tripped, *then* disarmed—so quickly that the siren hadn't had time to sound. That was disturbing enough, but the only person Devin had thought capable of completely disarming the complex unit was the inventor.

The system was almost one of a kind, a prototype. Her uncle, Eli Wingate, was a microbiologist, but he had a gift for anything technological. More than a gift; an absolute genius. To defeat a system he had designed seemed impossible. With the evidence right before her eyes, though, she had to believe it. One thing seemed certain; whoever had accomplished the feat, it sure wasn't an ordinary, everyday sneak thief.

The policewoman seemed to agree. "The only thing we can tell for sure is that it's been tampered with," she told Devin. "But apparently nothing is missing. You weren't confronted or harmed, didn't even see the person, in fact. The natural assumption is that either you scared the intruder off or we did. But if that was the case, why would he have taken the time to lock up on his way out?"

Devin struggled to control her temper. "Someone *was* here," she maintained.

"I'm not arguing that point," the woman said. "The question is, what was he after?"

"I have no idea."

She was a violinist, a classical musician, and as such had plenty of prestige but hardly what anyone would call a fantastic income. Her instruments were valuable, of course; that was one of the reasons Uncle Eli had installed the alarm system in the first place. But not one of them was a Stradivarius. Devin couldn't think of a single thing she possessed that would interest the caliber of thief who could have defeated such a technologically advanced alarm system. Indeed, he'd apparently left empty-handed, and calmly locked the doors on his way back out. What had he been after?

Even with every light in her apartment on, it still gave her a very eerie feeling to know someone had been inside her place while she slept. Possibly right beside her bed. Maybe he hadn't left anything physical behind to show his presence, but she had felt him there nonetheless. That feeling of waking up and sensing someone nearby had been intense and frightening.

The police officers were winding up their investigation. One of them said something about a failed burglary, and that a patrol would be added to the neighborhood, but Devin was only half listening. As if struggling with a difficult piece of music, she was going over the situation in her mind, looking for some kind of logic.

Why would someone break into her apartment? Eli had a key, and wouldn't scare her this way in any case, so he hadn't been the intruder. But the security system was his design, and the would-be thief had gotten past it handily. That brought to mind a very troubling question.

Could all this somehow be connected to Eli or his work? Although they often talked of his past accomplishments in the field of environmental science, they never discussed his actual research in progress. Could what he was working on be dangerous? Or valuable?

Devin only wished she could ask him. She hadn't spoken to Eli in days. He hadn't shown up as scheduled for their date Saturday, or even called to explain himself, and that wasn't like him at all. After making numerous calls of her own last night all she'd been able to find out was that he hadn't been home or at work all weekend.

Devin's life was normally so calm that two strange events happening one after the other was too much a co-incidence to be ignored. The apartment alarm hadn't gone off, but there was certainly one going off in her well-ordered mind.

Where was Uncle Eli?

Chapter Two

Devin elbowed her way past a perfectly coiffed, vehemently protesting secretary, opened the heavy wooden door marked President and stepped inside, slamming it shut behind her with a loud bang. After her early morning with the police, she was not in the mood for pleasantries.

"Where is Eli?" Devin demanded.

The man behind the massive desk stood up. Short black hair capped a tanned face, his blue eyes matching hers. His square jaw clenched as he spoke. "Devin, can't you see we're in a meeting? You'll have to wait."

"Not this time, Jay." Devin advanced toward his desk. "What's going on? Where is Eli?" She stopped between the two occupied chairs in front of the desk and looked down at the man seated to her left. "I can tell by your expression you know what I'm talking about, Richard. So let's have it."

Richard stood and enclosed her elbow in a tight hold, his fingers digging into her skin as he spoke softly in her ear. "We'll discuss this in private, Devin. Come with me."

She shook off his hand and stepped back, looking from one brother to the other. They could be mistaken for twins, the same five-ten height, weight and slender build. But Jay, at fifty-three, was ten months older than his brother Richard and ten times as cunning.

Standing her ground, she asked, "What's going on?"

"Exactly my question," the unidentified stranger occupying the other chair announced.

Devin looked at the man to her right. He had hazel eyes, a handsome face and light brown hair that just touched the collar of his white dress shirt. His suit was navy blue and well tailored. He was studying her intently.

"And you are?" Devin inquired.

He stood. "Nick Lang," the man told her, holding out his hand.

"Devin Prescott." She returned the firm handshake over the back of his chair. "What's your interest in this?"

Nick smiled. He liked her directness and the fire flashing in her pale blue eyes. "I'm responsible for the investment my company has in this firm. And you?"

"Eli's my uncle." She turned to face Jay again, her auburn hair brushing the shoulders of her loose-fitting, mustard-colored blazer. "My *favorite* uncle. Where is he?"

Jay sat back down, accepting the confrontation his niece was determined to have. "We're not entirely sure."

"Meaning you have absolutely no idea." Devin crossed her arms over her chest. "Have you called the police? Filed a missing person report?" She paused, rather enjoying the look of discomfort on Jay's face. "Have you told Grandmother?"

Richard pulled another chair up in front of the desk. "Take a seat, Devin. There are things you don't understand."

She ignored the plushly cushioned chair. "Such as?"

"You know Eli has taken off before unannounced," Jay began in a soothing tone. "He's—"

"A bit eccentric," Devin interrupted. "I know that. But Eli has never once missed a meeting with me without an explanation." She watched the brothers share a covert signal. "I see you've at least done some checking. So you know I wasn't listed in his daily appointment book. He called me the other night at home."

"Why?" Richard asked.

"We're fond of each other, for heaven's sake!" Devin shook her head at his puzzled look. "Unlike you two, some people meet to talk about things other than business."

Devin had had some time to think since her rude awakening that morning. In that time she had come to a few conclusions. While it was possible the intruder who had broken into her home was as smart as Eli technologically, it seemed more likely that he had somehow gotten inside knowledge of the alarm system. A friend or coworker, perhaps, to whom Eli had shown the security device. Or someone who would have had access to Eli's lab and work area, who knew how close he and Devin were.

The more she thought about it, the less she believed in the foiled burglary theory the police had come up with. Not a thing had been disturbed. Now her uncle had apparently disappeared. What made the most sense to her was that the intruder had either been looking for some trace of Eli or something Eli might have left with her. Something valuable.

"Why haven't you called in the police?" Devin asked.

Her question was met with stony silence. Richard sat in one of the chairs. "We can't," he finally admitted.

"Why not?"

"He's right," Nick Lang told her, still standing beside his own chair. "It wouldn't be advisable at this time."

Devin looked at him. "How do you know about this?"

"Eli canceled his lecture at a symposium I'd arranged for him to be a part of, and he didn't return my calls this weekend. I was concerned."

"For your stocks or him?" she asked tersely.

"Both."

Devin turned away from him, focusing her anger on Jay. Her question had been out of line and she knew it. But at the moment she didn't care whose nose she put out of joint.

"You'd better do some fast explaining or I'm calling the police," she warned. "Right after I call Grandmother."

It was the biggest weapon in her arsenal. The last thing her uncles ever wanted was for their mother to be meddling in company business. In her own way she could be even more ruthless than they were.

"That won't be necessary," Jay assured her. He leaned forward in the chair, his manicured fingers forming a steeple over the neat pile of papers on his desk as he chose his words carefully. "Eli has been under a lot of strain lately and—"

"Strain brought on by you two trying to get him to rush his experiments and research, no doubt," Devin inserted.

Jay ignored her outburst. "We believe he's just taking a little well-deserved vacation."

"And everyone else has to believe it, as well," Richard added. "The long-term financial success of this company depends on that."

"I don't care about the company!"

"But Eli does," Richard reminded her. "Devin, try to understand, we have a responsibility to our stockholders. They depend on us to make the right decisions. If rumors surface that Eli is missing, the public might jump to the same conclusion that you have, that something has happened to him. Our stock could go down the drain and the company along with it. We simply can't take the risk."

"But Eli is your brother! Can't you show even a little concern for him?"

"You're being totally unfair, Devin. Of course we're concerned," Jay said, his lips drawn into a tight, thin line. "But we're trying to protect his future, too. Which is why this has to be kept quiet."

Devin looked at Nick Lang. "Well?"

"It's a valid point, and part of the reason I'm here. Wingate has gotten most of its newer investors solely on the strength of your uncle's name and reputation."

"But this company is doing all kinds of research," Devin protested, looking at the brothers. "You have other scientists here. Successful ones, too."

Jay nodded. "Yes, but none have Eli's proven track record for coming up with new, salable results."

"There's more to it than that, isn't there?" Devin asked, her eyes narrowing. "What's Eli working on right now? Is it dangerous?" Jay would give nothing away, but she knew Richard wasn't as poised. She focused on him. "Answer me!"

Richard cleared his throat. "The work isn't exactly dangerous, it's more…" He trailed off with a shrug.

"What he's working on is quite valuable," Jay completed. "Both to the Wingate company and to the future of the world. His work is geared toward a better and safer environment."

"Save the PR crap for your investors. Spell it out for me in simple layman's terms." Out of the corner of her eye Devin saw Nick smiling, and turned her indignant glare upon him. "What's so funny?"

Nick laughed. "You've pinpointed the scope of Eli's research. Crap." Devin stared at him. "He's working on a faster-acting bacteria to break down sludge in municipal wastewater facilities, one without any potential harmful side effects of its own," he explained.

"Now I get it." But she wasn't smiling. "And I see why you are so worried about a leak. Couldn't the profit potential of such a procedure be worth millions if you sold it to every city and town in the United States?"

"Actually, billions, and distribution would be worldwide," Richard replied, his accounting background showing through.

Devin was so irritated by their attitude she wanted to scream. "Billions! If Eli's work could be worth that much, why aren't you more worried about his disappearance? He could have been kidnapped! Or worse!"

"That's a bit melodramatic, Devin," Richard said.

"Is it?"

Jay looked distinctly uncomfortable. "We're considering all the options," he told her. "But we have to keep this very quiet. If we don't, Eli won't have a company to return to at all. His ongoing experiments will be destroyed without someone to watch over them."

Always the smooth lawyer, her uncle Jay, trying to manipulate people into believing what he wanted them to. "Then what's your next step? A private detective?"

"Devin, this is a very delicate matter," Jay said, trying to reason with her. "Let's give Eli a little time. A full-scale investigation will only embarrass him when he finally does show up."

"You mean *if* he shows up." Devin stared at them in disbelief, scarcely able to believe her ears. "That's your plan? To wait and hope for the best?" she asked. Their silence was her answer. "Fine. If you're not willing to do anything about this, I will," Devin announced, turning on her heel. When she slammed the door on her way out it was even louder than before.

"Sorry about that, Mr. Lang," Jay said. Embarrassed, he chuckled softly and shrugged. "I assure you we're every bit as worried about our brother as Devin is. But she fails to see the big picture. And our niece can be . . . overly excitable on occasion."

"She's a performing artist, you see," Richard confided, as if that explained everything.

"I understand." Nick nodded at the two. "I have to be running along, as well, gentlemen. I'll be in touch."

When Nick Lang had gone Richard sat back down and glared at Jay. "Devin isn't going to give up."

"Relax," Jay told him. "Let her look around. She's a violinist, not a professional investigator. What does she know about looking for a missing person? Besides, Devin isn't stupid. She knows where we stand now. If she announces Eli is missing we'll simply refute the claim." He grinned. "And that would not only make her look foolish but anger Mother, as well. There's nothing worse in Mother's eyes than airing the family laundry in public."

"True. What about Nick Lang?" Richard asked.

"We'll provide him with any information he wants to keep him happy," Jay returned mildly. "He wields a lot of clout—once Lang bought in, others followed. But however much he might like Eli personally, he's a businessman first. He won't rock the boat if it means he'll lose money."

Richard still looked worried. "And Mother?"

"I'll call her this afternoon and tell her Eli is on vacation." Jay held up a hand to cut off his brother's protest. "With Mother's heart condition Devin won't upset her unnecessarily."

Richard knew his brother was right. He sighed. "Devin reminds me too much of Mother at times like this."

"Indeed she does." Jay chuckled, but without much humor. "Stubborn, meddling and pigheaded."

DEVIN WALKED DOWN the white hallways with their cheerful apple green trim, her rubber-soled shoes squeaking on the highly polished linoleum floor as she headed for Eli's office on the basement level. Once there, she knocked lightly on the jamb of the open door, then entered.

Myrtle, Eli's private secretary, was at her desk typing, the headset of a Dictaphone covering her ears. Her plump fingers flew across the computer keyboard, never missing a stroke as she smiled a greeting, revealing what she unabashedly referred to as her almost perfect false teeth.

Devin sat in a chair next to the desk, waiting for Myrtle to finish. She needed the time to calm down from her meeting with Jay and Richard, anyway. If she'd had her baseball bat in hand today, Eli's brothers would now be on the critical list at Phoenix General.

She gazed at her uncle's secretary, who always seemed able to calm the storms that occasionally raged between Eli and his siblings. Myrtle's short white hair, permed close to her head with waves and curves, complemented her pale, lined, paper-thin skin, which was highlighted by rouge on her cheeks and red lipstick.

Behind her neat, orderly desk, light and dark green ivy plant runners flourished under the bright fluorescent lighting, gracing the white walls in soft arcs. There was no way Devin would bring any more disharmony to this office than was absolutely necessary. She had decided to keep the break-in at her apartment a secret for now. Besides, she wasn't positive of the connection yet herself.

But if the woman across the desk from her couldn't shed some light on what was happening with Eli, no one could.

"There, it's finally safe to take a break," Myrtle announced, setting the headset aside. "I'll tell you, Devin, if anything ever happens to me, Eli will be completely lost. I've been with him twenty-three years now and he can still baffle me as to where he's going with a letter. Confuses himself, too, sometimes. Coffee?"

Devin smiled. "No, thanks."

"Eli's not in today." Myrtle looked away, straightening a pile of papers on her desk. "He's on vacation."

"Do you really believe that?"

Myrtle pushed her chair back, stood and poured a cup of coffee from the small machine in the corner behind her, adding cream and sugar. She was still stirring it when she sat down again. "No, I don't," she admitted at last, smiling nervously. "But how did you find out about this so fast?"

"Eli didn't show up on Saturday for our date."

"Oh, my!" Her bejeweled fingers reached for the large appointment book. "I thought I'd canceled—"

Devin reached over and placed her hands on top of Myrtle's, stilling them. "I'm not in there," she hastened to reassure her. "Eli called me at home last week."

"Oh." She sighed and leaned back in her chair. "Devin, I *am* worried. He can be flighty, but Eli has never, ever taken off without notifying me first."

"Did you tell that to Jay and Richard?"

"Hah! Yes, I told them, for all the good it did. Told them I was worried, too. But those boys don't care." She sighed. "Oh, I suppose they do care, but not enough. All they really give a darn about is making money."

Myrtle protected Eli from the world like a lioness with her cub, and she considered those boys, as she called Eli's brothers, a serious threat to her beloved boss. Their shabby treatment of him was a festering sore spot with her.

Not that she would speak of such things to anyone other than a member of the family, of course. She and Devin's grandmother were two of a kind in that department; it wasn't just bad business, it was bad manners. And after all these years, Myrtle considered herself a part of the family, too.

"Has anything in particular happened to upset Eli?" Devin asked. "Or has he been acting unusual lately?"

Myrtle smiled, then began chuckling and when it gave way to hearty laughter Devin couldn't resist joining in.

"Okay," Devin said, holding up her hands when their laughter had subsided. "I admit it, that was a pretty dumb question. Eli is always strange. But has he been any weirder than usual?"

"Not noticeably so." Myrtle was still chuckling softly. "He's been pretty excited by his latest work. Moody, too. Up one day, down the next. But that's normal for him when he's close to a breakthrough of some sort."

Devin frowned. "Any interesting phone calls?"

"Not that I know of." Myrtle sipped her coffee, then set it aside before opening the appointment book and showing it to Devin. "Eli didn't have much planned for the next month. I've canceled these two," Myrtle told her, sliding a red-tipped fingernail across the current week.

The two names weren't familiar to Devin. "Who are they?"

"Fellow employees here at Wingate. They were both dinner engagements. He likes knowing the people who work with him."

A disgusted sigh slipped out of Devin. This wasn't helping at all. "Where do you think he is, Myrtle?"

"I don't know, child. I wish I did."

Devin looked at the green metal door behind them. "I want to look through his office. Maybe I can find something, a clue as to where he is, where he might have gone."

"It's all right with me," Myrtle said, standing. She pulled a ring of keys from her loose-fitting red cardigan sweater, found the right one and unlocked the door.

Devin looked at her curiously. "When did you start locking his office during the day?"

"A few weeks ago. Eli said he was getting more forgetful and misplacing papers."

"But Eli isn't really all that forgetful, he just uses it as an easy way to cover for his mistakes. People expect him to be absentminded, so he plays the role."

Myrtle patted her on the shoulder. "I know that, and it does make you wonder what all's going on, doesn't it?"

Behind them, one of Wingate's security guards spoke loudly. "Are you lost, sir?"

They both turned. Nick Lang was standing in the open doorway. "No," he told the guard. "This is the office I'm looking for."

"Why, Mr. Lang, what a nice surprise!" Myrtle exclaimed.

She waved the guard off. He complied, and Nick stepped into the room. He was smiling at Devin.

"What are you doing here?" Devin asked. "Besides eavesdropping, that is?"

"The same as you, I imagine," Nick replied. "Looking for information on Eli's disappearance."

"Why?"

"Is she always so suspicious, Myrtle?"

Myrtle smiled. "It's understandable, considering the circumstances. You two know each other?"

"We met in Jay's office earlier," Nick explained. "If you ladies are going to search Eli's office I'd like to help."

"Thanks, but no thanks," Devin said.

Myrtle held up a hand. "Now, Devin, not so fast. We could use some help. We don't have any idea of what we're looking for."

"And he does?" she asked skeptically.

Nick grinned. "No, but I'm an interested party."

"Monetarily interested," Devin grumbled as she turned and walked into the inner office.

It was stark and simple, with white walls, four black metal filing cabinets and a large black metal desk, its surface unmarred by papers or clutter.

Covering one wall was a collage of Eli's lifetime of work—before-and-after photos of contaminated fields now green and growing, streams and ponds once dumped in, now sparkling clear, others in the process of being cleaned up.

Eli Wingate had been a pioneer in bioremediation, the bacterial cleanup of toxic waste sites. As others entered the field and research had become increasingly specialized, he had turned his genius toward what he considered an even more pressing problem. Garbage and waste materials. He had often said that garbage would bury the world long before any of the rest of its problems had a chance to kill it off.

"It can't help but move you," Nick said quietly.

He was standing right behind her, his breath stirring her hair, tickling her neck. Stepping away from him, she glanced at the spotless desk, then over at Myrtle.

"Where's the mess?"

Myrtle shrugged. "I found it this way on Friday. He's cleaned it up before a few times. But it's one more thing that doesn't seem right."

None of this seemed normal. "Where should we start?"

"I'll unlock everything and we'll have a go at it," Myrtle said, pulling her ring of keys out of her pocket.

Two hours later they were sitting in chairs staring at each other, dejected, at a loss as to what to do next.

"Well, did we come up with anything?" Myrtle asked.

"No," Devin muttered. "Even if a piece of evidence had bitten us on the hand none of us has the technological background to know she'd been bitten."

Nick rubbed his eyes. "You're right. There are plenty of things to see here, but I had only the vaguest idea of what I was looking at."

"Now, don't you two feel bad. I've been typing some of this for over twenty years and I still don't understand it. You know, I wanted to take some courses once to get a better grasp on what Eli was doing, but he was flat against it." Myrtle grinned. "He liked me not knowing what I was typing, so I couldn't change anything."

Devin returned her smile. It sounded typical of Eli. In her hand was a piece of paper with words and symbols quite foreign to her. "Then how do you decipher this code of his?"

"In the beginning Eli spelled them on the tapes for me and he's never quit. That way there are no mistakes, and if one does come up it's his fault." Myrtle stood and began locking the file cabinets. "I learned a lot over the years. This job has always been interesting. And I'm not ready for it to end. Sixty-eight is too young to retire." She grinned slyly. "Besides, my husband would drive me crazy."

Devin stood up. Her life had been disrupted by all this and she didn't like it. There was only one way to return things to normal. "Don't worry, Myrtle. I'm going to find him." To herself she silently added, *I only hope I'm not too late.*

Chapter Three

Eli's two chatty, sapphire-eyed Siamese cats greeted Devin as she entered his duplex, rubbing up against her calves with their sleek cream-and-brown coats, impeding her progress as they kept up their noisy, nonstop cat conversation.

"Come on, guys, don't try to con me, I know you've been fed. I talked to the people next door." Stooping down, she scratched both of them behind their chocolate-tipped ears, making them purr and rub up against her affectionately, demanding even more attention.

The chiming of the doorbell startled all of them. Devin was unsure who jumped higher. Cautiously she peered through the peephole. Then she sighed and opened the door.

"You again?"

Nick Lang was leaning against the doorjamb, hands thrust into his pants pockets. His suit coat and tie were missing, the cuffs of his white shirt folded up to show tanned, muscular forearms. "Is that any way to greet a guest?"

"You're not a guest, you're a pest. What are you—Oh, no! Quick, grab Hyde!" she yelled, grabbing the other cat as he tried to streak out of the house behind his brother.

Nick sprinted across the rock lawn after the Siamese, ducking under trees, around bushes and into the neighbors' yards. Suddenly the cat stopped in the middle of the fourth cement driveway, and Nick almost stomped on the chocolate brown tail it was flicking from side to side.

"Where were you going, fella?" he murmured, carefully picking up the big cat. It purred steadily against his chest as they returned to the house.

"Don't put him down yet," Devin warned. After closing the door she turned around. "Okay, it's safe now."

When he let go of the cat it ran out of the foyer right on its brother's heels. "They do this often?"

"Every now and then. Eli has never let his cats outside, and most of the time that's fine with them, but I suppose they get curious," Devin explained. "Besides, Jekyll and Hyde like getting into trouble."

"Interesting names."

"Eli's sense of humor. Although they can show signs of disturbing personalities." Devin leaned back against the door, hands resting on the knob behind her. "They're not the only ones. What are you doing here, Nick?"

He shrugged. "Same thing you are. Searching for clues."

"Then you're in the wrong place. The sort of clues you want are at Wingate, in the accounting department."

"This is getting so annoying!" Nick exclaimed. "Would you mind telling me why you're so intent on painting me with the same brush you used on Jay and Richard this morning?"

"You just answered your own question," Devin replied. "I'm well acquainted with the type. My impression of you was influenced by the company you keep."

"Is that so? My first impression of you wasn't so hot, either, Devin, and you made it all by yourself." Nick waved his hands over his head. "You act as if the sky is falling!"

She glowered at his antics. "I am not overreacting! Eli was working on a very important, extremely valuable project and now he's missing. Something may have happened to him. I'm his niece and I'm concerned."

"Well, I consider him a friend, and I am also concerned!"

"Hah!"

"Look, Devin, we do have a large stake in Wingate," he acknowledged, "but I also happen to like Eli and the work he's done. I agree that Jay and Richard might be taking his disappearance too lightly. You seem determined to do more than they're willing to, and I want to help. Why do you find that so hard to accept?"

"Because I don't know you, that's why!"

"Finally!" Nick grinned in triumph. "Let's start over, shall we? Pleased to meet you, Devin Prescott. I'm Nick Lang, businessman and all-around decent human being."

He held out his hand. Devin ignored it. "Maybe so," she said, "but in my experience I've found that those two things do not often come in the same package."

"That's some pessimistic attitude you've got there, lady. May I assume your dealings with Eli's brothers are behind it?" Nick asked.

"Assume whatever you like," she returned.

"Care to tell me about it?"

"Jay and Richard don't hold the patent on insensitivity," she told him, her jaw clenched. "For instance, how can a man who claims to be a decent human being ask such a rude question?"

"Me? Rude?"

"Do you really think I'd be so indiscreet as to discuss my family's problems with a stranger, especially one who is involved in a business deal with them?"

"I was just curious." Nick shrugged. "Jay and Richard don't seem like such bad guys. I understand their position."

"Sitting on their hands?"

"They don't want to jeopardize the company—a concern I readily admit I share. But before you bite my head off again," he added quickly, "I'm also worried about Eli. All I'm saying is that as an investor I can see both sides of the situation."

"Meaning I can't?"

"How could you? Emotionally, you're too close."

Devin let out an exasperated sigh. "So you're going to insist on poking your nose into my business, aren't you?"

"It's my business, too," Nick informed her. "That's what I've been trying to explain. Whether you like it or not, I'm involved. If you don't want my help, that's fine, but it sure doesn't make much sense."

It made perfect sense to Devin. She simply had a gut feeling that Nick still wasn't being straight with her. But then again, she supposed she really hadn't given him much of a chance to correct the situation.

"All right. We'll talk." Devin walked past him into the living room and sat down in a dark, velvet-covered chair. Once Nick was seated on the matching sofa she asked, "How did you meet Eli?"

"In college." Nick glanced around the room. It was simple yet elegant, with Oriental rugs, hardwood floors and a single vase with a lone flower on the glass coffee table. "I took a course he was teaching on environmental reckoning."

"Must have been some course."

Nick looked at her, puzzled. "What do you mean?"

"I take it you invested quite a bit in the company," she replied. "Why?"

Leaning back into the corner of the sofa he asked, "Are you always this direct?"

"Yes." She tilted her head to one side, studying him.

Nick hesitated. Unless he told her something she'd believe, he was quite sure Devin wouldn't allow him within ten feet of her again, let alone take him into her confidence. On the other hand, there was only so much he was willing to discuss, even with Eli's niece. But too much was riding on this to allow a loose cannon like her to go careening around.

"Eli's a good teacher and his work inspired me," Nick told her at last. He smiled. "You might even say he put me on the right track. I suggested the investment in Wingate and had to push hard for its approval. Biotech firms can be very risky investments. If they don't produce results, fast, they usually go bankrupt, or never show a profit."

"But you believe in Wingate?"

"I think eventually they'll show a very good return for the money," he replied honestly. "Eli isn't their only hope for new patents, either. I take it you're not that well acquainted with all that goes on there?"

"Just Eli's part in it, and only bits and pieces of that." She gave him a cool smile. "Eli can be eccentric, but he's a total professional. Contrary to what you may think, I *do* understand the need to filter what the public knows about Wingate. I'm part of the family, remember.''

Nick made a mental note to remain very aware of that fact. He had the feeling it could temper everything she told him, especially in the beginning. But at the moment he had neither the freedom nor the inclination to convince her to lower her guard.

''The bulk of the work there is geared toward agricultural advancements,'' he continued in a pleasant, informative tone. ''Improved seeds, new strains of crops resistant to disease so the use of expensive chemicals will be eliminated. Also, their study of new hydroponic gardening techniques shows great promise. Wingate's product line is already profitable.''

Devin frowned. ''You sound like a commercial. Exactly what firm do you work for, anyway?''

''Lang Inc.''

''Yours?'' she inquired, her eyebrows arched high.

''It's a family company,'' Nick replied. ''And I sound like a commercial for Wingate out of habit. It's the only way I could win approval for the investment.'' He shrugged. ''Not that it's difficult for me. As I said, the company had great potential.''

''But you pushed your family hard, and now that Eli is missing, their investment might be in jeopardy.'' She nodded thoughtfully. ''Now we're getting somewhere. What worries you the most, Nick? The money? Or what your family will think if the investment you recommended falls through?''

''Don't you mean what worries me the most *after* Eli's safety?'' he returned.

''Just answer the question.''

Nick shook his head and chuckled. ''You're really something else, Devin.'' He sighed. ''Okay. Naturally the money is a concern. But there's more than money involved here. I'm responsible, and I'm trying to protect myself.''

As he made this admission, Devin studied him intently. She didn't really know him, but she was starting to form a more educated impression of Nick Lang, and something didn't jibe. There was more to his motivation, she was sure.

Nevertheless, Devin was also getting the impression that Nick was genuinely worried about her missing uncle. Since concern for Eli—not just his work, but *Eli*—was in short supply at the moment, she could ill afford to dismiss Nick out of hand because of some vague suspicions.

"All right," she said. "I guess everybody has a right to look out for their own skin, especially when a family is involved. But just how far toward that end will you go?"

He smiled wryly. "I don't know, Devin. I suppose I'll find that out when we discover what happened to Eli.''

"Well, at least you're honest about it, which is more than I can say for Jay and Richard." Devin sighed. "What do you know about investigating a missing person?"

"About as much as a fiddle player does." He pointed to a gold-framed photograph on the black lacquer piano in the corner. In the photo, a younger Devin proudly took her first bow as a soloist with the local symphony. "Not much, in other words. But I'd say we're both open-minded and quick learners.''

"I am a violinist, Mr. Lang," Devin said coolly. "Not a fiddle player. If you're as quick as you say, remember that. There's a considerable difference.''

He shrugged. "I suppose there is, at that. Most fiddle players seem easygoing and pleasant, while you, Ms. Prescott, are too stiff by half."

"I am not!"

"Prove it. Quit wasting time with this silly third degree and admit you could use some help on this."

Devin fumed in silence. She didn't like having her nose rubbed in the obvious, but he was right—she could use someone's help. Even if he was a bit suspicious, and an amateur like her, there was no denying he did have a large stake in finding Eli. That alone could make him a valuable ally.

But he was also more than a little irritating, and she abhorred having to admit she needed help. "Be that as it may," Devin said, "the only thing I care about is finding my uncle, while you've made it quite clear you have ulterior motives. Why should I trust you?"

"Who else do you have?" Nick smiled. "And why should I trust *you?*" He leaned forward, forearms resting on his knees. It was time he gave her a dose of her own bitter medicine. "What's *your* real stake in this, Devin? Are you Eli's heiress? Will you profit if he's dead?"

"Well, we know you certainly won't." She felt the color rising in her face and struggled to calm her temper. It wasn't easy. "Not that it's any of your business, but Eli's entire estate will further his lifetime of research by educating future scientists," Devin finally told him.

"Knowing Eli, I'm not surprised," Nick commented.

Devin was beginning to wonder just how well he did know Eli. She could easily check and see if he'd really been a student of her uncle's. Unfortunately, it would be much harder to find out whether the two men had actually gotten close enough to become friends, as Nick implied.

Still, Devin intended to try. Myrtle was apparently acquainted with Nick; perhaps she would know. It might not prove his good intentions, but it would definitely provide an insight into his character. Uncle Eli did not suffer fools gladly. Neither did his niece.

She stood, having come to a decision. Eli and her mother had taught her to trust and believe in her instincts, and they'd rarely failed her. Besides, it was too much trouble to try to get rid of him. As long as Nick Lang was going to keep turning up, she might as well make use of him.

"I'm going to search Eli's office here. It won't be easy," she warned. "Help if you want to."

"I do."

"Suit yourself." Devin walked across the room, pulled a book out from the lined shelves, then opened it and removed a key. "Have you been here before?" she asked, pausing before a door at the end of the hallway.

"No."

"Well, you're about to see why he keeps this room locked." Devin turned the key in the dead-bolt lock, twisted the crystal knob and stood back as she pushed open the door.

Nick's startled gasp pleased her. "What a wreck!"

"Disgusting, isn't it?"

"It certainly isn't what I expected," Nick said. He glanced at her. "But disgusting?"

"Forgive me. For all I know your whole house looks like this. Eli is secretly a pack rat about his work, but at least it only shows in this one room."

"My house is spotless," he objected.

"Sure it is." Devin chuckled. "Once a week when your housekeeper finishes with it, right?"

Nick smiled. "How'd you guess?"

Entering the so-called office was like wading into a paper ocean. Except for a narrow path leading to the desk, every bit of floor space was filled. Piles of magazines and papers were stacked waist high and beyond, leaning precariously against walls and each other. The huge antique desk was overflowing with even more clutter, and behind that an entire wall of floor-to-ceiling bookshelves was also crammed full.

Scattered throughout were odd-looking devices, for the most part being used as paperweights, but all apparently designed to have a multitude of other functions, as well.

Nick studied one such thingamajig that was precariously perched on the near edge of Eli's littered desk. It seemed to be some sort of combination stapler, pencil sharpener and alarm clock. At least, he hoped that's all it was; it sat there ticking ominously, the little red light atop its shiny domed head staring back at Nick like some alert and malevolent eye.

"Are you sure it's safe in here?" he asked.

"Reasonably." Devin cleared off the chair behind the desk and sat down. "You can see why I decided to use you."

"I'll say," Nick said, still shocked by the mess. Eli's sharp, orderly mind obviously didn't extend to his filing habits. "How can he find anything in here?" He picked up a scientific magazine from the nearest pile. "This is over thirty years old!"

"You'll find things even older. Eli won't throw away anything pertaining to his work because it might come in useful someday. And there is a system to all this."

Nick shook his head in disbelief. "If you say so. Where do you want to start?"

"There are a couple of two-drawer oak file cabinets somewhere." Devin looked around the room, but didn't see them. "Why don't you try and excavate them?"

"If I start drowning you'd better save me, or you'll be out one helper," he warned, heading for the closest wall. "I could end up being paper-cut to death in here."

"I promise," Devin muttered, already reading the top sheet on a stack of papers near the edge of the desk. "Oh, and take care where you stick your hands. As you can see, Eli has a penchant for gadgets."

Nick didn't like the sound of that. "What do you mean, be careful where I put my hands?" he asked, looking askance at the little red-eyed guardian on the desk. "I thought you said it was reasonably safe?" Devin only nodded absently, her attention focused on her own task.

Gingerly Nick worked his way across the room and along the wall looking for file cabinets. Because most of the stacks were taller than the cabinets would be, it made the work time-consuming and frustrating. Every time he had to move part of a stack to look behind it—half expecting some gadget to leap out at him—another one fell over and he had to stop and straighten it before moving on.

"Have you ever heard of a company called TSA?"

Nick turned around. "Why?"

"Eli has a job offer from them," Devin replied.

"Let me see that."

When Nick reached the desk—causing a small avalanche of magazines in the process—Devin handed him the paper and watched his changing expression as he read the contents. Evidently Nick wasn't too happy with what he saw. Devin hadn't been, either; an already confusing situation had just taken on a new complication.

"Nice offer," she commented.

"A scientist's dream," he agreed, scanning the list of enticements. "No limitations on what you work on, no worries over funding your projects or managerial duties intruding into your personal life."

"No fighting with your brothers over every dime spent," Devin added dryly. Then she glanced at Nick, aware she'd let slip something that wasn't any of his business.

Nick leaned against the edge of the desk. "Do the three of them fight a lot?"

"Don't most business partners?"

"Come on, Devin," he said with a sigh. "I'm only trying to figure out what this might mean. Do you think it's conceivable Eli is considering this job?"

Devin frowned. "Qualify that question for me, Nick. Are you asking as a friend or an investor?"

"I've already told you. You can't separate the two."

She appreciated his honesty. The least she could do was be honest in return. "I don't know."

"Would you tell me if you did?"

"Nick . . ."

Just then the device on Eli's desk beeped loudly. Nick stared at it. "What the heck is that thing?"

"It's a jerk detector," Devin replied. "Works, too. You're being one right now." She had to laugh at his surprised expression. "Relax, it's just a clock. It beeps on the hour to help Eli keep track of time."

"Jerk detector," Nick muttered. "Very funny."

"I suppose even Jay and Richard were willing to admit that Eli's been under stress lately. But I really don't know whether he would seriously consider leaving Wingate or not. It's a possibility, okay?''

"Great." Nick rubbed his forehead, easing the frown lines across his brow. This whole situation wasn't making it any easier for him to repay the debt he owed to a friend. "Come up with anything else?" he asked.

"Not yet."

"Well, then. Back to the salt mines."

He headed carefully across the office to continue his search, while Devin resumed the tedious process of sifting through the mountain of papers on her uncle's desk. They worked in hopeful, methodical silence.

Finally Nick unearthed one of the file cabinets. He grinned. Progress at last! The drawers, however, were shut and locked tight. If he hadn't been crouched behind a huge pile of magazines he might have considered his next move more carefully. As it was, Nick hardly thought twice as he took a slender, well-worn sliver of metal from his shirt pocket and inserted it into the brass lock on the top drawer. Something clicked and he deftly opened the drawer.

Then he wished he *had* thought twice. With a loud hiss, a thin jet of menthol-scented shaving cream spewed out of a hole in the base of the cabinet, quickly coating his shoes and the surrounding floor in fluffy white goo.

"Oops!"

Nick wasn't sure which startled him more, the foamy assault on his feet or Devin's accusing voice, right behind him. "What do you think you're doing!" she cried.

Chapter Four

Nick quickly hid his lock pick and stood, an embarrassed smile on his face. "All I did was open the drawer! I guess Eli has a penchant for privacy, as well."

"Yes," Devin replied, gazing at him suspiciously. "He does. You have to push a concealed button before you open any locked drawer, or who knows what will happen." She looked down at his shoes. Under other circumstances she would have been laughing. But at the moment it didn't seem very funny. "The question is, how did you open it in the first place?"

"It wasn't locked."

"Is that a fact?" Devin reached past him and pushed the drawer back in. It shut with an audible click, and when she pulled on the oak handle, the drawer was again locked. She looked at him pointedly, her eyebrows raised. "They're automatic, so Eli didn't have to remember to lock them."

He shrugged. "Must have malfunctioned."

"Stay put while I get a towel or something. I don't want you tracking that stuff all over. Here," she added, handing him a small brass key. "I found that in the desk and the button is on the back of the cabinet. See to it there isn't another mysterious malfunction."

The first cabinet drawer yielded nothing of interest, at least not to Nick. In the second, however, he came across a gray metal lockbox. Luckily the key was in its lock, so he wouldn't have to explain how he opened it.

Inside were three envelopes. The first, addressed to Devin, was sealed and marked To Be Opened Upon My Death. The second, also sealed, was a copy of Eli's last will and testament. Nick put both of these grim documents back into the lockbox. The third envelope was an insurance policy. This one hadn't been sealed, so he unfolded the thick papers within and had a look.

Nick was staring at the document in his hand when Devin came back into the office carrying a towel. "Do you know an Yvette Soomes?" he asked.

Devin thought for a moment. "No. I don't."

"Well, Eli certainly must. He's named her as the beneficiary of a million-dollar life insurance policy."

"A million!" Devin dropped the towel on the floor and took the document from him. "Is this legitimate?"

"It's easy enough to find out," he replied, bending down to clean off his shoes. He covered the remainder of the foam with the towel. When he stood, Devin was scowling at him. Nick just smiled. "We can call the company and see if the premiums are paid up. I also want to check into that job offer."

"Wait a minute." Devin walked back to the desk and picked up a file folder. "As long as you're at it, there are four more offers in here from this year alone."

"He's a popular man," Nick muttered, taking the file she handed him. He sat on the edge of the desk and studied each letter in turn before closing the file with a sigh. "Eli has plenty to choose from. He can work anywhere in the world. The German and Japanese companies are offering him the most."

"They wouldn't kidnap him, would they?" Devin asked.

Nick shook his head. "I doubt it. Industrial espionage does exist, of course, and it can get ugly at times, but as a rule they're more likely to use payola than force," he informed her. "A happy scientist is a productive scientist."

Once again Devin shot him a sidelong glance. "You certainly have a broad range of interests, Nick," she noted suspiciously. "Investments. Environmental reckoning." She nodded her head toward the file cabinet. "Locks. And now industrial espionage. Just how do you know so much about the way it works?"

"All right. You figured me out." He held up his hands. "Caught red-handed by the lady gumshoe. Should I make a full confession, or would you prefer to beat it out of me?"

Her eyes narrowed. "What are you talking about?"

"I was ashamed to tell you, but...okay. Jack-of-all-trades, master of none, that's me. All sorts of interests, but I could never settle on anything. It's terrible."

"Oh, for the love of... Enough!" Devin exclaimed. "You're hiding something, Nick Lang, and so help me—"

"Hush!" He cocked his head and listened. "What's that ringing I hear? Is there a phone buried under all this?"

"It's in the kitchen," Devin said, tripping over a pile of magazines in her haste to get to it before the ringing stopped. She ran down the hallway, through the living room and into the kitchen just as the answering machine picked up. Myrtle's distinct voice rang out loud and clear.

"Oh, shoot! I was hoping you were there, Devin. Well—"

Devin grabbed for the white wall phone. "Don't hang up, Myrtle. I'm here." She reset the answering machine sitting on the edge of the counter. "Have you heard from Eli?"

Nick entered the room and sat on a stool at the counter. The kitchen was long, narrow and stark white. An old-fashioned green chalkboard hanging above the phone had a message written on it, he noticed. *Sat. — 7:00 pick up Devin.* She hadn't been lying about their date.

Devin was listening intently, unaware of his perusal. She tucked a strand of auburn hair behind her ear, revealing an oval face and large gold earrings. Dark eyebrows, drawn into a frown at the moment, contrasted with her pale skin and light blue eyes. That startling eye color, Nick observed, must run in her family. Every member he'd met so far had the same pale blue eyes.

An inch-wide, flat gold necklace followed the round neckline of her cream-colored, knee-length dress. If her calves were anything to go by she had nice legs. Sticking close to her certainly wasn't going to be a hardship for him.

"Thanks for calling, Myrtle. I'll keep you posted," Devin promised. Then she noticed that Nick had entered the room. "Oh, by the way, Myrtle. Just how did you meet Nick Lang, anyway?" She paused, looking at Nick and listening. "I see. Well, I'd better let you go now. Thanks."

"Satisfied?" Nick asked as Devin hung up.

"Not by a long shot. But she did confirm you were a student of Eli's. She also said you were a very nice man, and that she was happy you wanted to help me."

Nick smiled. "If Myrtle likes me, I must be okay," he said. Devin just scowled at him. "What did she call about?"

Devin pulled a stool out and sat. "The rest of the tape Myrtle was transcribing earlier today is blank, and one of Eli's many quirks is that he never gives her a tape until it's full. Myrtle believes it was erased. All the notes after the Monday before last are missing."

"What about the paper copies of his work?"

"I don't know. Myrtle never sees them. They're kept in the lab area where security is tight."

"Do you have access to the lab?" he asked.

Devin nodded. "Yes, unless the code's been changed recently. We'll go check it out." She glanced at her watch. "But it'll have to be later." The police weren't finished with her just yet. The way things were starting to shape up, though, Devin planned to try to put them off until she knew what was going on herself. "I have a one-o'clock appointment I can't miss," she informed him.

"How about tonight," Nick suggested, "after everyone at Wingate has gone home?"

"Okay." She didn't bother arguing. He certainly wasn't going to let her go alone. "What time should we meet?"

"I could pick you up."

"Thanks, but I'd rather meet you there. Say ten?"

Nick stood, not offended by her brusque manner. "Fine with me. I just had an idea, though. Switch on the answering machine. Let's see who else has called."

They listened to repeated messages from both of them, progressively more concerned as the tape ran on, and one from a woman Eli evidently hadn't been treating very well.

"I'm warning you, Eli!" The angry feminine voice sent Jekyll and Hyde scrambling for cover beneath the kitchen table. "If you stand me up tonight, you'll pay for it dearly! And I mean it!'' She then hung up with a loud bang.

''Recognize the voice?'' Nick asked.

Devin shook her head. ''It could be anyone. Eli has always had an eye for the ladies, as Grandmother puts it.''

''Ah, yes. I noticed that myself.'' Nick leaned against the counter. ''The voice sounds young, maybe one of his past or current students?''

''It's been known to happen with him.''

He looked at the spotless white counters. ''Does Eli keep an appointment book at home?''

''I don't know. I doubt it would be in his office if he does, though. Why don't you check out this room, and I'll search through the bedrooms.''

Nick found the black spiral-bound book in the second drawer he opened. He flipped through the lined sheets of white paper twice, staring at the pages thoughtfully.

With the book in hand he went looking for Devin and found her in the second bedroom, a huge orange cat in her arms. She was talking to it softly.

''I see you found a possible eyewitness,'' Nick said. ''Did he tell you anything?''

''She.'' Devin looked up to find Nick smiling at her. ''And Pumpkin would if she could, wouldn't you, honey?'' She carefully put the elderly cat down on the bed and stroked her one last time. ''What have you got there?''

''His appointment book, but the entire month of June is missing.'' He arched his eyebrows. ''Ripped out.'' Nick looked around. The room was just as spotless as the rest of the house—save the office, of course. ''Can you tell if this place has been searched?''

"No. I'm not here that much. But the older couple who live in the other half of this duplex keep house for Eli," she explained. "They haven't seen any strangers around recently and I don't think anyone could get in here without them knowing about it. Unless," Devin added, "they waited until they were gone."

"Either that," Nick agreed, "or we're dealing with a professional. Then again, a professional would have simply taken the whole appointment book, not rip out the pages in such an obvious manner."

"Oh, really? Professional thieves are another of your many interests, I suppose?"

"I read a lot. So sue me," Nick returned mildly. "It was just a supposition, anyway. I'm trying to make some sense from all this confusion."

Devin nodded. She was confused, too. The break-in at her apartment had been smooth and professional, and yet she felt sure the intruder was acting on inside information, so it might not have been a highly trained thief, after all.

For a moment Devin considered telling Nick about the break-in, but she finally decided it could wait. They had enough contradictory evidence as it was. Besides, she didn't trust her instincts about him *that* much. Eli's friend or not, Nick was still an unknown quantity.

She sighed. "This is all so strange."

"Isn't it, though. I guess we'll take it one step at a time. First we'll check out the lab, then go from there. I've always found complicated problems easier to comprehend if I break them down into their component parts."

"Funny. That's exactly the way a musician approaches an unfamiliar piece of music." Maybe they could get along, after all. Devin looked at her watch again. "I've got to get going." She headed for the front door. Nick followed her outside. "See you at ten?" she asked.

"It's a date."

WINGATE WAS QUIET except for a few odd, unidentifiable noises from various pieces of automated lab equipment and the soft sigh of the air-conditioning. Moving soundlessly on his crepe-soled shoes, a lone intruder kept one of the squat copper processing vats between himself and the heavyset guard. As he watched, the guard took a cursory look around, inserted a key into the security station, then removed it and continued across the lab to a door on the far side. As soon as the door closed, the man emerged from his hiding spot and, carefully skirting the television cameras, made his way toward the computer systems.

For a professional it had been easy to override this one remaining section of security cameras. Only someone paying very close attention would notice that the exact same thing appeared on every single computer screen, never changing, that instead of live action they were watching the same loop of a videotape over and over again.

It took consummate skill to be a thief nowadays with all the new technology—but the constant honing of those skills paid handsomely if you were successful at it. There were even fringe benefits, like this past weekend. It had been a pleasure to seduce the access code out of a young assistant who worked here. The right atmosphere, wine, dinner, dancing and then to bed. So far it had been a pleasurable job.

Unfortunately, this was the second time he'd broken into this particular lab. He didn't want to have to admit failure again, even if it was just to himself. Not that failure really bothered him so much. It was part of the job, a fact of life. Not getting paid, though, now that bothered him a whole bunch.

His gloved fingers flew over the keyboard with precise movements, a tiny, powerful flashlight held between his teeth making only a small puddle of illumination in the darkened room. A menu came up on the CRT and he began scanning the contents. The file he was looking to steal wasn't listed. He tried a few other tricks of the hacker's trade, to no avail. Perhaps he'd been given incorrect or inadequate data. It certainly wouldn't be the first time that had happened in his long career. But never say die, as the old saw went.

He returned the system to the task it had been performing before he'd interrupted it and looked around the small cubicle. There was no storage in sight. But something about the workstation didn't seem quite kosher.

After pushing the chair aside he knelt and crawled beneath the desk. The false front was open in less than a minute. With his flashlight he studied the neat rows of microfilm boxes. It was indeed a secret cache of information, but unfortunately none of the films were current enough to be of any use. Now he was starting to get worried.

Still perturbed by the desk's unusual design, he kept looking. Skillfully his fingers skimmed the top edges of the wood-grained metal desk. Then he crawled beneath the desk again, his fingers moving along the inside seams. Finally he came across a concealed latch and pulled on it, and the top of the desk popped up.

The sound of voices startled him, causing him to bump his head on the desk ledge in his haste to get out from under it. He had to get out of the room and into hiding. There was a coat closet on the other side of the lab, he recalled, and he made a quick but careful beeline for it, easing the door shut as the sound of approaching footsteps grew louder.

Who could it be? The guards weren't due to make their rounds again for another forty-five minutes, and according to his information there wasn't supposed to be any late-night work being done. Whoever it was, they had clearance to get past the guards and were heading straight for this wing of the lab. If he was caught he'd never live it down.

Then again, considering how fast and loose he was playing this game, he might not live through it at all.

Chapter Five

Devin drove along the deserted four-lane road that was the main approach to the Wingate labs. The wind blowing in through her open car windows was cool and soothing. Temperatures had topped one hundred earlier but were now in the low seventies, pleasant for a June night in Phoenix.

The breeze ruffling her hair helped her think. Was she doing the right thing by letting Nick Lang help her? Devin had the uneasy feeling that her uncle's disappearance might be just the tip of the iceberg, the most noticeable sign of a problem with even deeper implications. There was no telling what strange connections could turn up, and Nick, for all his evident concern, was still an outsider. Shouldn't she handle this on her own, both for Eli's sake and that of the company that bore his family name?

"Oh, please," she muttered to herself. "Don't let me start thinking like Jay and Richard."

Nick had a legitimate business reason for being involved, and that's all there was to it! Besides, he evidently had every intention of conducting his own investigation, anyway. She'd as soon have him where she could keep an eye on him.

It did unsettle her a little, though, that she found him strangely but annoyingly attractive. He wasn't her type at all. For the time being she supposed they could simply proceed as he had suggested; take things one step at a time and see what happened.

A block from the entrance to Wingate she found Nick waiting for her, sitting on the hood of his car, which he'd parked between two streetlights. He was dressed in jeans, blue T-shirt and tennis shoes. It was quite a change from his earlier businesslike demeanor.

Devin frowned. Just when she thought she had him pegged, he turns up in casual attire looking devil-may-care. Not that she disapproved, but she wasn't fond of surprises, especially not of the masculine sort. Just who was Nick Lang really, when he wasn't being an executive watchdog or helping find lost scientists?

When she pulled up, he slid off the car and leaned down to stick his head inside the passenger window. "Hello, Devin. I'm surprised you showed up."

She'd surprised herself, too. It wasn't like her to put this much trust in a man she barely knew. "Get in, I want to get this over with. And I'll do the talking."

"Fine by me. You seem pretty good at it."

She shot him a withering glance. "Just get in."

Devin drove them to the guarded entrance of Wingate and received clearance to enter. Nick did as she asked, not saying anything as Devin explained to a guard at the front entrance of the main building and then another one near the new addition that they were there to pick up something her uncle Eli needed. Obviously Jay and Richard were still keeping silent about Eli, even to the security personnel.

They encountered no one as they walked through the silent basement office area to the lab. Devin stopped at the end of the hallway, punched a code into the computerized entry pad on the wall, then pushed the solid steel door open.

"How often do they change the code?" Nick asked as he followed her into the lab.

"I have no idea. Eli gave me this one last week. We were going to a concert and I met him here."

The door shut quietly behind them. "I'm not complaining this time around," Nick said, "but it should be changed more often. Do you know where his work area is?"

"No, I just thought we'd wander around blind until we find it," she said dryly. "Of course I know where it is."

He shrugged. "Just asking. Nice touch of sarcasm, though. I didn't think you had it in you."

Ignoring him, Devin led the way past an array of huge stainless steel tanks as high as the ceiling, gleaming silver beneath the fluorescent lighting and resembling oversize test tubes. There were lots of gauges, different-colored hoses and other paraphernalia attached to them, hanging in what to their laymen's eyes seemed apparent disarray.

"What are these for?" Nick asked.

"Fermentation of some kind, but that's all I know about them." Devin turned left and wound her way through a row of squat copper vats. "This is a shortcut. Watch your step."

Nick was careful not to touch anything. "There are video monitors all over. Is it wired for sound?"

"No, that would create an invasion-of-privacy problem with the employees."

They were walking past more typical lab areas now, something familiar to any high school or college student, though the equipment was much more expensive looking.

Just as they were about to turn yet another corner, they ran smack into a young woman bustling along in the opposite direction. "Oh, excuse me." She stepped around them, still apologizing. "I didn't think . . . I'm so sorry."

"It was our fault," Devin said. "We didn't expect to meet anyone here at this time of the night."

"Neither did I." The tanned, leggy girl smiled, flipping her long blond hair back over one shoulder as she rearranged her sleeveless, low-necked red dress. "Well, no harm done."

"Were you working this late?" Devin asked.

"No, I, uh . . ." She blushed and began backing away from them, her small white purse held in both hands. "Actually, I left something here that I needed for my date. I've got to run, he's waiting for me. Sorry about the collision."

They watched her hurry away, the sound of her white sandals clicking on the linoleum floor. "Isn't it unusual for someone to be here at this hour?" Nick asked.

"Not really. When he's wrapped up in something, Eli works around the clock for days without much sleep."

"But she wasn't working dressed like that. Makes you wonder what she forgot that was so important to her date, doesn't it?" he asked thoughtfully.

Devin glanced at him. "Maybe she left her favorite perfume or something."

"Uh-huh."

"You have a suspicious nature, Nick Lang."

He laughed. "So do you. That's why we make such a good investigative team."

"If you say so," Devin commented, though she didn't much like the sound of the word. A team? She was a very private person and Nick was getting a bit too chummy for her taste. "Are you coming, or not?"

Nick was still looking in the direction the young woman had gone, though she was out of sight and earshot now. "Do you know her?" he asked.

"I've seen her here before, but I don't know her name." Devin turned and continued to lead the way. "Now, come on!"

Eli's work area, the size of a small walk-in closet, was windowless, neat and orderly. An impressive computer system monopolized half the space, apparently controlling some lab functions as well as data storage and processing.

"I expected chaos," Nick commented.

"Not here. That's only allowed in his home office. Shut the door." Devin knelt and crawled beneath the computer desk, hitting the chair with her hip. "Could you move that, please?"

He rolled the chair back against the door and watched as she opened what appeared to be a smooth wall beneath the beige desk, revealing storage area. Small, light blue square boxes were stacked neatly in rows on the narrow shelves.

"Microfilm," she mumbled, her backside to him as she crawled farther inside. It was a stretch for her to reach the tiny concealed latch in the far corner. The top of the desk popped up a quarter of an inch when she pulled on it.

After backing her way out from beneath the desk, she stood and raised the wood-grained metal top.

Nick stepped up beside her. "Is this where he usually keeps his papers?"

"His latest work, yes." She was staring into the shallow opening. "I can't believe it's empty."

"Who else knows how to gain access to this drawer?"

Devin tucked her shoulder-length auburn hair behind her ear and bit her lower lip. "No one, as far as I know. I only know about it because I found the latch by accident years ago when I was playing with it as a child. It was always our little secret, Eli's special hiding place that only we knew about. Sometimes he'd leave candy for me."

"No candy now," Nick observed. "Or anything else. Maybe Eli took the papers with him."

"Maybe." She lowered the desk top, pressed firmly until she heard a muffled click, then pulled upward on the edge. It didn't budge. Satisfied, she turned and sat on top of the desk. "But why would he do that?"

"Could be he suspected someone was trying to steal them." Nick snagged the chair with his foot and sat down, the position putting her torso at his eye level. Her blue jeans fit nicely. Even the oversize yellow T-shirt she wore couldn't hide her rounded, curving hips. He forced himself to concentrate on the matter at hand. "Then again, maybe I'm jumping to a false conclusion. Myrtle did say he'd been misplacing things. Those papers could be anywhere."

Devin crossed her arms and glared at him. "It's also possible someone really *did* steal them."

"Sure. As long as we're jumping to conclusions, let's do it with both feet. Are you always such a pessimist?"

"I'm a realist. His latest notes aren't here, the tape Myrtle was working with was partially erased and there is no sign of Eli. Even if he did take the papers with him, where is he? Why hasn't he called any of us?"

Nick rolled his chair back and forth as he thought about it. "Let's stick to what we know for sure, okay? Eli's missing, the circumstances of his disappearance are odd and he hasn't contacted anyone we know of to explain things. That's not good. As for the missing notes, though, we can't be sure of anything yet." He thought for a moment. "Could one of his assistants have taken them, maybe even with his approval?"

"No," Devin returned adamantly. "Where work is concerned Eli trusts no one, and those notes are the key to explaining his work in progress. Years ago he had a problem with someone who acquired his data and beat him to a patent. Since then he's careful almost to the point of paranoia."

"Oh?"

"His work is recorded on tape, and then put into a re-stricted-access computer file by an assistant. Certain key elements are always missing, however. Myrtle gets part, the assistant gets part, but no one has everything except Eli himself."

"And this project, according to Richard and Jay, could be worth billions eventually." Nick shook his head. "That certainly gives someone a reason to steal his notes, kidnap him, or both."

"Yes, it does," Devin agreed quietly.

He leaned back in the chair. "This is all supposition, of course. But the motivating factors are certainly there. Now, who do you think would do such a thing?"

She shrugged. "That's the big question, isn't it? After all, Eli isn't a rocket scientist, or a semiconductor wizard. This is hardly a matter of national security. But his work could have great profit potential. A rival company, maybe? Or just some greedy soul who somehow learned of his research and the money to be made?"

"Those are the obvious answers," Nick said. "But the motive might not be entirely profit. This all could be the work of a disgruntled employee, past or present."

"Revenge?" Her eyes widened. "That's possible, I suppose, but why pick on Eli? He's something of a hero figure around here. Jay and Richard easily make an enemy a day, but not Eli. Now, a disgruntled peer of his, someone working in the same field, that I just might buy."

"Have anyone in mind?" Nick asked.

Devin slipped off the desk and stood. She sighed, clearly disgusted. "No. I don't know, Nick. We're grasping at straws, and it isn't doing any good at all."

Her worry, concern and love for Eli were easy to see. "Tomorrow we'll check into the other leads we have. Yvette Soomes and those job offers. If nothing else, maybe we'll accidentally shake the right tree and somebody will fall out who can help us." Nick stood and opened the office door. "Come on, Devin, time to go home."

They headed back out of the lab the way they had come, Devin in the lead. The sound of their footsteps echoed off the copper and stainless steel fermentation vats, making it seem as if there were several people moving around in the deserted wing instead of just two.

When the last of those echoes had died, a door across the lab from Eli's cubicle swung open and a man emerged, glancing nervously at his watch. Only ten minutes remained before the guards made their next rounds. Skirting the security cameras again, he returned to the office he'd been forced to vacate so hastily, and had the trick desk top open in seconds.

He cursed. Somebody had beaten him to the contents, and he had a pretty good idea of who that might be. One of the people who had just visited this office. The only name he had heard wasn't that common. Devin. It had to be the same one. The time had come to pay Eli Wingate's niece a more in-depth visit.

Chapter Six

Bright and early the next morning Nick sauntered into the accounting division of Lang Inc., knocked on one of the office doors, then entered without waiting for a reply.

"I need a favor, Jerry," he announced, closing the office door behind him.

"Yeah? What I need is a lock on my door."

The man with the carroty-red hair who was sitting behind the desk had been Nick's best friend since junior high school. The pair knew just about everything there was to know about each other, which would be either an asset or a liability, depending on the situation. At the moment Nick thought it was probably a bit of both.

"A lock wouldn't stop me," he said.

Jerry watched, frowning, as Nick took a seat in front of his desk. "True. But I do my best to forget that facet of your character." He sighed. "What sort of favor?"

"Just a little one." Nick held up his right hand, the thumb and forefinger about an inch apart. "No problem."

"No problem, huh? The last time you said that, I ended up in the unemployment line, old buddy."

"Hey! I was only doing what I'd been hired to do," Nick objected. Then he looked around the nicely appointed office and added, "Besides, I made up for it, didn't I?"

A few years ago Jerry Wilson had been unable to find work after a scandal hit the accounting firm he'd been working for back East. Though not involved in the actual mess, Jerry's resumé was still tainted by the work experience. Nick had hired him as an accountant and tax specialist for Lang Inc., creating a position for him. Taxwise, it was a move no one in the family firm regretted.

Jerry didn't regret it, either. He was happy to be at Lang Inc. and Nick was well aware of that fact. But of course, he also knew Jerry was right; it was Nick who had exposed the scandal at his former firm in the first place.

"Oh, please," Jerry said in a long-suffering tone. "Please don't tell me you're into that stuff again? You were doing so well!"

"You make it sound like an addiction."

"It is! You're not fooling me with this security consultant bit. I know you too well, Nick," his friend returned. "They ought to have a hotline for you guys. Midnight skulkers anonymous or something."

Nick laughed. "Enough, already! I come in to ask for a simple favor and get nothing but grief. Will you help, or not?"

"What's in it for me this time? A jail term?"

"That's a heck of a thing to say to a pal! This is legit, Jerry. I have a friend who's in trouble and I need you to dig up some information for me. That's all."

He scowled at Nick. "Which friend? What sort of trouble? And why do you need me?"

Now came the tricky part. Jerry was a friend, but he was also a Lang employee. "It's a touchy situation, Jerry. I'm really not at liberty to discuss all the details. As for the information, I'd get it myself but there are other things I need to attend to. Time is of the essence.''

Jerry put his feet on top of the cluttered desk and laced his fingers behind his head. "Are you going to tell me what's going on? Or are you still mad at me over that Wingate matter? Remember, I didn't vote against it. I simply played devil's advocate.''

"No, I'm not mad at you. You were only doing your job." While Nick had pointed out all the positive aspects to the prospective investment, Jerry had skillfully pointed out all the possible pitfalls, and quite eloquently at that, considering the short amount of time he'd had to prepare his presentation. "But that's what I'm saying, Jerry. If I tell you everything, you might consider it your job to interfere.''

"Meaning you don't trust me to keep a secret?" Jerry asked. "That hurts, Nick! It really does! If you ask me not to say a word, I won't, and you know it!''

In spite of the histrionics Nick could tell that Jerry actually was wounded by his implied accusation. And in point of fact, Nick *did* trust him—up to a point.

One way or the other, he supposed he'd have to let Jerry in on at least part of this. His friend would now consider it his sworn duty to find out what he was up to, and Nick already had one pesky inquisitor in Devin Prescott.

"I'm sorry, Jerry," Nick said. "But when you hear what I have to say, you'll understand why I'm edgy.''

"Apology accepted. Now spill your guts!''

"Eli Wingate is missing.''

"Holy smoke!" Jerry nearly fell out of his chair as he swung his legs off the desk and leaned forward to stare at Nick's face. "Are you sure? I haven't heard anything.''

Nick grinned. "Just because you can gossip almost as well as a woman doesn't mean you're blessed with feminine intuition, as well. Things do happen without your knowledge."

"I resent that remark. I'm as good a gossip as any woman. Most men are. Just ask my wife."

They both laughed, easing the tension in the room. Still, Nick told him, "This can't leak out, Jerry. Not around here, especially. In fact, not even the people at Wingate know about it, except for a few members of the immediate family."

"Don't worry," Jerry assured him. "I have stock options too, you know. And seeing as how your father has been known to shoot the messenger on occasion, I have no desire to be the bearer of bad tidings, either—too many payments left on my Porsche to risk that. Now, I think you'd better tell all, my friend."

Nick had no intention of doing that. Having a best friend like Jerry was something akin to having a second mother, and an overly protective one at that. But he did fill him in on the recent events, knowing he would keep this confidence to himself.

Jerry sat up straight now, all business. He muttered a curse under his breath. "I didn't exaggerate one bit about the pitfalls to this investment, Nick, and your old man is still chafing about being overruled. He made his money by investing in safe, steady, well-established companies and solid real estate. A venture capitalist he's not, nor will he ever be. And he'll never admit that he hasn't lost money because of the tax breaks involved in this limited partnership."

"Isn't that the truth. Dad's never going to change. He still hasn't gotten over my starting the security consulting division, either. It even galls him to see it making money."

"As your accountant, the more you make the happier I am. But as your friend," Jerry said, "I'm not too thrilled with your pet project myself. It's too close to that other crap you were involved in."

"That's over, Jerry."

"But you can't resist dipping your hand in, right?"

Nick grinned. "It's not a matter of choice this time. I have to find Eli. You could say it's even poetic justice."

"I suppose. He found you, in a way. Or so I thought."

"Would you stop clucking like a mother hen?" Nick demanded. "And don't worry about my dad, either. If you haven't already figured it out, he likes being unhappy."

"Yeah." Suddenly Jerry grinned like a little kid, raising his red eyebrows repeatedly, his freckled face red from too much sun. "So tell me, what's this Devin Prescott like? Is she gorgeous?"

Nick laughed. "Dad's not the only one who'll never change. Devin isn't gorgeous, exactly, but there's something about her I like. She's very direct."

"Does she work at Wingate?"

"No, she's a concert violinist." The price for Jerry's help was answering personal questions, but it was worth it. Right now he needed certain information fast, and Jerry had the skills to locate it for him. "Remember that, should you ever meet her. Violinist. Call her a fiddle player and she's likely to hand you your head."

"Oh, ho! La-di-da, is she?"

"She can be a bit stiff," Nick admitted.

Jerry shook his head and chuckled. "You always did have strange taste in women. But then, you've also never been able to resist a challenge, have you?" A soft beep sounded from the watch on Jerry's wrist and he pressed one of its myriad buttons, stopping the noise. "That's to remind me that I have a meeting in ten minutes. Now, what exactly do you want from me?"

"Do you still have the data you compiled on the bio-tech firm comparisons?" Nick asked him. He nodded. "Does it include any newer start-up companies?"

"Some, but not that many. Why?"

"I need a list of companies working on projects similar to Eli's. Focus on the newer start-ups to begin with."

"Why?" Jerry repeated bluntly.

"Just a hunch. According to Myrtle, some of Eli's papers have been misplaced lately. If someone is selling information belonging to Wingate, I think that's who'd be buying it, thereby saving themselves years of research and a ton of money. If we can find the firm, we might find Eli."

Jerry shrugged. "It could be an established company, too. The pilfering of data to get ahead faster is a standard way of doing business for many firms," he pointed out. Then he uttered a short, curt laugh. "Hah! What am I saying? You know all about that. In fact, why don't you just get in touch with some of your old buddies and find out who's in the market?"

"That's a myth, Jerry. There's nothing even resembling a network in that business," Nick informed him. "If there was, don't you think I would have plugged into it rather than come here and put up with your sneaky third degree?"

"Excuse me?"

"I already told you those days are over. Now, are you going to help me or torture me?"

"Take it easy! I'll begin with the start-ups as per your request," Jerry assured him. "Anything else?"

Nick took a sheaf of papers out of his inner suit-coat pocket and handed them to him. "Check into these job offers, see if they're still open."

"You're just full of happy news, aren't you?" Jerry muttered, glancing at each page. "This is not a good sign. But it should be interesting." He looked up at Nick. "Find any counteroffers by Wingate?"

"No."

Jerry shuffled the papers, frowning. "Definitely not good, but I'll see what I can find out."

"Thanks." Nick stood up. "I'll keep you informed."

"You'd better, or I just might start gossiping about you and a certain fiddle player."

"Yes, indeed," Nick said. "I really will have to introduce you to her. You'd look great in a body cast."

Nick left Jerry's office smiling, as he usually did. After informing his secretary that he'd be gone for the day he headed for Devin's place. She wasn't in the phone book but Myrtle had been happy to give him her address.

Devin's apartment complex was exactly what he had expected, older but well maintained and on a quiet back street. Through her closed front door he heard the faint sounds of violin music. At anyone else's home he would have assumed it was a recording, but in this case he couldn't be sure. If it was Devin practicing, there was no doubt she'd entered the right profession. The music was sweet, clean and played with such assurance that Nick couldn't help listening a moment longer. Finally he pressed the doorbell, then stood right in front of the peephole, smiling.

"My, my. What a surprise," she said, opening the door wide to let him enter. The sleeves of his light blue shirt were cuffed up on his forearms again, and caramel dress slacks hugged his hips. That shade of blue looked good on him with his light brown hair. "It's Nick, the intrepid sleuth."

Nick stepped inside. "Sarcasm becomes you, Devin. How lucky you are that I'm around for you to use it on."

"Oh, yes. Lucky me."

While she closed the door he looked around curiously. To his left, a carved Oriental coffee table held center attention, a modern cushy sofa behind it against the wall, with a big antique rocking chair beside it. Doors leading to the bedroom and bathroom were beyond that.

To his right, overflowing bookshelves flanked a tall armoire that housed her television and stereo. The armoire was painted the color of desert sand, with zebras, lions, giraffes, elephants and birds meeting around a pool of blue water.

In the dining alcove the only piece of furniture was an ornate, claw-footed buffet set against the far wall. On top, a case lined in gold crushed velvet lay open. Nearby, a highly polished wooden violin sat on a silver stand, a sheet-music holder beside it.

"So that was you playing. It sounded very nice."

"Thank you." Devin accepted the compliment with a graceful nod of her head as she moved past him. "It should. I practice everyday. To what do I owe the interruption?"

"Sorry. But I thought you'd want to know what I've found out so far," Nick replied. He watched her as she crossed the room. Her silky peach T-shirt was tucked into off-white slacks, a multicolored scarf wrapped around her waist serving as a belt. Tiny gold heart-shaped earrings were her only jewelry. "The premium on that million-dollar life insurance policy is paid up."

Devin picked up her violin and glanced at him, her eyes wide. "That *is* worth an interruption."

She carefully put the violin into the case and snapped the locks shut. With case in hand she knelt in front of the buffet and slid a wooden door aside. After putting the instrument away she closed the door and stood to face him, her attention now completely on the matter at hand.

"I'd say we need to find out who and where this Yvette Soomes is. Do you agree?" Devin asked him.

He nodded. "I do. I'm hoping that Eli keeps a personal address book that will have a current listing on her."

"He does, and I hope so, too," she said. "Of course, we'll have to find it first."

"I was afraid you were going to say that."

"Give me a few minutes to get ready."

By TAKING THE BACK streets they were at Eli's in five minutes. Devin turned her key in the front lock and slowly eased the door open, ready to stop the cats if needed.

Jekyll and Hyde did race up to greet them, but then they immediately turned and ran down the hallway, stopping at the closed door to Eli's office. They pranced back and forth in front of it, meowing loudly. When that wasn't enough to get Devin to follow them, both cats ran back up to her and Nick, talking all the way, seemingly scolding the two humans for their inattention.

"What's wrong with them?" Nick asked. Their constant, wavering yowls sounded remarkably like a pair of babies crying. "Did the neighbors put catnip in their kibble?"

"I'm not sure." Devin watched them repeat their run up and down the hallway twice more. Suddenly she smiled. "Eli must be home! He never lets them in that room."

Devin hurried out of the foyer and down the dark hall. Jekyll and Hyde were ecstatic. But Nick wasn't. He went after her, an uneasy feeling plaguing him.

"Devin, wait," Nick ordered.

She ignored him. Twisting the knob of the office door she stepped inside before he could stop her. "Eli! It's about time— What are you doing in the dark?"

Devin reached for the light switch. She never made it. The shadowy figure beside the door grabbed her hand and pulled. She slipped to the floor with a thud, screaming all the way.

Chapter Seven

"Devin!"

Nick raced in after her and found himself being shoved sideways by strong hands. He struggled to stay upright but lost his footing, slipping on the slick magazines that had been tossed all over the office floor. The unseen hands pushed him again. It was a losing battle. Floundering, he toppled over, falling on top of a pile of papers not far from where Devin lay. Another pile tumbled down with him, covering them both.

The shadow was slipping out the door. Nick rolled over and made a slithering dive for him, but missed and ended up facedown on the carpet in the open doorway. He groaned.

So did Devin. "You okay?" he asked, finally pulling himself into a standing position by using the doorknob.

"I'm fine," Devin muttered. She sat up, rubbing her left elbow. "Don't just stand there! Get him!"

The sound of a door slamming echoed through the quiet house and Nick took off. He ran down the hallway, through the living room, dining room and into the kitchen. Flinging the back door open, he ran outside as a white car roared down the alley away from him.

"Dammit!" He'd been too late to see the license plate number and from the back all new cars looked the same to him. Disgusted, Nick checked the back door for signs of forced entry, but didn't find any.

Near the kitchen and dining-room juncture he crouched down to look at the alarm system. The orange lights were off, indicating that the system had somehow been disarmed. No, not just disarmed. Tripped and then disarmed. This guy was bold, fast and either better than Nick had been in his glory days or in possession of inside information on Eli's clever design. Maybe even both.

"Who are you and what do you want?" Nick wondered aloud as he went back to the office. The lights were on now and he'd expected to find Devin waiting for him there, but the room was empty. A total disaster area, but empty. Where was she? Had there been more than one intruder?

"Devin?" he yelled. "Devin! Where are you?"

She poked her head out of the middle bedroom, the big orange cat in her arms. "Calm down, I'll be right there."

Carefully she placed the cat on the bed and took one last look at the alarm system identical to her own. This system had been overridden just like hers. Perhaps it was time she told Nick about the break-in at her apartment.

Then again, why tell the story twice? He'd learn of it soon enough, when the police arrived. Devin turned on the hallway lights and went to join Nick. Bruises were already forming on her wrist where the man had grabbed hold of her to fling her aside, and she massaged them gently.

"Are you hurt?" Nick asked, standing in the doorway of the office.

"No, but this room sure is."

She and Nick surveyed the damage. There weren't any pathways to the desk now. Every stack of magazines had been pushed over, creating a solid, knee-high sea of paper. Books from the shelves were flung everywhere, their colorful covers perched like little boats dotting endless waves.

"Messy burglar," Devin murmured.

Nick looked at her. "Did you get a look at him?"

"Barely." Devin leaned against the wall. "He has dark hair, is taller than me and was wearing gloves. Lot of help that is."

"It's more than I saw," Nick commented sheepishly.

She moved past him toward the living room. "I'll go call the police."

"No."

The sharpness of his tone made her turn and stare at him. "Why not?"

"For all the same reasons as before. What if Eli is just on vacation?"

"You don't believe that any more than I do."

"No," he admitted. "I don't. But what we believe and what we know are two different things. Until we have proof—"

"That doesn't matter now. A crime has been committed. Someone broke into Eli's home and he could come back."

Nick sighed. "If he didn't find what he was after, calling the police won't stop him from trying again."

She stared at him, puzzled. "You say that with such conviction."

"Devin," he began, speaking softly, "all I'm trying to do is make sure that whatever we do, it's the best thing for Eli in the long run."

"For Eli, is it?" She crossed her arms under her breasts. "And what about your reputation with your family?"

The stubborn set to her chin told him he wasn't getting through to her. "Okay. Let's say we do it your way. What do we tell the police?" Nick asked.

"The whole story, of course!"

"They'll want to know why we haven't reported Eli as missing yet, and saying he's an eccentric who takes off whenever he feels like it won't make our case top priority, now, will it?"

"I suppose not," she admitted. "But this—"

"This?" he interrupted, pointing at the office. "You said the guy was wearing gloves, so there won't be any fingerprints. What are they going to find here, besides a very messy room?" Nick arched his eyebrows. "A room they'll want to sort through and catalog, I might add."

"I hadn't thought of that," Devin muttered.

"And are you going to tell them about Yvette Soomes, too?" Nick continued. "It's the best lead we have, and they'd think so, too. They'll go and talk to her. When they get through, she might not be in the mood to even speak to us, let alone tell us anything useful."

Devin wasn't so sure they could do any good with Yvette Soomes in any case. But Nick had made one point she couldn't ignore. As strange as Eli could be, she knew he wouldn't want the contents of that room revealed to the general public. And it would show up in the police report, along with the fact that he was missing. Jay and Richard would be furious, and so would Eli—if he was in any condition to care, that is.

She still had the feeling something was terribly wrong. But what if her instincts were off this time? The two break-ins were connected somehow, she was sure, but they might pertain to the sludge project or Wingate in general and not Eli in particular.

And what if Eli really had just taken off to be alone? Was she overreacting? More to the point, was she willing to jeopardize what Eli lived for, his work?

Devin shook her head and groaned. "Oh, no. Something's wrong here, Nick. You're starting to make sense."

Finally. "Maybe it's because I'm right."

"Maybe." Whoever had overridden the alarm system was not your everyday petty thief, and other than this room being a mess there wasn't any evidence of a break-in. Calling the police now would only cost precious time, and maybe even get them a stern warning to stay out of the way. That she would never agree to. Devin sighed. "Okay. I don't like it, but for now we'll do it your way."

"Thank you." He rubbed his hands together with mock enthusiasm. "Okay, let's dig into this disaster and find that address book. Do you know what it looks like?"

"Yes, its the size of a credit card and covered in black leather."

Nick made a face as he looked at the sea of magazines. "Great, like looking for a needle in a haystack."

"I didn't see it in here yesterday. I'm going to check his bedroom first." Devin walked past him and went back into the second bedroom.

A minute later she came back carrying a small, black leather book, a gold pen sticking out of the top. "Saved!" she exclaimed triumphantly. "And this is interesting."

"What?"

"The pen was inserted between these pages." She held the tiny book open for him to see. "Yvette Soomes. I'm going to call these phone numbers, see what I can find out.''

Nick followed her slowly into the kitchen. With a good set of picks the lock on the office door could be opened in seconds by any run-of-the-mill burglar. But the alarm was another matter, even for a skilled man with inside knowledge of the unique system.

Was this industrial espionage? Nick was predisposed to believe it, but that didn't make it so. And if it was, it still didn't necessarily mean there was a connection to Eli's disappearance. The inside-information angle was another big problem, mainly because it expanded the range of possibilities. Anyone who knew Eli knew his interests had never been confined to one subject. The thief could have been after any number of things. But what?

Devin was already on the phone when Nick joined her. ''Personnel, please,'' she said. ''I need a verification of employment. Yvette Soomes. Yes, I'll hold.''

Nick grinned at her. This unusual woman had a few tricks of her own, evidently. That intrigued him. *Devin* intrigued him. She was sitting on a stool in front of the kitchen counter, the gold pen in her hand. Nearby both Siamese cats were sprawled out beneath dining-room chairs, watching her while they cleaned themselves.

''Yes, I'm still here. No, no, I don't need to speak with her,'' Devin said in a soothing tone. ''All I need is verification that she is employed by NHS, and what her classification is. Yes, thank you.'' She placed her hand over the bottom of the receiver. ''I think the business world would come to a screeching halt if it wasn't for hold.''

''Probably,'' Nick agreed.

Devin held up her hand. "Yes, I'm here." She jotted something on a scratch pad. "I see. Can you also give me your address there, please?" she asked politely. "Thank you, you've been quite helpful."

Devin set the receiver in its cradle, then looked over at Nick, who had taken a seat on a stool at the end of the counter. "Yvette Soomes is a scientist for a company on the outskirts of Los Angeles, California."

"And the other number?"

She punched in the same area code and a string of digits. On the second ring an answering machine came on and Devin held the receiver out between them so Nick could also hear.

"Leave your name, phone number, today's date and the time you called. I'll get back to you eventually."

"Well, she's brief and to the point, not unlike Eli," Devin said, hanging the receiver up on the wall base. "I wonder what else they have in common?"

"Only one way to find out." Nick glanced at the address she'd written down. "Want to go to California?"

"Go there!" Devin stared at him. "We can't do that!"

Nick chuckled at her stunned expression. He'd figured that would be her reaction. He was quite sure the idea of just picking up and going anywhere on a moment's notice was totally alien to her. If so, the rest of his plan would probably send her into a conservative tizzy.

"Of course we can," he assured her. "In fact, I'd say we have to. It's the only way we'll be sure."

"Why don't we just call her?"

"Because if she does have anything to do with Eli's sudden disappearance a phone call might spook her. And besides, you miss so much when you can't see how a person reacts to your questions." Devin wasn't convinced. "What do we say on the phone?" he asked. "Sorry to bother you, but we can't find Eli Wingate. Have you seen him? Oh, and by the way, what is your connection to Eli? Why is he leaving you a million dollars when he dies?''

Devin grimaced and held up her hands to stop him. ''All right, you made your point. But we can't really come right out and ask her those things face-to-face, either.''

''No. I don't know how we should play it, but we'll have time to think on the way out. Let me have your seat.'' Devin stood and Nick took her place on the stool by the phone before punching in a number. ''You're going to love this.''

Devin eyed him warily. ''Who are you calling?''

''A friend of mine. He only uses his plane on weekends.'' Her eyes widened and her lips parted slightly in reaction to his words. Nick smiled. ''Don't worry, I've borrowed it before, and I have a pilot's license.''

She was shaking her head. ''No. If we have to go, then we'll go, but not in a private plane.'' And certainly not with an enigma like you at the helm, she added silently.

''Anything else would be too much trouble.'' There wasn't an answer at the first number, so he hung up and dialed another. ''This way, we can be back here before nightfall, depending on what we run into.''

Run into? ''I wish you hadn't used those particular words. No, I don't think so, Nick.''

''Trust me.''

''Trust you! I don't even know you!''

Nick grinned. ''We can remedy that situation,'' he assured her. ''It's your choice, Devin, because I'm going, with or without you.''

Chapter Eight

Franklin Delano slouched down lower in the front seat of his rental car, cursing his luck, the heat and this whole convoluted situation. He may not have brought much honor to the memory of his namesake over the years, but at least he had always been good at the dirty games he played. This job, however, was going so badly he was tempted to call it quits and retire to Tahiti.

He was parked between two other cars in the quiet apartment complex lot, waiting for Devin Prescott and her friend to come out. Sweat was dripping down the sides of his face, his clothes sticking to his body whenever he moved. At only eleven in the morning the temperature had already topped one hundred. It was probably one hundred and twenty in his car, even with the windows open.

But Frank supposed he should count himself lucky. If he hadn't had a flat tire on the way there, they would have caught him inside. And if they had caught him at Devin's just after nearly catching him at Eli's, he'd have booked that flight to Tahiti.

What he needed was air-conditioning, but running his car engine would draw too much attention. Whatever those two were doing in there, he wished they'd hurry.

Inside that apartment was an oasis of cool air, and plenty of ice-cold water. The thought made him even more uncomfortable.

No doubt about it, he was getting too old for this kind of thing. When he'd started out, stealing was simple, easy work for an intelligent person. Nowadays you practically had to have a degree in computers to acquire anything worth the risks. Just staying up with the constantly changing technology was a never-ending challenge, only he didn't enjoy the challenge as much as he used to. The money was better than ever, but he'd made plenty through the years and wasn't desperate for more. Why he kept doing this he didn't know.

Frank tensed and slipped lower on the car seat when he saw the apartment door opening. Peering over the edge of the dashboard, he watched as an auburn-haired woman locked the door while a tall, light-brown-haired man looked on.

When they drove away, Frank got out of his car, pulling his wet shirt away from his chest as he walked to her front door. Getting inside her place was child's play for him now, but after disarming the alarm he spent a moment studying and admiring the system. It really was ingenious. Without inside knowledge, bypassing it would be close to impossible. Lucky for him he had that information.

Slowly he pushed himself up to a standing position beside the claw-footed buffet. The arthritis in his knees was acting up again, his bones creaking more loudly than usual. According to his doctor the dry desert climate was supposed to be good for his condition, but he sure hadn't felt any improvement since he'd been in town.

Between the dust, the heat and this job, all he'd felt was frustrated and thirsty. The kitchen sink, only a few feet away, would take care of one of his problems. With his gloved hand he turned the water on low, and drank greedily from the faucet until he had his fill.

"Now get to work, you lazy old hound dog!"

He went back to the buffet, pulled open a drawer and looked inside. It was filled to the brim with sheet music, as were the three other drawers.

Frank groaned. "Great! It couldn't be normal stuff, like silverware, could it?" he groused, grabbing a thick sheaf of the black-lined paper. "I'll be here forever!"

Page by single page he went through the stacks of sheet music. An hour later he was working on the bookshelves, thumbing through each book slowly, then shaking it to see what fell out. Next he went into the bedroom, continuing to work methodically until he had been through the entire apartment. On his way out he was his usual courteous self, making sure the door was locked behind him, but his temper was as hot as the asphalt beneath his feet.

Not far from the apartment complex he found a relatively quiet pay phone and made a call, leaving a message along with the number. If she didn't call back within five minutes he'd be long gone. He was already sweating profusely again.

As if on cue, the phone rang just as he'd been ready to return to his car. Without preamble he spoke. "No luck."

"I am getting sick and tired of hearing that." Her voice, sharp and cutting, came through the long-distance line clearly. "Try again. And do it right this time."

Frank shrugged. "It's your money, but I'm telling you it's not in any of the places I've already looked. Doing it over and over isn't going to make anything appear."

"Then find a new place to look. I want the missing piece to that formulation and if you want the rest of your money you'll get it for me."

Frank quickly dropped the pay phone receiver into its cradle before she could slam hers down in his ear as she always did. He wasn't any happier with this situation than she was. First the scientist, now those papers. In a way, though, this latest failure had actually rekindled his desire to succeed. The notes were becoming like the Holy Grail to him, his pot of gold at the end of the rainbow.

But it wasn't just the money anymore, it was the fear of defeat. A double defeat. The woman he could deal with. But the others would deal with *him*. Harshly.

For the time being, though, they were merely upset, and would still come in quite handy. Frank smiled. There were other places to search. Less likely locations perhaps, but they were possibilities. He dialed another number, this time waiting until someone answered.

THE SMALL CONFERENCE ROOM at NHS headquarters in California was simply furnished with a round white table and four bright blue cushioned chairs. No Smoking signs were the only art on the bold blue-and-white-striped wallpaper.

Devin sat calmly at the table, watching Nick as he prowled restlessly around the room while they waited for Yvette Soomes to show up. A tweed silk blazer hugged his broad shoulders, the tie he'd had in the back seat of his car blending perfectly with the caramel-colored slacks.

There were two doors into the room, and he stopped at the one marked Not An Exit. It was almost directly behind her and Devin turned her padded chair around to get a better look at what Nick was doing.

He was hunched down before the odd, smooth, silver doorknob, studying it. She watched as his fingers curled around the knob, then slowly he turned it to his right and pulled. Nothing happened. He then twisted it to his left and pulled again. It didn't budge, and he stepped away from the door with a wide grin on his face.

"Clever," Nick murmured, looking at Devin. They'd stopped at her apartment before leaving town, and over her peach top she'd put on a bone white jacket that matched her slacks. The same curved gold necklace she'd worn at their first meeting added a finishing, classy touch to her outfit. "The door's locked, and no keyhole. They don't trust us."

"All visitors, or just us, I wonder? Nick, you don't suppose..." Her voice trailed off as the door he'd just tried to open swung their way.

A tall, slender woman entered the room and closed the door behind her. Her light blond hair was cut short in layers, with the front swept back from her forehead and possessing a two-inch-wide streak of white. High cheekbones were prominent in her long pale face, her skillful makeup hiding all but a few age lines at the corners of her large brown eyes. She was wearing a knee-length white lab coat over baggy green slacks and top.

"You wanted to see me?"

Nick stepped forward and held out his hand. "Nick Lang." Yvette shook his hand. "And this is Devin Prescott," Nick said, introducing her.

Yvette nodded at Devin, who had risen from her seat at the table. "Ms. Prescott," she said, then stuck her hands into the pockets of her lab coat. "What's this all about?"

"We're here on behalf of Wingate," Devin explained. The other woman remained standing, all business. Devin did the same. "The company is planning a testimonial dinner for Eli Wingate. They'd like you to be one of the guest speakers."

Her expression didn't change. "I see," she said.

Devin smiled, hoping for some kind of reaction out of the woman besides calm nothingness. "It's a surprise for Eli. He's such a dear man," she continued. The other woman neither agreed nor disagreed. Devin tried again. "As well as a top-notch scientist, of course."

"Of course," Yvette said.

She was studying Devin intently now, with bright, intelligent eyes, but there was still no emotion apparent on her face. Though it wasn't easy, Devin kept smiling. It suddenly seemed very close in the small room.

Quietly Nick stepped back to stand near her, in an attempt to save her from the woman's scrutiny. For once, cool, direct Devin seemed at a loss, and he didn't blame her. She'd met her match in Yvette Soomes. Then again, if this was Yvette's normal personality, she probably didn't get invited to many parties, so perhaps that accounted for her odd behavior.

In a way, though, her behavior was also a revelation in itself. He'd seen robots with more warmth, which led him to believe this had to be an act—or a total shutdown of emotion. But why? Was it because of them and some threat she perceived in their presence, or simply the mention of Eli's name? One way or the other, Nick felt she definitely knew Eli Wingate as more than a peer, but their connection was a puzzler.

At last the uncomfortable moment passed and Yvette shifted her gaze from Devin to Nick and back again. "Unless Wingate has taken another bite out of the industry, you two certainly came a long way to make a simple invitation. Why didn't you just call me from Phoenix?'' she asked.

Devin blinked. "Well..."

"We were already in Los Angeles on other business," Nick inserted smoothly. He placed his hands lightly on the back of a chair. "Since we were so close it only seemed appropriate to ask you in person. If you would, we'd also like to request that you keep this quiet until everything is arranged. We do want it to be a surprise for him."

"All right," Yvette told them with a nod of her head. Her eyes narrowed slightly. It was the most animation they'd seen from her. "As for my attending, though... When is it going to be?"

"The third weekend in September," Devin replied. She knew from Eli's previous travels that September tended to be a free month for him and other scientists.

"I'm sorry, but I won't be available at that time."

Devin was growing tired of playing cat and mouse. Any response, even frustration or anger, would be preferable to this. "I know you're a busy woman, Ms. Soomes, but it would only be for one evening, after all. Couldn't you at least consider trying to change your plans and attend?" she asked, then decided to press even more. "For Eli's sake?"

Nick covertly touched Devin on the back, not as a warning, but to urge her onward. He was watching the way Yvette's hands, stuck deep in the pockets of her lab coat, clenched and unclenched unconsciously every time Eli's name was mentioned. Her face, meanwhile, remained a study in indifference.

"Yes," Nick said. "Think of Eli."

The woman shook her head, curtly this time. "No. I'm sorry. My plans can't be changed."

Like Nick, Devin saw a chink in the armor. Yvette's voice held hints of agitation now, and she took advantage of it. "I know Eli would want you there. Are you positive it can't be arranged?"

"Yes!" The harshness of her own voice made Yvette pause for a moment to regain her composure. When she was once again the perfect picture of an icy Nordic queen, she added softly, "I'm very positive. Now, if you'll excuse me, I must be getting back to my lab."

Yvette's cool facade had shown signs of melting, but it had just as quickly refrozen. What was she hiding? "I hope you're not reluctant to attend because your research is so similar to Eli's," Nick said. "We have every intention of making this a festive occasion. Shoptalk will be held to a minimum. Wouldn't you like to get together with old friends and have a good time?"

"Please!" Clearly on the verge of losing control again, Yvette turned away from them and placed a hand on the knob of the door through which she had entered. For her, the knob turned. "I don't wish to be rude, but I really do have urgent work to do." She opened the door. "Your exit is through the other door. Good day."

Devin waited until Yvette was out of the room before speaking. "Interesting."

"Very," Nick agreed.

"Did she seem—"

Nick held up his hand to cut her off. He walked over to the door Yvette had exited through and tried to open it as she had. It wouldn't budge. "Keyed to fingerprints," he told Devin softly. "Deceptively simple but very high tech, like the lady herself, I'll bet. Let's get out of here."

Once out of the building and back on the highway in their borrowed car, Devin completed the question she had started to ask Nick earlier. "Did Yvette seem hostile to you at the end?"

"Quite. I got the impression she would have cheerfully wrung our necks if we mentioned Eli's name one more time." Nick paused as he changed lanes in the heavy traffic. Then he added, "Good move, by the way. If you hadn't gone on the offensive, she wouldn't have let even that much show."

"The question is, what set her off? She's an attractive woman. Maybe Eli dumped her and wasn't nice about it."

He glanced at her. "Eli?"

"You're right," Devin admitted with a sigh. "He's the only man I know who remains friends with all his ex-lovers, and he has plenty of them." Devin cringed. Without thinking she'd revealed another family secret to Nick. By the way he was smiling, though, perhaps it wasn't such a secret to him, after all. "Yvette's animosity *must* be work related. Eli probably beat her to some kind of patent or breakthrough."

"Maybe." Nick slowed down to take the exit for the small airport where he'd landed his friend's plane. "Whatever it was, Eli evidently feels he owes her a million dollars to make up for it. That's quite a business debt, don't you think?"

"Still, it is possible," Devin said. "The scientific field is like any other as far as women gaining advancement is concerned. We have to work harder and be better to get the same promotions. A small setback early on could have delayed the progress of Yvette's career for years."

"Are you speaking from personal experience?" Nick asked.

"Mine, Yvette's, my mother's and probably yours, too. It's the same for all women." Devin shifted in her seat. Nick was quite good at turning the slant of a general discussion to personal matters. In fact, she was sure he was quite good at a whole bunch of things he hadn't owned up to yet. "Now," she continued, returning to the original subject. "What we have to figure out is what her grievance against Eli is."

"Any ideas?"

"Well, it did seem to upset her when you used that prod about her research and Eli's being so similar," Devin replied. "I wonder if that might be the key."

"It's possible. I know that the two companies are working in related directions. I have a friend looking into the specifics," Nick told her.

Devin arched her eyebrows. "A trustworthy friend, I hope."

"To a point. And I only gave him enough leash to take him to that point."

"How sly of you," she said. "Why do I get the feeling this is a game you've played before?"

"I told you I was a fast learner."

"Sure you are." Devin didn't believe his innocent routine for an instant. Her curiosity was growing by the hour. But the mere fact that he could bend the truth so smoothly made it an itch she couldn't scratch. "Okay. I think Eli and Yvette have more in common than their profession, but for now that's all we have, so let's go with it. What I do know for sure is that for Yvette to have gained the title and position she enjoys, she's had to publish a certain amount of her work."

"Then one of Eli's scientific journals will have her work detailed in it," Nick said. Then he frowned as he remembered the condition of Eli's office.

Devin noticed his expression and laughed. "Relax," she told him. "I know an easier way to find out her specialty."

"How?"

"You'll know soon enough," she replied, enjoying the act of frustrating his curiosity for a change. "I'm a fast learner, too, you know. And I can play my cards as close to my vest as you can."

Nick parked the car near a small hangar where they'd found it and got out, leaving the keys inside. "I liked it better when you were direct and open."

"Tough." Devin grinned broadly, thoroughly enjoying herself for perhaps the first time since this mess started. "We should also talk to Eli's assistants at Wingate," she said as they walked across a gravel parking lot to the one-room airport office. "They should know exactly what Eli's been working on recently."

"Good idea. We'll head for Wingate when we get back to town. We can check with Myrtle, too. But first," Nick said, holding the office door open, "let's tell the manager of this place his car is back safely. With the rates he charged us I'm tempted not to, but he'd probably call out the air police to hunt us down if we don't."

"That's the price you pay for desperation," Devin told him, laughing at Nick's indignant tone of voice. "And for dealing with these little fly-by-night operations instead of a real airport with real planes and real car-rental services."

"Admit it, Devin. You kind of like flying in a private plane, don't you? On a real plane, as you put it, they don't let you pester the pilot."

"Very funny. Just make sure there's a barf bag on board for the flight back," she returned. "Or I might have to show you how much of a pest I can really be."

Chapter Nine

Devin's threat aside, the air-sickness bag remained unused and the flight back to Phoenix was uneventful. She wasn't sure if Nick could necessarily take credit for the smooth ride, but he did seem to be an accomplished pilot. Not that she would ever tell him so, of course. He might decide she actually liked flying in a noisy little tin can and expect her to do it again.

As a mode of transportation, however, she had to admit it was fairly fast and convenient, which was more than could be said for driving a car in Phoenix. They encountered the heavy evening rush hour traffic on the freeways, slowing down their return to Wingate considerably.

When they finally entered Myrtle's office it was almost six. She stood up and looked at them expectantly. "Did you find him?"

"No, Myrtle. I'm sorry," Devin said, stopping beside her desk. Myrtle looked so worried and hopeful at the same time that Devin wished she had more to tell her. "But we're working on it."

Myrtle was rubbing her hands nervously. "Together?"

"It seems that way," Devin replied dryly.

"Well, that's just fine! You know, I always think two heads are better than one. What one misses the other catches."

"We're in this together, Myrtle," Nick assured her.

Devin nodded encouragingly when Myrtle looked at her. "And we're doing everything we can to find him."

"I know, child. It's just that I'm..." Myrtle let out a deep sigh and sat back down. "I'm so very worried. This just isn't like Eli. He can be inconsiderate when he's working, but he knows how I worry about him, and ever since that first time he's always let me know where he'll be." Tears glistened in her eyes. "I shouldn't be such a Gloomy Gus. But I think something awful has happened."

Devin patted Myrtle on the shoulder, trying to console her. "Actually, there is something you can do to help if you have the time."

"There is?" Myrtle straightened up. "What?"

Nick looked as puzzled as Myrtle did and Devin surprised herself by winking at him before returning her attention to the older woman. "It's still possible that Eli just took off on one of his little trips, you know. He may even have left the particulars for you on that tape that was erased."

"Devin, you always were a terrible liar," Myrtle told her. "But go on. Speak your mind."

Devin smiled. "If he did leave town, we need to know how. If we can find some sort of paper trail leading us in a definite direction it would be a tremendous help. But," Devin warned her, "finding his starting point will be very time-consuming, since we don't know when he left, where he might have been headed or even what means he would have used."

"Land sakes! Why didn't one of us think of this sooner?" Myrtle pulled a phone book out of her bottom desk drawer. "Don't you worry. I have plenty of time. I'll start with the airlines he usually flies with." She already had the yellow pages open and was scanning the listings. "Don't you two have something better to do, some lead to check out? I'm doing my part."

Nick laughed. "Yes, you are, and you're right—we have lots to do. Let's go, Devin."

They were walking side by side to the main labs when Nick spoke again. "Think you're pretty smart, don't you?"

"As a matter of fact, I *am* smart," Devin told him smugly. "The search will keep Myrtle occupied and she won't fret herself into a tizzy. Besides, it really is a good idea, one we should have thought of before now."

"She's right. You're not much of a liar. The reason we didn't think of it is that neither of us believe it," he said. "But it was nice of you to put on a show for her."

Devin wrapped her arms around her middle. "I was doing it for myself, too. I don't know what to believe. Eli wouldn't have taken off like this unless it was an emergency, but if that was the case we'd know about it. If he'd been kidnapped we'd have a ransom demand by now. The longer he's missing, the more I think that he's met with foul play."

Since he couldn't disagree with her Nick made no comment. At the main lab entrance Devin punched in a code and the doors slid open, allowing them to enter. She quickly led him to Eli's lab area. But it was obvious the trip was useless.

"We're too late," Devin said, standing in the empty room. "Everyone's gone home for the day."

Nick glanced at his watch. "It is after six. We'll have to talk to them tomorrow. Are you hungry?"

"Ravenous. You could have at least provided a bag of those little peanuts for your passenger."

"Sorry. Allow me to make it up to you by inviting you to dinner." He linked his arm through hers and started to lead her back the way they'd come. "How about Chinese?"

As they rounded the corner, however, they found their exit blocked by a pair of beefy, stern-faced young men.

"Excuse me, Ms. Prescott. Mr. Lang," one of them said brusquely. "Would you come with us, please? Mr. Wingate would like to see you."

Devin and Nick looked at each other, then at the two uniformed guards standing in the entrance to the glassed-off lab area. The request was polite enough, but somehow, Nick didn't think it would stay that way if he and Devin refused.

"Do we have a choice?" he asked.

"Not really. Our orders are not to let either of you wander around here by yourselves anymore."

Devin scowled. "That does it! It is time Jay and I had another chat. Come on, Nick."

She started off in the direction of Jay's office. Nick fell in step beside her. The guards escorted them there, saw them inside and then left.

"Have a seat," Jay offered pleasantly from behind his desk as they entered the room. Richard was seated in a chair to their right in front of the desk.

Devin remained where she was, standing beside Nick near the open office door. "Did you tell security Nick and I could no longer come and go as we please?"

Jay managed a small smile. "Even as a child you were direct, always wanting to get right to the heart of the matter."

"The complete opposite of you," Devin returned. "I'm warning you, Jay. I haven't had dinner yet and I'm in no mood for one of your snow jobs. Answer the question."

"We decided it would be best if a guard accompanied you while on company property from now on, yes," he told her, still smiling. "Just a necessary precaution."

"Against what? The truth?"

Nick leaned casually against the doorjamb, rather enjoying the confrontation. It was obvious Devin was trying to needle Jay, and from his pinched expression it was clear she knew all the right buttons to push. They didn't like each other and tonight they weren't bothering to hide it, which could prove very educational.

The two were glaring at each other. Richard spoke up to break the deadlock. "Now, Devin. There's no need for this animosity. Jay and I are simply looking out for company interests, as always."

"What's that supposed to mean?" she demanded.

"It means you've been going places you have no business going," Jay said. "The video monitors showed you two entering the secure area last night. Why?"

Devin's eyes went wide. "I beg your pardon!"

"I said—"

"I know what you said," Devin interrupted. "I just can't believe you said it! Who do you think you are?"

"I'm the president of this company," Jay replied, his jaw clenched in anger. "Wingate has government contracts, Devin, and those people like to think we take them seriously."

"You'd better take *me* seriously," Devin said, stepping closer to his desk. "I told you I was going to find out what happened to Eli and I meant it. Nick is helping me. We were in the lab last night looking for clues as to where he might be. If necessary, we'll go there again, or anywhere else we want!"

"Not without a guard, you won't," Jay informed her.

Richard cleared his throat. "Honestly, Jay. On occasion you have all the tact of a charging rhino." He shot his brother a stern look, then turned to Devin and Nick. "It's kind of you to help, Mr. Lang. How is the search for Eli coming? Did you find anything in his lab?"

"No, we didn't," Nick replied before Devin could open her mouth. Then he stepped farther into the room and stood beside her. "But while we're on the subject of security, I have a bone to pick with you two."

Nick didn't much like the way the two brothers were behaving this evening, either. Judging by the spots of color on Devin's cheekbones, though, she might explode at any moment, and inadvertently divulge more than he wanted them or anyone else to know just yet. It was time for a diversion, and luckily he had one made to order.

"As an investor," Nick continued, reminding them of his position, "I take Wingate's government contracts seriously, as well. And what Devin and I were doing in Eli's lab is secondary to the fact that we were there at all. If you're so concerned about security, I think the first thing you'd better do is take a look at your systems. The code we used to gain entry to the lab is over a week old, and we used the same one again today. How often are they changed?"

The question, and his air of authority, put the pair on the defensive just as Nick planned. Richard was looking at his brother for an answer. Jay had a blank expression on his face. They were both clearly at a loss.

"I don't know," Jay finally admitted. "The security department deals with that aspect of our business."

"Well, gentlemen, I suggest you call the head of that department, give him or her a royal chewing out, and then get the whole crew busy checking *all* your security. Don't you train your people? I had a pass to look around Wingate, but not to enter a secure area, and yet I waltzed right in without a question asked."

"That's only because you were with a member of the immediate family," Jay informed him.

"Members of the family can be bribed," Nick returned. "Or threatened. Last night the guards at your gates didn't even check my pass. What if I'd had a gun aimed at her, forcing her to do whatever I wanted?" He shook his head in disgust. "The one thing Devin and I have discovered is that something strange really is going on around here, so you better get with the program. Eli has better security at his own home and even that was bypassed this morning."

The way Nick's mind worked intrigued—and bothered—Devin no end, but his final announcement truly shocked her. How had he known about Eli's alarm system? She hadn't mentioned it to him. More to the point, his suspicious expertise would have to extend much deeper than a jack-of-all-trades' for him to know that the intruder had bypassed it.

Richard was also shocked by this announcement. He was staring at Nick, mouth agape. "What did you say?"

"Someone broke into Eli's house?" Jay asked.

"Yes. We interrupted him as he was trashing Eli's home office," Nick informed them. "He got away. Neither of us got a good look at him. It could be a coincidence, but I doubt it. I think there's more to your brother's untimely disappearance than meets the eye.''

Jay was outraged. ''Why didn't you call me right away?''

''What good would that have done? Like I said, the guy got away. There are no clues as to what he might have been after. Besides, I thought you were convinced Eli was just taking a little vacation?''

''He still might be,'' Jay said frowning. ''Maybe it was just a burglar.''

''Did you call the police?'' Richard asked.

''We didn't see any reason to,'' Devin told him. ''There was nothing to check out but a messy room, and you know how protective Eli is about the things in his office.''

Jay nodded curtly. ''Good decision, Devin.''

''No telling what kind of publicity that might have generated,'' Richard agreed.

Their obvious relief made Devin both mad and curious. This was different from not reporting Eli missing. An actual crime had been committed. Not calling the police still bothered her and she was surprised it didn't bother Jay and Richard, as well. They were hard-nosed businessmen, not above bending the rules to fit their cause, but as far as she knew they had always been law-abiding.

What was the real reason they were so worried about police involvement? Were they concerned about the company? Or were they actually hiding something?

''You two believe what you want,'' Nick told them. ''All I know is that Wingate seems to have plenty of problems, and you'd better start addressing them. Eli is missing, and I think someone is actively looking for whatever he's been working on. I wouldn't be surprised if they hadn't already managed to get inside Wingate to Eli's work.''

Jay picked up the phone and pressed a button. ''I want you in my office, now!'' He punched another button and yelled a similar demand to someone else, cut the call short by hanging up and then dialed an outside line.

Richard, meanwhile, had gotten quickly to his feet and was busy at the file cabinets in the corner, presumably looking for information on the security personnel at whom Jay would soon be bellowing.

Devin nudged Nick and together they backed out the office door. Jay took no notice. Richard glanced at them but he didn't say anything as they left. Word must have traveled quickly along the Wingate grapevine that a storm was brewing, because two guards picked them up immediately and did a properly conscientious job of escorting them to their car. Even the guard at the gate looked at them suspiciously as they drove past on the way out.

Devin sighed. ''I have the funny feeling we've made our last foray into Eli's lab. Not that it matters much. I'm not sure his assistants would talk openly to us, anyway, but they sure won't with a pair of guards standing by.''

''It won't be easy,'' Nick said. ''But I think something can be arranged on both counts.''

''Oh?'' She arched her eyebrows. ''Now I suppose you're going to tell me you've dabbled in breaking and entering?''

Nick smiled. ''It really has you worried, doesn't it?''

''What?''

''The things I know and how I might have learned them.''

''You bet it worries me,'' Devin replied. ''Just how did you know about Eli's alarm, anyway?''

''He told me about it.''

"Okay. But I can't believe he told you how it works, and even if he did, it would take a scientist to understand the explanation." She frowned. "Or a crook."

"Well, a scientist I'm not. And that system is far above the head of your garden-variety crook," Nick told her.

Devin's eyes widened and she turned in the passenger seat to stare at him. "What are you saying, Nick?"

He was laughing softly. "*I'm* not saying anything. As usual, you're the one doing most of the talking, and all of the jumping to conclusions."

"You're skating on thin ice, buster," she informed him. "I'm hungry, frustrated and more than a little confused. If you don't start giving me some straight answers, I'm going to beat out a pizzicato tempo on your nose!"

To Nick, the threat sounded almost tantalizing. But one glance told him she was serious. Her graceful, long-fingered but very strong-looking hands were clenched into fists and there was an unmistakable fire in her pale blue eyes. Now, he decided, was not the time to tell her how lovely she looked when she was mad.

However, it was time to tell her a few things. Just a few. "All right," he said in a placating tone. "I'll talk. But first I'm going to feed you. You're getting cranky."

"Just drive." She crossed her arms and stared out the windshield. "I want food and I want it fast. But no fast food. And you're buying. Got it?"

He chuckled. "Your wish is my command."

Rather than Chinese, which he didn't think would fill either of their appetites any longer, Nick took her to a Mexican food place he knew of, with great food, fast service and dim lighting. Best of all, the green chili was even hotter than Devin's temper. Ice-cold *cerveza* managed to take the bite out of both, and before long she was actually smiling again.

But her curiosity was still intact. "Well?" she demanded. "Just what are you really, Nick Lang?"

He pushed his plate away. "Oof! Full!"

Devin threw a tortilla chip at him. It was so unlike her that it caught him by surprise and bounced off his chin. The stunned expression on his face made Devin laugh gleefully.

"For one thing, I'm obviously a good influence on you," Nick said. "Another few days with me and you'll loosen up so much your own conductor won't recognize you."

"It's not you, it's the beer," she returned haughtily.

In fact, she was surprised herself at the effect Nick had on her. His loose, easygoing style was infectious. And he wasn't half bad to look at, either.

She brought herself up short on that thought and cursed inwardly. Consuming the first drink on an empty stomach while they waited for their food hadn't been such a smart idea. Odd, though. She didn't really *feel* tipsy. Just happy. That was a strange enough emotion to deal with under the circumstances without delving into its true cause.

Back to business. "You'd better start doing some fast talking," she warned. "Or the hot sauce is next."

Nick didn't doubt it for an instant. "I haven't really been lying to you," he began. "I just haven't told you the whole story. You see, it's my job to know about things like locks, industrial espionage and alarm systems."

"Aha! So you're *not* an investment consultant."

"You jump to so many conclusions it's a wonder you don't have flat feet," Nick remarked. "I am *so* an investment consultant. I help my family research and keep track of the places they put their money—and we do have a lot of money in Wingate. But my main function at Lang these days is as a *security* consultant."

Devin was bewildered. "For your family firm? What do they do that would require security?"

"Everybody needs some protection in this day and age," he replied. "However, my security division is a separate business within the company. I hire out to other firms, help them determine their security needs and advise them on the best method to handle those needs, things like that."

"Well!" Devin exclaimed. "That certainly explains a great deal!" For a moment she felt relief wash over her. Then she frowned again. "Why didn't you tell me before?"

Nick took a sip of his drink before answering. There was still only so much he felt he could say. "I wasn't sure how far your family loyalty extended, that's why. If Jay and Richard knew about my other occupation, they might have spruced up Wingate's security system before I had a chance to check it out." He shook his head. "Good thing I did have the chance. Brother, does it need work!"

Something still didn't quite ring true to Devin, but his explanation did give her some satisfaction. He hadn't told her all this before because he didn't trust her. Now he did. She realized she was coming to trust him, as well.

"Why didn't you tell Jay and Richard what we'd found out so far?" Devin asked.

Nick shrugged. "I don't know. In my line of work you have to be perpetually paranoid. But they were acting sort of strange this evening. I didn't particularly like the way they sicced the guards on us, either."

"Neither did I." Devin leaned back in the booth and sighed. "And I suppose I should tell you that it's not just this evening. Those two have been acting strangely for quite some time."

"Oh?"

"As if we needed one, there's another aspect to this situation you should know about," she said. "Eli doesn't get on well with his brothers. They do fight a lot, and according to my mother they always have."

"About what?" Nick asked.

"You name it. All three are fiercely competitive in their own way. Lately, though, things have been even more strained than usual between them. Tension is high all over Wingate, in fact," Devin informed him. "Eli's dissatisfaction with his brothers and the way they run things is apparent to most at the lab, and he's always been a champion of the underdog. Their latest fight concerned Jay and Richard's decision to dilute employee medical benefits, a move which prompted Eli to say he was quitting, something he'd never done before. They backed down. But Eli meant it."

Nick was gazing at her thoughtfully. "Thanks for confiding in me," he said. She was getting more comfortable with him. That was good. Very good. "As an investor in Wingate, it's information that doesn't exactly thrill me to hear. But it could work in our favor."

"How so?"

"I'm even more inclined now to believe that Jay and Richard aren't being straight with us about what Eli was really working on," Nick said. "If his assistants don't like the way they're running things, they might be more willing to open up to us."

"True," Devin agreed. "But after your little tirade, security will be stout at the labs, so how do you propose we get in to ask them anything?"

He smiled enigmatically. "Don't worry. We'll find a way."

"But—"

"Right now, though," Nick interrupted, "I think we should go home and get our beauty sleep. We will undoubtedly have a busy day tomorrow."

Devin didn't like the sound of that, but she had to admit she was tired. As they left the restaurant she glanced at her watch and was surprised to see it was after nine. They had actually enjoyed a reasonably quiet dinner together. There was a degree of trust building between them she couldn't deny, as well as something else she couldn't quite put her finger on.

Liar, Devin told herself. She wasn't blind. Nick found her attractive and the feeling was mutual. When he pulled into the apartment complex parking lot, a number of things raced through her mind.

Her life, full of music, intense concentration and self-discipline, could also be seen as rigid and barren. Without a doubt there were few opportunities for romance. At this moment in particular, with her uncle missing and that normally peaceful life in turmoil, Devin felt the need for the sort of companionship Nick had been providing.

Perhaps she even felt the need for more than that.

Still, when he switched off the engine, Devin looked at him with suspicion. "You don't have to come in," she said.

Nick ignored her. He walked around the car and opened her door. "I'm going to see you safely inside."

Devin thought about the intruder at Eli's, and the mysterious break-in of her own apartment, and decided to acquiesce. In fact, it was high time she told him about the break-in. Given the profession he had confessed to this evening, she should probably even invite him in to take a look at her own alarm system.

After unlocking her door, she slipped a hand inside and turned on the overhead lights in the living room. "It's been an interesting day, Nick," she said, turning to face him. "At the risk of giving you the wrong idea, I have something I want to show you, as well as a confession of my own to make."

"Do you ever!" Nick was looking over her shoulder into the apartment, a shocked expression on his face.

Devin spun around. "Oh, no! It can't be!"

Chapter Ten

Devin's apartment was a disaster area. Her living-room floor was covered with the entire contents of her bookshelves. The extensive collection of sheet music that had taken her years to compile had been tossed everywhere like confetti, along with the sofa cushions and small pillows from the rocking chair.

"My violins!"

She ran across the living room, trying not to step on books and sheet music in her haste to get to the buffet that housed her most prized possessions. All four of her violin cases were out on top and open. She picked up her favorite, checking it over carefully before stroking the strings.

"He's all right," Devin murmured, hugging the wood against her chest for a moment. These polished pieces of wood were her livelihood, her friends.

Nick shut the front door and watched as she lovingly put the instrument back in its case and picked up another one, then another. "Are they okay?" he asked as she put the last one back into its case.

"Yes." Devin started to turn around but stopped when she saw the condition of her kitchen. Grimly she reached around the doorjamb and flipped the switch for the overhead light.

The cupboard doors were all open, the shelves inside bare, their contents now sitting on the counter or piled on the floor. It was a mess, but nothing appeared damaged or broken. Just thoroughly, completely searched.

"Two break-ins might be a coincidence," Devin muttered, turning back to face Nick. "But not three."

"Three? What are you talking about?" Nick demanded.

"That confession I was going to make." Devin bit her lower lip. "The morning you and I met in Jay's office, I awoke very early, thinking someone was in my apartment. My alarm system—one identical to Eli's—had been disarmed and I called the police, but when they got here and looked around, they found no one."

"Why didn't you tell me this before? Like this morning when we interrupted that guy at Eli's?"

"I was going to, but..." She shrugged. "The first time nothing was disturbed, so I couldn't even be sure the two were connected."

"Give me a break!" Nick advanced into the room, trying not to step on anything. "Your alarm system is the same as Eli's, you knew his had been bypassed, probably by the same person, but you didn't see a connection?" He tossed a pillow up onto the couch to give him more room to pace. "What else haven't you told me?"

Ignoring him, Devin grabbed hold of a piece of wire that was plugged into an outlet near the kitchen. She followed it across the room, going beneath papers, books and another pillow before she found the phone at the other end, near the entrance to the bedroom. The darkness of the room didn't hide the chaos inside, but she wasn't ready to face it yet.

"What are you doing?" Nick asked.

The phone unit in hand, she sat in the rocking chair, which had been haphazardly placed in front of the bedroom door. "Calling the police."

"Why?"

"I don't believe you! Look at this...this...disaster in here! It'll take me days, weeks to get things back in their proper place."

Nick shrugged. "How will calling the cops help that?"

"What's your problem, anyway? You know it's past time we called them. I'm beginning to think you just don't like the police."

"They'll only come in here, poke around and ask a bunch of stupid questions, then forget the whole thing and go have a doughnut somewhere," Nick said sourly. He couldn't help his animosity toward the authorities. It was a normal reaction considering his previous occupation. In his own mind his earlier jobs had always been quasi-legal, but in the minds of the police they weren't. "Worse, they might leave the water even more murky than it is already."

"I don't care what you think," Devin told him, punching in the number with angry jabs. "This is my apartment, and I'm calling the police."

Granted, things were getting out of hand. Nick was surprised by the anger he felt when he looked around, but he still didn't see how calling the police in was going to help the situation any. Professionals didn't leave calling cards unless they were stupid or just plain careless. This one was neither. But he was certainly messy.

"They'll be here soon," Devin informed him, setting the phone down beside the chair. "Don't disturb anything."

Nick resumed pacing in front of the couch, trying to get everything straight in his mind. "Why didn't you tell me about the first break-in right away?"

Devin rocked her chair gently. "Because I didn't think it was any of your business."

And she still wasn't sure it was. She knew from experience that hormones weren't a good gauge to judge someone by and Nick Lang was too easy for her to like. What did she really know about him? There had been a surprisingly sour note in his voice when he talked about the police. A lot of people didn't like them, or were uncomfortable around them, but Devin felt it went deeper than that with Nick. What was he hiding?

"None of my business? Wake up, Devin." Nick yanked off his tie and stuffed it into his coat pocket. "Until now this was all about Eli. But the condition of these rooms means you've been drawn right into the middle of whatever is going on. Not telling me things isn't helping you or Eli."

"Or yourself."

Where was the funny, increasingly agreeable woman he'd had dinner with? He wanted to shake some sense into her, but realized that this was all completely new to Devin. He could hardly expect her to react like a hardened veteran of the industrial espionage wars.

"Devin, either way, I won't lose money on this deal, but Eli is my friend, and he has plenty to lose. You—"

A loud knock on the door interrupted him. "Police," a gruff male voice called out.

"They sure got here quick," Nick muttered.

Devin let them in, and introduced Nick as a friend. The questions were endless, especially since once again, after a thorough inspection with the police by her side, she found nothing missing. She honestly didn't know what the intruder's real motives were, and wasn't sure she'd tell them if she knew. Protecting Eli had to come first.

Nick had carefully avoided as much of the proceedings as he could. After the police left she found him in the kitchen by the phone outlet.

"You have a message on your answering machine." He glanced at her. "Mind if I hear what it is?"

"Go ahead and turn it on."

He pressed a button and the tape rewound before playing the message. "Hi, Devin. This is Jerry, a friend of Nick Lang's. You have a very nice voice. Do you sing, too? I have some answers, so tell Nick to give me a call. Toodles."

Nick looked at his watch. "It's after eleven, and Jerry and his wife are no night owls. We'll have to wait until tomorrow morning to talk to him."

"Fine with me. It's past my bedtime, too."

Nick's thoughts wandered to the condition of her bedroom. The comforter and sheets had been stripped from the bed, her clothing pulled out of the dresser drawers and tossed about, the nightstand overturned. It would be quite a job putting things back into a state where she could even go to bed.

Besides that, there was always the possibility the intruder could come back. "You can't stay here," he said.

The more she looked at the mess in her apartment the more upset she became. Her entire world had been turned upside down, her daily routine thrown completely out of whack. And none of it was her doing. "I don't intend to," she replied, yawning. "I just remembered I have an early-morning appointment tomorrow. I've got to get some sleep."

"There's a spare bedroom at my house. You're welcome to stay with me."

The fluttering of her pulse at his invitation convinced Devin it wasn't a good idea. Maybe a physical attraction did exist between them, but she wasn't ready to add any fuel to what might be a smoldering fire.

"Thanks for the offer, but I'll stay with my grand-mother."

"Isn't it a little late to be disturbing her?"

Devin smiled. "She's the only one I would disturb now. Grandmother is an insomniac. She'll love the company."

"What are you going to tell her?" Nick asked, watch-ing as she bent down and picked up a cushion from the floor.

Walking over to the couch, Devin put the cushion back in position before picking up another one. "Not the truth, certainly. She has a heart condition." Pausing, she thought for a moment. In the quiet of the apartment a soft hum suddenly filled the room. "I'll tell her my air conditioner is broken. That's a serious crisis when tem-peratures are breaking one hundred every day."

"Do you want a ride?"

"No, I'll need my car tomorrow morning, anyway." Devin placed the last of the cushions back on the sofa. "You can go on home. I'm only going to pack an over-night case, then head over there."

Nick pulled the rocking chair farther away from the entrance to the bedroom and sat down. "I'm going to make sure you get there safely. Take your time pack-ing."

"I don't have much choice in either case, I suppose."

She was too tired and disgusted to argue with him. If he wanted to follow her, fine. He'd found her address and could find Grandmother's too, if he wanted.

After Devin left the room he picked up the phone and put it in his lap. The soft muttering curses drifting from the bedroom assured Nick she was well occupied trying to find things. After inspecting the bottom of the phone, he unscrewed one end of the receiver and cocked it toward the overhead light.

To the inexperienced eye nothing looked amiss. The tiny round transmitter fit in as if it was part of the inner workings. Most likely the sole purpose of the first break-in had been to place it there. But why?

He heard Devin drop something in the bathroom. There was no reason to worry her about this now; she was upset enough already. Quickly removing the bug, he twisted the mouthpiece cap back into place. He crushed the bug under his foot. A bit of fine electronic dust wouldn't be noticed amid all the rest of this mess.

"I'm ready," Devin announced, coming back into the room with an overnight case in her hand. Odd, she hadn't heard him talking to anyone, so why was the phone sitting in his lap? "Is something wrong with it?"

Nick bent over and put the phone on the floor. "No, I was just trying to get hold of someone."

"Don't let me keep you from her."

He stood and took the overnight case. "I'm not married and I don't have a steady girlfriend."

"I didn't ask," Devin said, moving past him to the door.

Nick laughed at her perturbed expression. "No, I guess you didn't. Ready?"

"Just a sec." Devin walked back to the phone and picked it up. "I need to give her a quick call first."

Since Nick didn't know where her grandmother lived he stayed within a car length of her at all times. A fiery, independent woman like Devin might just try to lose him.

He liked those sterling qualities in her, just as much as he liked upsetting the routine-loving side of her nature. When she was angry he saw glimpses of the passion she kept so tightly under control. It was undeniably attractive, but he couldn't let it get in the way of the job he had to do. He had a debt to pay.

She pulled into the driveway of a rambling, ranch-style house, got out of the car and waved to Nick as he slowed to a stop near the curb. The porch light was shining like a beacon in the dark. Still, Nick waited until she was safely inside before he drove off.

As Devin locked the front door she heard the shrill whistle of the teakettle, then silence. It wasn't the greeting she'd had in mind. Grandmother was making tea, which meant she was ready for a nice, long chat. Maybe if Devin feigned exhaustion she could go right to bed.

"I'm in here," her grandmother called out.

A lamp near the door was turned on low, casting enough light for her to find her way through the living room to the hallway that led to the bedrooms. Accepting the inevitable, Devin set her overnight case down and went into the kitchen at the back of the house.

Her grandmother was swathed in a high-necked, royal-blue-and-white robe that swirled around her slender figure as she walked over to the kitchen table with a tray.

"I have tea ready for us." With wrinkled, steady hands she poured golden liquid into the two cups, then sat down. "Who's the man who followed you here?"

Devin managed to hide her dismay. But she wasn't all that surprised. Grandmother still had the vision of an eagle, and the curiosity of a cat—especially where matters of the heart were concerned.

Devin sat in the chair across from her. "He's just a friend," she replied.

"You didn't want to spend the night at his place?"

"Grandmother! I barely know him."

Pale blue eyes that matched her own were filled with curiosity. Thick white hair, pulled back into an elegant chignon, flattered her grandmother's classically oval face that was only lightly lined by eighty years of full living. Her cheekbones were dusted with rouge, and lipstick lined her thin lips. Never once had Devin seen Lucinda Wingate without makeup on.

"First date?"

Not quite, Devin thought, but it sounded good, and would be an easy way to explain why she and Nick were going places together. "Yes."

"I want to meet him." Lucinda sipped the steaming tea and set it down. "I like his making sure you got here safely. He has good manners."

Devin picked up the small china cup and held it between her hands. "I may not be going out with him again."

"Don't lie to me, child, or yourself. Your interest in him is obvious to me."

As Lucinda admonished her granddaughter with a thin, narrow index finger, the heavy gold and diamond rings on the others slipped sideways, clinking softly. "All right, I probably will see him again, but that doesn't mean you're going to meet him," Devin told her firmly.

Her grandmother acted as if she hadn't heard. "How did you two meet?" she asked. Devin's strong character had always been a source of pride for her. It was a trait they shared, along with the pale blue eyes and the gloriously rich auburn hair that had been Lucinda's color when younger.

Devin didn't bother trying to hide her impatience. It was too late for this third degree. Maybe she should have gone to her mother's; the inquisition couldn't be any worse. "We met at Wingate," she answered around a showy yawn.

"Oh? Does he work there?"

Devin sighed. "No, he doesn't. His name is Nick Lang and he's a friend of Eli's. He works for Lang Inc., a family company, but I don't know what he does there. We went to dinner, had some Mexican food and then he drove me home, which was when I found out about my air conditioner. And no, I didn't invite him into my apartment for more than a cup of coffee. Anything else?"

"Don't take that tone with me, young lady," Lucinda returned sharply. "And sit up straight!"

Years of training by that voice made her automatically square her shoulders and sit up. "I'm sorry," Devin said, and meant it. "I've had a full day and this is a bit late for me to be talking to anyone."

"Apology accepted." Lucinda sipped her tea. "What you need is a vacation. Jay called to tell me Eli has gone on one. Made it sound like a crime. At times it's hard for me to believe those three boys are all my own flesh and blood."

"They are opposites," Devin commented, ready to change the subject away from herself. Obviously Grandmother wasn't quite ready to let her go to bed yet, so she might as well make the best of it. "Eli does like needling them every chance he gets, too, doesn't he?"

"Oh, my, yes!" Lucinda smiled. "Not that they don't deserve it on occasion. When they were younger, the little scamps used to fight like cats and dogs, always plotting and scheming to put something over on each other. Jay and Richard worked as a team, of course, they had to. Eli was so bright it was the only way they could best him.'' She laughed out loud. ''But he usually got the last word!''

''Oh, really?''

''I remember one time.... It wasn't funny then, of course, but I'll never forget the afternoon he blew them up!''

''Blew them up?'' Devin asked, startled. She'd known they had fought, but wasn't aware the hostilities had gotten quite that vitriolic. ''You're kidding?''

Lucinda shook her head. ''Not a bit. They were in high school at the time. I forget what started it off. There were so many things.'' She paused, thinking. ''Oh, yes. Eli built a telescope from scratch, just got the idea, read a book and made one from a big piece of pipe and heaven knows what else. He was so proud! Won an award at school for it and all. Naturally, Jay and Richard were envious.''

''They didn't break it, did they?'' Devin asked.

''Those two? My word, no. They sold it.''

Devin gasped. ''That's terrible!''

''Yes, indeed,'' Lucinda said. ''Of course, I grounded them for months and made them give Eli the money— even then they tried to keep a broker's fee, if you can imagine.''

''I can.''

''It was a nice telescope, and naturally Jay and Richard had made a real killing on it. So Eli was able to build another, even better one. But with Eli it was always the principle of things that mattered.''

''It still is,'' Devin agreed. ''So he decided to get even, I take it?''

''Well, he said he wanted to teach them a lesson, but he could be just plain mean in those days. Thank the stars he grew out of that so nicely!'' Lucinda exclaimed.

"Anyway, what Eli did was mix up some kind of explosive. I don't know what it was. The whole house smelled awful for days afterward, though, that's for sure."

"I can't believe he used it on them."

"Not literally, of course. Still, it wasn't nice."

Devin could tell her grandmother was trying her best to be stern and disapproving, but couldn't quite manage it. "So what did he do?" she asked.

"Got 'em good, that's what!" Lucinda replied, chuckling. "You see, Jay and Richard came home from school and went to their rooms, as usual. They were grounded, remember, so that was about all they could do, and they let me know how boring it was by flopping down on their beds as noisily as they could. It had become a ritual—I swear they even had it timed so they'd hit the beds at once. Bang!"

"You don't mean..." Devin trailed off and closed her eyes as Uncle Eli's plan became clear to her. "He didn't!"

"I suppose I'll never know what he did for sure. But they both had those heavy brass beds, you know, and evidently Eli had put some of that explosive on each one, at the bottom of the two posts nearest the headboard," Lucinda explained. "That afternoon, when Jay and Richard did their belly flops onto their beds, they got the ride of their lives!"

Devin's eyes popped open. "Oh, no!"

"Oh, yes! I heard the explosions and came running, but it was all over. There was this thick, smelly smoke billowing out of both their rooms, and as it cleared I could see that Richard's bed had flipped all the way over on top of him. He was pinned under it and yelling bloody murder, though neither of them were hurt too badly," Grandmother noted. "But Jay got the worst of it. Eli must have put a bit extra on his bed, because poor Jay had gone flying across the room and ended up in the closet—and let me tell you a teenage boy's closet can be a real horror. Jay won't wear a pair of tennis shoes to this day."

It felt good to laugh after all Devin had been through today. "Oh, Grandmother!" she said at last. "You must have made that up."

"Cross my heart." Lucinda set her empty cup on the tray and stood up. "Well, I'm ready for bed now. Thank you for keeping me company, dear."

"I always enjoy your company, Grandmother."

"Always? Bosh. You were never much of a liar, Devin."

She smiled. "Leave the tray. I'll clean up."

Devin kissed her lightly on the cheek and watched her leave the room. Her heart attack ten months ago hadn't slowed her down much, but it did keep Devin from confiding in her, and that was a shame. She could use her grandmother's levelheaded advice right now.

After quickly cleaning up the kitchen, Devin headed for a bedroom to grab a few hours' sleep. It was too late to cancel her early-morning appointment, and she really didn't want to. Tutoring an eleven year old on the violin was always a constant challenge, and one she enjoyed immensely.

What she wasn't looking forward to was waking up to more of Grandmother's probing questions about Nick. She had to admit, though, that Lucinda had given her food for thought in another area. At the moment those thoughts were hazy, but as she drifted off to sleep, Devin wondered if that story about Eli could help explain the mystery confronting her.

Boys would be boys. But they grew into men, and all too often carried with them their past hatreds and grudges. In fact, Devin was of the opinion that they didn't get more civilized, as much as the means of their revenge simply took on more subtlety.

How far would Jay and Richard go to pull a fast one on Eli? Conversely, just how far might Eli go to make his brothers suffer for their sins?

Chapter Eleven

The university was an excellent setting for private lessons. In the classroom the school provided for them, Devin was gazing out the window at the people passing by, all the while listening carefully to every note the eleven-year-old boy played.

When she'd first been approached to privately tutor a child, she'd hesitated. The demands on her time were already tight. But her friend from high school who was now a social worker had convinced her to at least hear the boy play before making a decision.

At nine years old, the heart and soul that had flowed from Mario's fingers was intoxicating. His playing had been raw and unpolished, of course, just like his little fingers, but his potential had been unmistakable. Her heart had opened for this child, who had auditioned on a borrowed instrument because his mother couldn't afford to buy him one or even provide lessons. Devin provided both, and at times she wasn't too sure whether student or teacher got the most out of their sessions together.

"Again, please," she murmured quietly when Mario came to the end of the passage he'd been playing. "And remember, the signature shifts at measure twelve. You played C-sharp."

Soft, romantic violin strains filled the room as she returned her visual attention to the hot, sunny outdoor scene beyond the window. Concrete pathways were woven through the rocky, naturally landscaped area outside the classroom, a few big cacti the only greenery.

Among the casually clad young people hurrying to their morning classes were two older men in light-colored suits. Startled, Devin leaned closer to the window to get a better look at them as they headed for a nearby entrance. No, she wasn't seeing a desert mirage—it was definitely Jay and Richard. What were they doing at the university?

Devin glanced at her student. "Excuse me, Mario," she said, truly sorry to interrupt his playing. "Would you mind if we quit a few minutes early today?"

He grinned at her mischievously, his big brown eyes barely visible through the thick veil of black hair hanging down across them. "Not a problem." Mario winked at her. "See someone you'd like to know?" he asked.

"Someone I do know, you impertinent thing."

Mario clasped his hands together over his heart. "Tell me it isn't so! I can't bear it!"

Devin had to laugh. She'd given up trying to make him more respectful. The kid was sharp, irrepressible and an incurable flirt. He was serious about his music, but that was about all. She wagged a finger at him, then picked up her purse and headed for the classroom door.

"Same time next week?" she asked.

"Yeah, you can tell me what happened with this hunk you're chasing after then, too."

"You keep your mind on music, and practice. I heard those slips you made," she told him in parting.

Devin left the room and ran as discreetly as she could to the end of the hallway. They'd entered through the doors on her right and hadn't come past the classroom, so that left only one other direction.

Summer school was in session and a few people roamed the hall with her as she made her way toward the center core of the building. She spotted them easily, their suited bodies sticking out like flares in a clear sky among the T-shirts and shorts of the students.

At the end of the hallway they swung right toward a row of offices. Staying back, she watched as they entered one, then slowly moved in closer to find out who they'd come to see. It was the chancellor's office. What sort of business could Jay and Richard possibly have in there?

Farther down the hallway there were chairs against the wall between two large potted palms, and Devin sat down in the one next to the first plant, using it for cover. She peered through the narrow, needle-tipped fronds, wondering how long they'd be in there, and what she was going to do when they came out.

Under the circumstances, Devin decided to find out what the pair was up to. With all the confusion and loose ends in this situation, one never knew what might help solve it.

A few minutes later the door opened and Jay and Richard emerged, along with another man and woman. As she'd thought, the foursome headed in the opposite direction away from her, because on this end of the corridor were only more offices.

What was she going to do now? Go scurrying after them, hoping to get close enough to find out what they were doing? That didn't seem likely. How many palm trees could she hide behind? It was possible that evidence of whatever business Jay and Richard were conducting with the university could be found in the chancellor's office. But that idea didn't exactly appeal to her, either. It wasn't her way to depend on anyone, but right now she wished Nick was there.

That thought, so unlike her, forced Devin to her feet and across the hall. If Nick had been there, this is just what he would do, and she was every bit as capable of poking her nose where it didn't belong as any man.

Nevertheless, as she reached the office door she found that her palms were damp and her heart was thumping in her chest. Silly. If the office was occupied, she would simply apologize and find some other way to snoop.

But what if it was empty? Then she would have to go in and look around. Maybe the door was locked. She twisted the knob and it turned easily in her hand. Devin closed her eyes for a brief moment before she pushed it inward.

The office was empty.

Scarcely breathing, Devin stepped inside, firmly closing the door behind her. If they came back, she'd be trapped in a very embarrassing position. Who could tell? What with some madman on the loose trashing places, and million-dollar bacteria and insurance policies involved, this might even be dangerous!

Forcing herself to calm her vivid imagination and think only about the task at hand, Devin took a deep breath and turned to look around the small office. To her left were filing cabinets, and adjacent to them a copier, typewriter and word processor. But what caught and held her attention was the secretary's desk, where four neat piles of papers were sitting.

Devin hesitated, her pulse leaping at the thought of being caught while going through them. The notoriety from such an incident would certainly damage her relationship with the school, possibly even her career. No matter how good her intentions, regardless of what Jay and Richard might have to do with all this, the fact remained that she had absolutely no right to be in this office reading private papers.

Then she thought of Eli, and her resolve became as hard as concrete. If something was going on that involved Eli, or if something had happened to him, her life could be changed forever, anyway. Helping him was worth the risk.

How much time did she have? How soon would they return? If she was going to do this, she first had to make sure that the inner office directly in front of her was empty, as well. The door was partially open and Devin walked over to it, braver now but still hesitant.

"Quit wasting time," she chastised herself softly.

With a damp hand she pushed on the door and it flew back, hitting the wall with a thump. Devin cringed at the noise, but stepped forward into the room. Sheer curtains over a large picture window behind the desk muted the brilliant sunshine, but it still exposed every nook and cranny in the room, which was void of people.

Relieved, she went back to the secretary's desk. Her hands were trembling as she began thumbing through the papers in the first stack. There was no mention of Wingate, or Jay and Richard among them, or in the next pile, either. Great. She'd risked a heart attack and being caught for nothing.

Suddenly, loud male voices echoed into the room from the outside hallway. Startled by the sound, Devin dropped the sheaf of papers in her hand and then watched in horror as the loose pages floated to the floor, some gliding beneath the desk as they landed. Her veins surged with a fresh dose of adrenaline, making her pulse race wildly.

Without thinking she dropped to her knees and crawled under the desk, her nose almost to the floor in order to see the hallway door. When it didn't open she gathered up all the papers and backed out from under the desk. Sitting down on her heels she shuffled the pages, at last managing to get them into a neat pile, then returned them to the top of the desk where she'd found them.

Her heart was pounding like a gong going off at dinnertime, her pulse racing away at twilight speed, and when she stood her knees almost buckled beneath her. So far she'd been lucky. She wasn't cut out for this, but she felt as if the inner office was beckoning to her, asking her to come inside and discover its contents.

The lure was too great. Devin entered the room, ignoring the rows of floor-to-ceiling bookshelves on two of the walls, instead heading for the front of the massive desk dominating the room where a thin stack of pristine white papers sat all alone. She turned them around to face her.

The name Wingate almost leaped off the typed pages to grab her. After reading the first paragraph she realized she didn't have the time to try to figure out what the legal mumbo jumbo typed on them meant. What was she going to do? She couldn't steal them; snooping was one thing, thievery quite another. Besides, they'd notice the papers were missing right away.

"Think, darn you!" Devin muttered to herself.

The copier! Picking up the papers she went back into the front office to the copy machine. She removed the paper clip holding them together and set the first page facedown on the glass surface, then closed the lid. With a quick prayer that this was one of the quiet models, she hit the print button. The noise gave her already over-loaded nervous system yet another jolt, but it wasn't too bad.

Twenty excruciating pages later she reclipped the papers together and returned them to the desk where she'd found them. Her heart was still pounding as Devin realized she was going to get away with her little heist.

Then, as she was reaching out for thc knob, the door suddenly opened without her help. Devin jumped backward, stifling a scream.

So did the older woman who entered the room. "Oh! You startled me!" she exclaimed. "Can I help you with something?"

Devin opened her mouth but couldn't speak. She had the illicit copies clenched tightly against her chest with both hands, afraid she might drop them. The woman was well dressed, her short brown hair sleekly styled, suiting the half-rimmed gold glasses she wore. She seemed un-fluttered to find someone in her office. But she was a bit perturbed.

"Do you have an appointment?" she asked.

Devin watched as she sat behind the desk. "Oh, no, I—" Had she heard the noise? "I was just using your copier."

"There is one in the faculty lounge," she said, peering over the top of her glasses. "Are you a guest teacher?"

"Yes, and I know where it is, but...there was a line for it and the student I'm tutoring has a bus to catch. Sorry, I've got to run or I'll miss him. Thank you for the use of your machine."

Devin strode quickly down the hallway, heading for the nearest exit. She didn't want any more encounters right now, especially not with her uncles. Once outside she ran to her car and got in, locked the door and promptly collapsed on the driver's seat. But her paralysis didn't last long. The heat was stifling and she started the engine, turning the air-conditioning on full blast as she tried to calm down.

"Of all the stupid, crazy things to do!" she muttered.

Seconds, mere seconds and she would have been caught in the act. She didn't like this skulduggery. There was an almost pleasant tingle in the pit of her stomach, but it had to be bad for a person to accelerate their heart to such quantum-leap speeds. Devin held out a hand, and found that she was trembling and weak all over. How could anyone do this for a living? How did a thief take it, withstand the pressure? Could danger be addictive, as she had heard?

Devin didn't know and didn't want to find out. This one time had been enough for her. She sat up, placed the papers on the other seat and put her car in Reverse, backing out of the parking space. It didn't make sense to hang around here, and besides, she had another appointment to keep. Surely she'd stop shaking by the time she got there.

Chapter Twelve

Nick stepped into the elevator at the high rise that housed the Lang Inc. offices and thumbed the button for his floor. Just as the doors were sliding shut he saw an auburn-colored streak flash in front of his eyes, and Devin slipped in beside him.

"You're late!" she groused. "Your secretary assured me you'd be in by ten."

"What are you doing here?" Nick asked.

She'd surprised him, all right. "We're supposed to talk to Jerry this morning, remember?"

"Actually, I don't remember inviting you," he replied. Then he grinned at her outraged expression. "Cool down. It slipped my mind, that's all. You're welcome."

"I'd better be," Devin returned. But she grinned, too. "Looks like you've had a good morning so far."

Her grin broadened. "I have, thank you." The elevator stopped and took on a few more passengers, then resumed its upward climb. "I'll tell you about it later," she said.

He nodded. The other people in the elevator were listening and watching them with interest, their attention keeping Nick quiet, too. "This is our floor," he said at last, stepping aside to let her exit first. The elevator doors slid shut behind them. "Our offices are this way."

"That's what the sign indicates," Devin quipped. Now that she'd calmed down she was feeling good, and quite pleased with what she'd done. A bit guilty, but pleased.

Nick glanced at her. Her cheeks were pink and flushed, her pale blue eyes seeming to sparkle. "You really are in fine fettle today, aren't you?"

"Yes, I am."

What had made her so cocky? In her hand she held some papers rolled into a tight round tube. "Did those papers say something you liked?" Nick asked.

They were alone as they walked along the carpeted hallway with its textured grasslike wallpaper, but she wasn't taking any chances, not after what she'd been through to get them. "I'll tell you in your office," Devin said.

"Okay." When she looked up at him her auburn hair slid backward exposing large, fan-shaped, green-and-gold earrings. A silky cream T-shirt was tucked into tailored mint green slacks. She wasn't just perky this morning, she was sexier than he'd ever seen her. "You've definitely aroused my curiosity," he admitted. *And that's not all,* he added silently to himself.

"Good."

They paused before a door marked Lang Inc. Nick opened it for her and they went inside. The receptionist smiled a greeting as they passed her desk, then resumed typing. From the reception area the hallway branched off in five directions. Devin realized the firm probably took up a good portion of this floor. Impressive for a family company.

"We'll talk to Jerry first. He has to leave here by eleven today." Nick led them to a solid-looking wooden door

PLAY HARLEQUIN'S

LUCKY CARNIVAL WHEEL

scratch-off game
and get as many as
SIX FREE GIFTS...

HOW TO PLAY:

1. With a coin, carefully scratch off the silver area at right. Then check your number against the chart below to find out which gifts you're eligible to receive.

2. You'll receive brand-new Harlequin Intrigue® novels and possibly other gifts—ABSOLUTELY FREE! Send back this card and we'll promptly send you the Free Books and Gift(s) you qualify for!

3. We're betting you'll want more of these heart-warming romances, so unless you tell us otherwise, every month we'll send you 4 more wonderful novels to read and enjoy. Always delivered right to your home. And always at a discount off the cover price!

4. Your satisfaction is guaranteed! You may return any shipment of books and cancel at any time. The Free Books and Gift(s) remain yours to keep!

NO COST! NO RISK!
NO OBLIGATION TO BUY!

FREE "KEY TO YOUR HEART" PENDANT NECKLACE

*The Austrian crystal sparkles like a diamond! And it's carefully set in a romantic "Key to Your Heart" pendant on a generous 18" chain. The entire necklace is yours **free** as an added thanks for giving our Reader Service a try!*

(PLAY THE LUCKY)

"CARNIVAL WHEEL"

Just scratch off the silver area above with a coin. Then look for your number on the chart below to see which gifts you're entitled to!

YES! Please send me all the Free Books and Gift(s) I'm entitled to. I understand that I am under no obligation to purchase any books. I may keep the Free Books and Gift(s) and return my statement marked "cancel." But if I choose to remain in the Harlequin Reader Service®, please send me 4 brand-new Harlequin Intrigue® novels every month and bill me the subscribers-only low price of $2.49* per book—a saving of 40¢ off the cover price of each book. And there is no extra charge for delivery! I can always return a shipment at your cost and cancel any time.

181 CIH AGPK (U-H-I-11/92)

NAME _____
(Please Print)

ADDRESS _____ APT. NO. _____

CITY _____ STATE _____ ZIP CODE _____

39	WORTH FOUR FREE BOOKS, FREE PENDANT NECKLACE AND FREE SURPRISE GIFT
15	WORTH FOUR FREE BOOKS, FREE PENDANT NECKLACE
27	WORTH FOUR FREE BOOKS
6	WORTH TWO FREE BOOKS AND A FREE SURPRISE GIFT

*Terms and prices subject to change without notice. Sales tax applicable in NY.
© 1989 HARLEQUIN ENTERPRISES LIMITED

CLAIM YOUR "FREE GIFT" TO MAIL THIS CARD TODAY!

More Good News For Subscribers Only!

When you join the Harlequin Reader Service®, you'll receive 4 heart-warming romance novels each month delivered to your home. You'll also get additional free gifts from time to time, as well as our subscribers-only newsletter. It's your privileged look at upcoming books and profiles of our most popular authors!

If offer card is missing, write to:
Harlequin Reader Service, 3010 Walden Avenue, P.O. Box 1867, Buffalo, NY 14269-1867

marked Accountant, knocked on it and opened it for her to enter.

A man with carrot-red hair was sitting behind a cluttered desk, his attention on a computer screen to his right. He was dressed casually in a short-sleeved blue-and-yellow-plaid shirt.

"Be with you in a minute," he murmured, not looking up.

Devin sat in the chair Nick indicated before the desk. A short row of bookshelves behind Jerry held family photographs, the striking resemblance impossible to miss. On the white walls were framed photographs of cars, all of them Porsches.

"Gotcha," Jerry muttered, pressing another button. "Now, what can I— Well, well! You must be Devin," he said, focusing his attention on the woman sitting in front of his desk. "The fiddle player, right?"

The man hit a raw nerve of hers right off. She made a sour face. "You *must* be a friend of Nick's."

Jerry laughed. "Sometimes I am. How about you?"

"I'm a classically trained violinist."

"And I'm a classically trained accountant," he returned, nose in the air in an uppity pose. "Big deal. You play a fiddle, just a different way."

Devin frowned. "Has anyone ever told you that you're irritating?"

Jerry looked at Nick, who was standing near the lone office window, smiling. "You did warn me she was direct." He suddenly grabbed his own chest, placing his hands over his heart. "And I already have holes in me to prove it. A few more and I'll be like Swiss cheese." Jerry slumped sideways in his chair.

"This is your accountant?" Devin asked doubtfully.

Nick thought it best to intervene before she really let Jerry have it. "All right, you two, settle down," he said, chuckling. "I got your message, Jerry. What did you find?"

"Lots of stuff." Jerry straightened up and pointed to a pile of papers near the edge of his cluttered desk. "For starters, all those job offers are valid and still open. Eli Wingate is very much in demand."

"Has he contacted any of the companies?" Devin asked.

"No," Jerry replied. He saw the concern on her face and added quickly, "Or at least not yet."

"And the list of other labs pursuing projects similar to Eli's?" Nick asked.

Jerry looked pleased with himself. "No need for a list. While there are a few doing research along similar lines, as far as I can tell only one has the personnel and financial backing to be even distant competition for Wingate in the area of, uh, garbage reduction." He handed Nick a piece of paper. "That explains the focus of their project. It's a place out of California by the name of—"

"NHS," Devin inserted. "Right?"

"Yeah," Jerry replied, slack jawed. "How'd you know?"

She shrugged. "Just an educated guess."

"They have an employee by the name of Yvette Soomes," Nick informed him, "who just happens to be the beneficiary of a million-dollar life insurance policy Eli carries."

"Man oh man!" Jerry exclaimed. "I'm beginning to see why you like all this spy stuff, Nick. Heck of a lot more exciting than double entry bookkeeping. I called Wingate and told them I was verifying their insurance policy on Eli. It took some wheedling, but I found out the policy *they* carry on him is also quite sizable.''

Devin was confused. ''They who? What kind of policy?''

''Jay and Richard Wingate. Life insurance,'' he replied.

''Did you know about this, Nick?'' she demanded.

He shrugged. ''I knew it was a good possibility,'' Nick admitted. ''It's not unusual for a company to carry a policy on a vital employee.''

She still didn't like the sound of this. ''How large?''

''It is higher than usual,'' Jerry informed them, ''and it was only taken out three months ago. Wingate stands to collect enough to help them weather any bad times because of Eli's untimely demise. But that's only if something actually happens to him and they can prove it.''

Devin felt the blood draining from her face as his words sank in. Would Jay and Richard do something so heinous as to kill their own brother for money? And if so, why? Was Wingate in fact in some sort of dire financial position?

''What you're saying,'' Nick concluded grimly, ''is that, given enough time, they could buy a good replacement for Eli.''

Jerry nodded. ''The stock would plummet, but with the right replacement it would shoot back up again. Attracting new investors might be a lot tougher without Eli, but that much cash gives them a nice cushion to work with. From an accountant's point of view I found the news encouraging.''

''You would.'' Devin turned sideways in her chair to glare at Nick, her pale face turning pink with color as her temper heated up. ''And you. If Jay and Richard were overstating Eli's importance to the company all along and you knew it, why didn't you tell me?''

"I didn't *know* it. But I knew if there was a panic that Eli's work could be in jeopardy. And we both know he lives for his work," Nick told her, sidestepping the actual question. "Besides, I'm not the only one with a penchant for withholding information, now am I?"

Devin stood. "Thanks for your help, Jerry."

"Call me anytime."

"Thank you." With that she walked out of the office.

"It seems you're in the doghouse, chum," Jerry noted.

Nick grimaced. "So what else is new?" he muttered. "I've been in there so often since I met her it's a wonder I don't have fleas. Could you get my appointments canceled for me, Jerry? This could take a while."

"Will do."

"Devin, wait up," Nick yelled down the corridor, then dashed past the startled receptionist and out the door, hot on Devin's heels. "We need to talk."

She ignored him, striding quickly down the hallway. "I have nothing to say to you."

Nick grabbed hold of her arm and pulled her to a stop. "Devin, listen to me."

"Are you working for Jay and Richard?" She shook his hand off her arm. "Being paid to keep an eye on me?"

Nick couldn't have been more stunned if she'd actually hauled off and slapped him. He even took a step backward, reeling with the verbal blow. "What! Where did you get that insane idea?"

"Lang Security. Ring a bell?"

He wanted to shake her. "We're a consulting company, Devin. We make recommendations. We don't sell any products, nor do we have detectives who follow people.''

''And you expect me to believe you?''

''Follow me back to my office,'' Nick said, angrily shoving his hands into the pockets of his khaki pants. ''I'll show you my books and prove it to you.''

''Forget it.'' Devin walked over to the row of elevators and punched the button. ''That wouldn't change the lie you've told already.'' She glanced at him. ''Or is it *lies?* What did Jerry mean when he said you loved 'this spy stuff'?''

Nick blew out a deep breath. There were things he was keeping from her and she knew it. This business was starting to get messy.

''I am *not* working for Jay and Richard.'' Nick paused, debating with his conscience. ''I'm working for Eli.''

''So you've been telling me.''

''No. I mean Eli hired me as a security consultant when papers started getting 'misplaced,''' Nick informed her.

Devin turned and stared at him incredulously. ''He what?''

''Hired me. To look into security at Wingate. Without the knowledge of his brothers, I hasten to add,'' Nick said.

''But—''

''Wait,'' he interrupted. ''Before you jump to any of your famous conclusions, Eli and I really are friends and I really did invest in Wingate. I'd been wanting to for a while, anyway, and it was a made-to-order cover as far as getting me on the inside. I'd just started poking around when Eli turned up missing himself.'' Nick frowned. ''And it's beginning to look like I may have been a bit hasty with the family funds, after all. Take my word for it, Devin, I'm just as confused as you are about what's going on.''

The elevator arrived. Devin ignored it. When the doors thumped shut again, she leaned her back against the nearby wall, all the while looking at Nick.

"Confused doesn't even begin to describe what I'm feeling at the moment, Nick.'' She shook her head. "How am I supposed to take your word for anything? You're like a chameleon that keeps changing colors all the time.''

"I'm sorry. But Eli swore me to secrecy.''

"Then why tell me now?'' she asked.

Good question. "Because it's the only way I could think of to make you listen to me. No offense, Devin, but I need to keep you under control,'' he told her honestly.

"Meaning you still don't trust me.'' Devin uttered a short, curt laugh. "Look who's talking!''

"Actually,'' Nick returned in a quiet tone, "I do trust you. But you have to admit you can be volatile. For instance, what are you planning to do now? Confront Jay and Richard?''

The elevator doors opened again. It was empty, and this time Devin stepped inside, with Nick right behind her. "No, I'm not. I'd like to, believe me, but they wouldn't tell me anything.'' She pressed the button for the underground parking garage. "And you can rest easy because I'm not telling them anything, either. If you must know, I intend to go question the lab assistants.''

Nick couldn't prevent a smile from lifting the corners of his mouth. "And just how do you propose to get in?''

Devin glared at him. "I'll figure something out.''

"Remember what Myrtle said. Two heads are better than one.'' He continued to smile, knowing it made her mad and rather enjoying the spots of color that appeared on her cheeks. "Come on, Devin. Play some other tune for a while, will you? I'm getting tired of this one."

He was still hiding something from her, she was sure of it. She couldn't verify his story about working for Eli, either. In addition, he was making her so crazy she would gladly shove him down this elevator shaft.

The doors slid open and they walked out into the cool, dimly lighted parking garage. Their footsteps echoed in the dusty oil-and-exhaust-scented air.

In the final analysis, Devin knew nothing had changed. She still needed someone's help. Even in a fit of temper she also knew that finding Eli was the most important thing to her. At this time she was persona non grata at Wingate, she hadn't figured out what her papers meant and didn't know where Eli was. As usual, Nick seemed to be the only one offering any help. What choice did she have?

"Okay," Devin said at last. "We'll try the cooperation concerto in D major. Now wipe that smug grin off your face and help me figure out what these mean."

She stopped behind her car and held up the hand in which she still held the papers. Nick saw that her knuckles were white from the grip she had on them.

"Where'd you get them?"

"At the university. I was there tutoring a boy on the violin and I saw Jay and Richard on campus." Quietly Devin explained to him just what she'd done to get hold of the papers.

Nick whistled when she finished her story. "I didn't think you had it in you, Devin."

"Nor did I." At last she'd done something that really impressed him. It made her feel proud, and that worried her. She didn't want to care what he thought, and after all, what she'd done had been vaguely illegal. A change of subject was in order. "I don't suppose there's a lawyer in that jack-of-all-trades tool kit of yours?"

He laughed. "Not even close. But let's see if we can make any sense of what you've got."

Devin handed him the first half of the papers—her trust only went so far—and looked askance at her own share. Reading legal stuff like this always gave her a headache. "Well, then, start interpreting. I'd hate to have to explain to someone else how we acquired them."

"That would be tricky. But let's go back and use Jerry's office. He's gone by now and no one will look for me there. And it's air conditioned."

While Nick began reading, Devin used the phone to make a few calls. Then she forced herself to at least skim over the papers she'd stolen. Fifteen minutes later they were facing each other, Devin behind the desk in Jerry's chair.

"Well?" she asked.

Nick shrugged. "The bare bones is that Wingate and the university have agreed to a joint research project. From what I can tell it's a purely agricultural study, which, if anything is discovered, will result in a shared patent. Dry stuff. But very interesting nonetheless."

"And how!" Devin exclaimed. "I haven't heard anything about this."

"Me, either. But it's a good move for the company."

Devin frowned. "How nice for the company. Why are they keeping it so quiet?"

"Beats me. It's a great publicity tool to get new investors." He paused thoughtfully. "But on the other hand, the papers aren't signed yet," Nick continued. "If something happens to sour the deal it could be embarrassing."

"Especially if Eli Wingate has disappeared and his two brothers are implicated," Devin added.

"You're jumping to conclusions."

"And you're talking like a lawyer."

He smiled. "Who were you calling earlier?"

"Oh, just a couple of friends of mine. They both work for phone companies," she explained. "It occurred to me that a record of Eli's long-distance calls from that Thursday or Friday might prove interesting. But there were none, not from work or his home."

"Too bad. Good idea, though." Nick sighed. "I guess that leaves us with only one direction. We need to know the focus of Eli's project to see if it matches the one at NHS."

Devin nodded. "Which means we go talk to the assistants."

"Right. Of course, that means that on the way over, we have to figure out how we're going to break in." He smiled. "It's about time we got to do something fun for a change!"

Chapter Thirteen

The thought of climbing over a nine-foot metal chain-link fence that had been baking all day in one-hundred-and-five-degree heat had about as much appeal to Devin as having herself branded. After that, they'd have to run the length of a football field across the dusty desert, dodging the natural vegetation and thorny cactus in order to get to just an edge of the building.

Hot, sweaty, dirty work. That plan made Nick's first suggestion sound perfect. His bold idea was to drive right up to the gate and see if they were turned away. While Devin was skeptical, she found herself agreeing with him since she didn't have any better ideas of her own.

Which was why she was driving them to Wingate in a four-door sedan that Nick had borrowed from Lang. They'd agreed it was best to leave her car at her grandmother's just in case her uncles recognized it in the parking lot.

Devin slowed to a stop in front of the white wrought-iron barrier blocking the entrance to Wingate. The palms of her hands were damp, her heart beating rapidly as she waited, wondering what was going to happen.

A uniformed guard stepped out of the small, glass-fronted building, and stared at her for a moment before smiling. He was waving her through, the barrier gliding backward as he spoke. "Go right on in, Ms. Prescott."

The parking area reserved for visitors was up front by the main entrance, but Devin avoided it, not wanting to draw attention to herself. Instead she began driving up and down the rows of parked cars in the employee section, looking for an empty space.

"That was easy."

"I thought it might be. You're still family," Nick muttered, rising up from the back-seat floorboards. "It wouldn't look good to turn you away at the gate, but the front desk will be different. They'll shuttle us right to Jay's office, which is the last place we want to be."

"Oh, I don't know. I wouldn't mind getting in there to have a look around—without them there, of course."

"One thing at a time, Devin," Nick said. Then he chuckled. "Starting to like this spy stuff?"

"Well... It is rather exciting," she admitted sheepishly. "Like the way I feel the moment before the curtain goes up on a performance, only extended." She drove into a space on the last row and turned off the engine. Her eyes met his in the rearview mirror. "Come on, I'll show you a little secret that will get us past the front desk."

Shimmering heat rose from the hot asphalt, casting apparitions into the wind, desert mirages not to be believed. They were only halfway to the building and Nick was already sweating in the hundred-plus heat of the noonday sun, his thin, white cotton shirt damp in spots.

"Where are we going?" he asked irritably.

"We're headed for the far side of that wall. It'll lead us to the middle of the building where the new addition joins the old," Devin said, brushing a film of perspiration off her upper lip.

The pink adobe wall was as tall as the building and ran in a semicircle, the center almost touching the parking lot before it curved back in to rejoin the building.

They stepped up over the cement curb and followed the curve of the wall around to an area landscaped with rocks, the different kinds and colors producing an appealing scene that ran all the way to the end of the building.

"What's behind the wall?" Nick asked.

"Employee patio. It's shaded from the sun, but rarely used in the summer months."

There was no shade in sight on their side of the wall, or any windows, either. The wall itself was so hot it burned Nick's skin when he brushed against it. Devin led them across the colorful rocks and up to where the wall joined the side of the building.

Placed about three feet apart were two lengths of brown rain gutter that ran from the roof down into the ground. They were there because Phoenix was hit from time to time by torrential rainfalls that caused flash flooding. But their placement, so close together, made Nick wonder if there was another purpose for them. There weren't any doors on this side of the building, so how were they going to get inside?

He leaned closer. Hidden by the shadows of the guttering were two lengthwise seams. Upon even closer inspection he located another at the top. What looked like cracks in the pinkish adobe finish actually outlined a door.

"Excellent design," he whispered, quite impressed. He was studying the bottom of the door and the way it was hidden by rocks when he noticed Devin bend down and run her hand along the shadows at the base of the wall.

"Got it."

The L-shaped piece of shiny metal she was holding was about six inches long. He watched as she slid it under the bottom of the door before turning it upward.

Devin pulled with all her strength, but the door wouldn't budge. This was one of the reasons she knew she'd need help; even Eli had trouble opening it on his own.

"Help me pull, but don't touch the door. It's solid metal beneath the fake adobe facade and so hot from the heat of the sun that it will blister your skin."

Nick squatted down beside her on the rocks and put his hands over hers. Together they pulled and tugged until the door slid open, a refreshing cool wave of air drifting out.

"Go on in," Devin urged. She returned the metal piece to where she'd found it and slipped inside, pulling the door shut behind them, engulfing them in total darkness.

"What's next?" Nick asked. Luckily he wasn't claustrophobic. The passageway was about two feet wide, and he couldn't see even a glow of light from around the closed door behind him. "I've got a little flashlight in my pocket if—"

"No. I don't think we should risk it. Just follow me." Devin tried to squeeze past Nick without touching him, but her breasts brushed against his chest as she moved around him. "It's narrower than I remembered. Sorry."

"Don't be. I enjoyed it," Nick said, his deep voice soft in the total darkness. "Do you know what this exciting spy stuff reminds me of?"

"What?"

"Rub past me again and I'll show you."

Devin cleared her throat. "Yes, well, I think we'd better get on with this, shall we? We'll walk forward about five feet. It'll be even narrower—you'll have to turn sideways to get through," she warned. "At that point a door leads into a closet and we'll be in the janitor's area."

The coolness of the enclosure felt good to Nick and he knew the air had to be the result of the thickness of the adobe walls. "Was this part of the original plans?"

"No, it was a miscalculation on the builder's part, and leaving this almost wedge-shaped passageway in was the architect's solution to the problem. My uncles had the door installed as an emergency exit," she explained. "Eli uses it now and then—he calls it a shortcut. But I think he just likes it because it's different."

It would also be an excellent way for someone to get inside without using the main entrance. In his former profession, Nick would have loved it. Now, it seemed an outrageous security risk. But they had camouflaged it quite well, making the detection almost pure luck since it wasn't even on the original blueprints.

"I'm at the closet. Stay here until I call you."

Devin pushed on the panel, easing it open without a sound. Overhead a dull yellow bulb highlighted the interior of the storage closet. The shelves had seldom-used supplies, bug sprays and other items not often in demand.

She moved into the large closet. "Come here."

Nick did as she asked, then stood back studying the panel curiously as she firmly pressed it closed. He touched the finished curving lip around the notched shelves, noticing how it hid any signs of an opening.

Devin spoke in a whisper. "Neat, isn't it? Richard came up with the design around this door, and he made it. Woodworking is his hobby."

"How many people know about this entrance?"

"Me, Eli, Jay, Richard, Grandmother and Harry. Harry's a trusted friend of the family and is in charge of maintenance for the plant. He put in the door. The builders and architect assume we left it as they did, closed off."

"Then you must trust me to show me this."

"Not really. There's a hidden lock that opens this panel. If your fingerprints don't register an alarm goes off that's so loud it would force you out of the passageway."

So much for his judgment of the security risk. He really should get out in the field more; his instincts were getting rusty. But then, he had an excuse. "This is the weirdest system I've ever encountered. Elements of high-tech detail surrounded by lots of great big gaps. The Wingate security department needs a complete overhaul."

"You've got that right. Now that I got us into the building, do you have a better way to get us into the lab besides using Myrtle to get the access code for us?"

"Hey! You stole my idea!" Nick accused. "The question is, can you get us to Myrtle without getting caught?"

"We'll find out." On the lower third of the door there were shutters for ventilation, and Devin hunched down in front of them, easing the top one up to peek out into the hallway. "It's clear."

Nick followed her out and shut the door behind them. It was nondescript except for the word Chemicals stenciled in red. They were at the end of a short hallway, and up ahead another one split off into two directions. Even here the windowless hallways were painted white with that cheerful apple green on the trim.

Devin started to move forward, then suddenly stopped. Nick bumped into her. "What's wrong?" he asked.

"Shh!" A young man in a tan uniform was whistling a current hit song as he passed their corridor with a lunch bag in his hand. "We'll get caught doing this. I've got an idea. Maybe we should find a phone and call her," Devin suggested.

"I thought about that," Nick whispered in her ear. "But it'll take time to find an empty office. We can't ask to use someone's phone, either. I don't have a visitor's pass for the area and you might be recognized."

As the whistling became fainter Devin moved up to the end of the hallway. "Then let's get out of here."

They turned left, walked around another corner and then up a short flight of metal stairs. At the top, Devin eased open another solid steel door to peek out into the corridor.

There were a few people in the halls, one wearing a lab coat and a couple of office workers Devin recognized, but no guards in sight. She looked over her shoulder at Nick and waved him forward. "Let's go."

Devin strode down the hall, her flat, crepe-soled shoes not making a sound. Her hands were damp again, her heart pounding away. Oddly enough, though, she wasn't worried about herself this time.

If they were caught Devin knew the police would never be called in for a family member, but she wasn't so sure Nick would get the same treatment, large investor or not. Jay and Richard would probably charge him with trespassing and whatever else they could think of, and unfortunately she was really beginning to care about what happened to Nick Lang. She didn't know why. Maybe because she was finally accepting the fact that he really did want to help Eli.

Nick seemed to care about her, too. That was a fairly novel experience for Devin, and she decided she liked it.

But she had no idea what it would all amount to, just like the situation they were in right now. Devin hated leaving things to chance; but again, she didn't have much choice.

Myrtle's office door was open and they found her inside at her desk, talking on the phone. She looked puzzled when Nick closed the door, but held up a finger indicating she'd only be a moment longer. Her cheerful red-and-white-striped dress filled the room with color.

"What's wrong?" Myrtle asked, setting down the phone. "Why close the door?"

"Because we're no longer welcome at Wingate," Devin said, sitting down. "We had to sneak in here and we don't want to get you in trouble."

"Don't you worry about me, child. You two worry about yourselves and Eli. I can take care of myself."

Nick sat in the other chair by her desk. "Did you get the access code to the lab?"

"They did change it this morning," Myrtle said. She leaned forward and put a piece of paper on the desk in front of them. "I didn't even have to arouse suspicion by asking for it," she announced proudly. "I wheedled it out of someone over coffee instead. Pretty good work, I'd say."

Nick smiled. "Very good."

Myrtle grinned and winked at him. The whole exchange had Devin's mind in motion. When had Nick called Myrtle? Why hadn't he told her about it? What was Nick keeping from her now?

Then she shook her head, cursing her overactive imagination. Myrtle part of some scheme? That was crazy!

"Devin?" Nick was touching her on the arm. "Did you get too much sun?"

She pulled away, the tingling sensation left from his touch unnerving her. "I'm fine."

Nick frowned. Now what was her problem? "Myrtle just said they're taking lunch breaks right now," he told her. "That'll make it easier to talk to them one by one."

"Then what are we waiting for?" Devin asked.

"After you, your royal highness."

"You two be careful. And stop picking on each other, for heaven's sake!" Myrtle said, chuckling as they left the room.

Devin strode to the lab, expecting Nick to keep up with her. The whole situation made her uncomfortable, and Nick was adding elements she didn't need right now. At the end of the long hallway she stopped and peered around the corner at the entrance to the main lab.

"Rats!" she exclaimed softly.

"Where?"

Devin looked perturbed. "Would you get serious? I mean there are guards in front of the entrance to the labs." Devin peeked around the corner again. "We need Myrtle."

"What for?"

"As a distraction." She waved him off. "Go get her."

"Yes, ma'am."

Nick did as she asked, returning with a huffing Myrtle a few minutes later. She was rubbing her pudgy hands together, rings clinking as they touched. "What's wrong?"

"We need you to distract the guards for us."

Myrtle looked shocked. "Guards!" She clasped her hands over her bosom and looked around the corner. "Well, I'll be, this place is changing all the time. What should I do, Nick?" she asked, looking to him for guidance.

That rankled Devin. "It's my idea! Why ask him?"

"Because he's more experienced, dear," Myrtle replied.

"How did you know?"

"Because I told her what I really do at Lang," Nick said. "I had to. It was the only way she'd help me do this, since you were coming along."

"But the whole thing was my idea, too!" Devin objected.

"Then let's get on with it!" Nick exclaimed quietly. "Do whatever you can to get them away from that door, Myrtle. Maybe you could pretend to fall or something."

Myrtle smiled at Devin. "I told you so." While Devin did a slow burn, Myrtle patted her white hair, preparing to meet the enemy. "Are you two ready?"

They nodded and watched as Myrtle walked over to the guards in her colorful muumuu-type dress, pausing for a moment to speak to them. Then she strolled on toward the employee patio at the end of the corridor. After a moment there was a thump, followed by a moan.

"Oh, my," Myrtle yelled loudly, her voice booming down the corridor. "I need help!"

Devin risked a peek, and saw that she was sitting on the linoleum-covered floor. Her position was a little too carefully arranged, with her flowing dress tucked in by her legs, but otherwise convincing.

The older guard rushed over to help her. "What's wrong, Myrtle?"

"I think I've sprained my ankle. Oh, John, can you help me back to my office?" Myrtle pleaded.

"Hey, Billie," the guard named John yelled. "I've got a lady in distress over here. Come give me a hand, will you?"

"Stay put," Nick said, before rushing over to the digital pad inset in the wall. He quickly punched in a sequence of numbers with one eye on the guards that were helping Myrtle. Or rather, trying to help.

Myrtle wasn't cooperating and they were having a devil of a time getting her up off the floor. He heard the whoosh of the security doors as they slid open, but as he turned to motion Devin to join him she streaked past him and was inside before he could stop her.

Nick dashed inside, grabbed her hand and pulled her back against the wall between two large vats. He whispered in her ear. "We have to avoid the cameras, let them shoot only the backs of our heads if possible. Or we'll be out on our butts before we learn anything."

Devin nodded. "Do you want to take the quickest route?"

"Lead on."

She led them through equipment, over wires, past the various work areas and employees who were concentrating much too hard to be curious, until they were inside a section of Eli's lab area. A pretty woman with short, curly brown hair that just touched the shoulder of her white lab coat sat on a stool with her back to them, looking into a microscope.

"This is good," Devin whispered. "She's all alone in here and I know her, too."

They walked farther into the room. "Hi, Mary Ann," Devin said cheerfully. "Have you met Nick Lang? He's a new investor in Wingate. Richard and Jay asked me to give him the grand tour."

"Nice to meet you," Mary Ann said, smiling.

Nick shook hands with her, and looked around as if he'd never been here before. "So! What are you doing?"

"Cataloging the results from our latest test run."

"What happens after that?" Nick asked.

Mary Ann folded her hands on the countertop. "After that someone else will put the information into the computer and we'll compare the results."

"Are you close to a major breakthrough?"

The eagerness in Nick's voice made both women laugh. "I'm sorry, Mr. Lang, but we're not even close. This type of research is slow going, but when we do make our breakthrough it will be big." She gave him a wide, sunny smile. "And quite profitable, I'm sure."

"Those are the very words an investor likes to hear," Nick said. They chatted for a few more minutes but found out nothing startling from the conversation.

"If you don't have any more questions," Mary Ann said, "I'll be taking off. It's lunchtime for me."

"Don't let us keep you," Devin told her. "Thank you for your time."

They only had to wait a few minutes for someone else to show up, and as they talked to more employees in the various sections a definite pattern emerged.

Eli hadn't been working on the sludge project at all.

That, however, was about as much as they could learn. None of his assistants so far were able to give them a clue as to what he *had* been doing before he disappeared.

Frustrated on that front, they looked for the leggy blond woman they had almost collided with in the hallway the other evening. But that, too, was a frustrating search.

At last Devin muttered, "It's about time! I was beginning to think she'd taken the day off."

Nick spotted her entering the room as well. Today her shining blond hair was pulled back into a tight bun, and a white lab coat hid her figure completely, but it didn't hide her tanned beauty.

Devin walked over to her and launched into the same spiel she'd given everyone else. The woman smiled, showing pearly white, perfect teeth. Devin certainly hoped she was guilty of something.

"I'm always pleased to meet investors," Natalie said, concentrating completely on Nick. "How may I help you?"

Nick smiled engagingly. "Oh, I'm just satisfying my curiosity about my investment. Eli Wingate has made such a difference with his work so far, and I'm interested in what he's up to next. Hence my investment here."

"I agree with you, of course," she said, although there was a slight edge to her voice. "But you realize that Eli can't do all this on his own. As a matter of fact, he isn't even currently involved in our sludge project."

Nick played her along. "No! Then what's he doing?"

"I don't know. He's working on some kind of secret project that's taking up all his time."

She said the words *secret project* as if it were some stupid game Eli was playing. Obviously, Natalie was irritated not only by Eli's actions but by his stature as a scientist, as well. But why? "Sounds intriguing," Nick said. "Are you sure you don't know what it is?" he asked with a sly grin.

"Oh, I'm sure. I've tried to find out but Eli locks the door to the lab when he's working on it."

Again, she sounded as if Eli had done something to put her nose out of joint. Devin was just about to come right out and ask her about it when a faint beep sounded from the black, very expensive-looking watch on the other woman's narrow wrist.

Natalie smiled, showing those teeth, and just the tip of her tongue as she looked at Nick. "Excuse me, Mr. Lang, it's time to check on my bugs. But feel free to call on me any time, if you have more questions."

He watched her walk away, then looked at Devin. She had a puzzled, annoyed look on her face. "What's wrong?" Nick asked. "Did she leave a bad taste in your mouth?"

Devin shook her head slowly. "Yes, but that isn't it. There's something I can't put my finger on." She shrugged and headed out of the room beside Nick. "It'll come to me."

"Good. It's past time we were out of here."

She led them back to the main entrance without a single problem, save the logistics of making sure the cameras only caught the backs of their heads. At the entrance, however, Devin pulled him aside. "Do we just walk out?" she asked.

"Let's wait until someone else is leaving and go out with them. If we're lucky the guards won't notice us."

They stayed behind a tall copper vat until they heard voices near the door. When it slid open Nick and Devin stepped in behind the two men leaving, making themselves seem as if they were part of a group. The men turned right and Nick and Devin went left, striding away before they were noticed.

"What now?" Devin asked, keeping up with his fast pace.

"Back out the way we came in, I'd say."

"Suits me. You're the expert," she said sarcastically.

They rounded a corner and almost ran smack into a waiting Myrtle. "Oh, my! I'm glad I caught you two. Come this way. We must talk!"

Myrtle checked each doorway before they passed it, almost walking on tiptoe as she led them away from her office.

"What's going on? Where are we going?" Devin asked, unnerved by her strange behavior.

Myrtle held up a hand to silence her as she stopped in front of an office. The lights inside were out and Myrtle pressed her nose against the long, narrow strip of glass to look inside. Then she reached into the pocket of her cardigan sweater and pulled out a key.

"Eli's master key," she told them, opening the door. When they were inside, she sat in a chair behind the nearest vacant desk with a big sigh. "Oof! I'm not used to this! Close the door, Nick, but don't turn on the light."

Nick did as she asked, and leaned back against it. The fluorescent light from the corridor poured in through the narrow strip window, leaving most of the room in shadows. But neither of them had to see Myrtle's face to know there was a problem. Her voice was taut with worry.

"What's up?" Nick asked.

"I just left Jay's office. They've given me a paid leave of absence until Eli returns. I have until three o'clock to tidy things up and leave."

Stunned, Devin sat down in a chair with a thump. "Why, those two... Can they do that?"

Myrtle took a deep breath. "Yes, I am paid by the corporation. They also want to make sure I don't take any work home with me, seeing as how it's classified stuff. There's a guard sitting in my office." Myrtle smiled. "I'm in the ladies' room right now."

"I'm sorry about this, Myrtle," Devin said. "It's our fault. We've been snooping around, making them nervous about security." There was more to it than that, but

Devin didn't think Myrtle needed any more worries right now.

"Don't blame yourselves for the actions of those two boys," Myrtle replied sternly. "Besides, I could use the time off. All this excitement! I found Eli's paper trail, or at least part of it."

Devin moved to the edge of her chair. "Go on."

"He took a shuttle flight from here to Las Vegas late Thursday. Actually, it was very early Friday morning. However," Myrtle said, holding up a hand, "I haven't found out where he went from Las Vegas. Nor might I, ever. Planes leave there at all hours of the day and night, for all over the nation, and there are so many other kinds of transportation out of that city, too. It's daunting."

"It's a start, Myrtle," Nick said.

"I'll say!" Devin agreed. "Now we know Eli left of his own accord." Even in the darkened room, she saw Nick shake his head, and realized he was right. "Or at least under his own power," she amended. "That's encouraging news."

Myrtle clasped her hands together. "I know, and I can keep looking for where he went next from my own home. Did you two find out anything useful in the lab?"

"More puzzling than useful," Nick replied. "According to Jay and Richard, Eli was working on the sludge project. But everyone else says he wasn't. In fact, no one seems to know just what Eli was doing recently."

Myrtle sighed. "I've always teased Eli about being secretive, even told him he should change his middle name to that."

No one laughed. At this moment all three were keenly aware that Eli was still missing, and that none of what they had learned so far put them much closer to finding him. As time went by with no word, the question they didn't dare speak aloud came more often to mind.

Was Eli Wingate still alive?

Chapter Fourteen

"Look at that guy." Devin pointed out a well-developed young man in a tight blue T-shirt and shorts jogging on the sidewalk. She shook her head as they drove past him. "Only a muscle-bound idiot would be out running in this heat."

The mood Devin was in made her ready to pick on anyone and anything, but Nick couldn't disagree with her. Heat stroke was a reality in their desert climate and the guy wasn't even carrying water. "It's not too smart."

"I can't believe they're making Myrtle take a leave of absence," Devin said, returning to what had her so mad. "I'm tempted to tell Grandmother everything."

Nick slowed to a stop in front of the sprawling ranch house and turned off the engine. Getting out of Wingate had been as easy as retracing their steps, but Devin was still upset over the things they had and hadn't discovered. "I thought you said she had trouble with her heart?"

"She does," Devin replied, disgusted. "And it's the only thing right now that's stopping me from bringing her incredible wrath and temper down on Jay and Richard."

Nick grinned. Devin had a pretty hot temper of her own. If her grandmother's was hot enough to impress the likes of this fireball, he would take extra care to stay on her good side should they ever meet. "We don't know if they've done a thing to deserve anyone's wrath," he reminded her.

"Oh, they deserve it, all right! Can you believe their gall?" She slammed the car door shut. "The sleaze bags!"

Nick looked at her over the roof of the car. "You're more upset about it than Myrtle is."

He started to join Devin on the sidewalk but stopped, his attention drawn to the long black limo gliding slowly to a stop just past him. The windows were so darkly tinted he couldn't see inside.

As soon as the limo stopped moving, the rear door closest to him opened and a huge young man stepped out. He was wearing a blue T-shirt and skimpy shorts that showed all his overdeveloped muscles.

A warning bell went off in Nick's mind. He took strong men seriously. Fast men worried him. But the scariest guy he'd ever met was a pro football player who was strong and fast at the same time. This guy had the same look.

"Something I can do for you?" Nick asked.

The man didn't say a word. He just took two lightning-quick steps toward Nick and grabbed him by the arms. Nick felt himself being spun around, then he was pushed headfirst into the limo, all in a matter of seconds.

At the same time, the identically clad jogger they'd seen earlier ran up and grabbed Devin from behind. Muscular forearms wrapped around her, pinning her arms to her sides. Then he lifted her off the sidewalk and carried her to the limo. It happened almost as fast, but she managed to protest.

"Let go of me!" Devin yelled. "You muscle-bound creep! Put me down this instant!" She fought, kicking any part of his bare legs that she could while trying to claw his hairy arms. None of it seemed to bother him. When he got to the limo, his partner got hold of her ankles and together they stuffed her feetfirst into the back seat.

Doors slammed shut. Devin fell across Nick's lap as the big black vehicle took off, her nose brushing across the rich gray velour of the seat as they rounded a corner at high speed. When the limo slowed down she managed to raise her head and peer through tousled strands of auburn hair. Two elegant-looking men were studying her with keen interest, but there wasn't a weight-lifting thug or gun in sight.

Of course, that didn't mean one of these gentlemen wasn't capable of pulling out a weapon and using it. That, obviously, was Nick's opinion, as well. As he helped her to a sitting position beside him, he looked at her, his eyes full of silent warning. But he also seemed as puzzled as she. Devin combed her fingers through her hair, trying to return some sense of order to it—and everything else.

The two men sitting calmly on the bench seat across from them were well-groomed and clad in very expensive off-white suits. Though dressed for the heat, however, they were either hermits or from out of town; no one who spent much time in Phoenix could manage to keep that pale indoor look to their faces.

Devin looked around. All the windows were covered with a film so dark that you could barely see out of them. Everyone was silent. There was only the slight sensation of motion as the limousine glided smoothly along.

"Who are you?" she asked.

"That's not relevant," the man with the short gray hair opposite Nick replied. "Just cooperate with us and we'll return you to your grandmother's house, Ms. Prescott. Where is your uncle, Eli Wingate?"

"You're well-informed," Nick observed.

"It would amaze you just how well-informed we are, Mr. Lang," the other man said. He was younger, maybe late forties, his black hair also cut short in a style as conservative as his vanilla-colored suit and tie. "And if you knew how much more we could learn about you if we really tried, you would be appalled." He looked at Devin. "Answer the question, please. Where is Eli Wingate?"

Devin spread her slender fingers out straight and wide, then balled them into tight fists, feeling for the slightest pull or damage. "How am I supposed to know?" she said. She leaned forward and tucked her silky blouse back into her mint green slacks. "I'm not his keeper."

The gray-haired man cocked his head slightly. "Perhaps not. But we know the two of you are looking for him."

"Then your question isn't relevant, either. If we knew where he was, we wouldn't be looking for him, now would we?"

Nick had to smile. These two men weren't worrying Devin at all, her usual direct manner out in full force. Actually, he wasn't terribly concerned at the moment himself. If this was an abduction, it was a strange one. There was a smoked-glass partition separating them from the driver's compartment, and both he and the two goons were facing straight ahead. They seemed unconcerned and as nonthreatening as their employers.

Still, that situation could change at any moment, so Nick divided his attention between the trio up front and the distinguished pair doing all the talking.

"Do you know what his latest project is?" the younger one asked Devin.

"Crap."

The man raised his eyebrows. "Really, Ms. Prescott—"

"He's working with sludge," Devin interrupted, wrinkling her nose up at them. "Lovely job. You should look into it. With any luck you'd fall in."

The gray-haired man's thin lips turned upward just a tiny bit. "Come now, Ms. Prescott. We all know that Eli was working on another project entirely. What did you find out at the lab today?"

That one shocked her. "You have spies working inside Wingate?" she asked incredulously.

"Nothing so melodramatic," he assured her. "But we do have our sources."

Nick frowned. "In that case, gentlemen, you're already aware that no one at Wingate knows what Eli was doing behind locked doors. So why ask us?"

The younger man shifted in his seat. "It never pays to assume, Mr. Lang."

"It's a fact," Devin said. His legs were close enough for her to kick him in the shins and she was sorely tempted, considering his snobby, superior air. "No one knows!"

Nick couldn't be sure their soft touch would continue, especially with Devin around irritating them. Apparently she didn't realize what was going on. Nick thought he had a pretty good idea. It wasn't information they were after as much as the assurance that Devin and he didn't have any.

"This is a waste of all of our time," he said. "What do you really want from us? Why does Eli's disappearance have you so worried?"

"I'll tell you something that does worry us," the younger man returned. "Your involvement in this, Mr. Lang. Why are *you* so interested in finding Eli?"

Nick didn't flinch. But only his years of subterfuge, role-playing and bald-faced lying made it possible. Just how much did they know about him and his past? "I'm an investor in Wingate, for one thing. And a friend of Eli's."

"If you say so." The gray-haired man stared at Nick for a moment before turning his attention to Devin. As he did so, his entire demeanor changed. "I saw you massaging your little finger. It's not hurt, is it?"

Devin was baffled by the turn in the conversation. "No, it's fine."

"Good. We certainly wouldn't want to get on the bad side of Eli by injuring his niece." He paused for a moment. "I heard your solo last month. It was exquisite."

"Superb," the younger man added. He, too, had undergone a sudden personality change. "I hope this situation with Eli hasn't upset you unduly. Artistic temperament is so delicate."

Devin glanced at Nick, but he appeared just as confused. She scowled. "Excuse me, but did I miss something? We were just being interrogated, were we not?"

"Oh, interrogation is much too strong a word," the one with the gray hair told her. "We simply wanted to find out how much you know."

"And since we don't know anything, we're all friends now?" Devin shot back irritably. "I don't think so. Just because you like classical music, that doesn't make what you're doing all right with me."

"We don't simply like classical music, we're absolute aficionados," the younger one said. "And we will make full restitution for any inconvenience we have caused you." He withdrew a business card from a silver case he kept in his coat pocket and handed it to her. "Just send us a bill. It will be paid promptly."

Devin scanned the card. All it had on it was an odd company name and the address of a post office box in Aspen, Colorado. "What the heck is C Group?"

"A think tank."

"What do you think about?" Nick asked.

"We have interests in many areas," the gray-haired man replied. "However, our specialty is finding quiet solutions to delicate matters of industry and government."

The light was dawning in Devin's mind. "And which one is Uncle Eli?"

"Neither," the younger one said.

"At least not yet," his companion corrected. "You see, the project your uncle has been working on was commissioned by us. With his help, we intend to solve an embarrassing governmental problem."

Nick raised his eyebrows. "What kind of problem?"

"That, I'm afraid, is classified information," the older man told him. "In fact, if we're successful, the nature of it will never be publicly known." He smiled. "That's the whole point of C Group, you see."

If there was anything that rankled Nick more than the police, it was government toadies. "What I see is a couple of pompous jerks in white suits who just abducted two people right off the street. That's illegal, you know."

The younger one smiled. "Then I suggest you call the police, Mr. Lang," he said, sarcasm dripping from every word. "After we speak with them, I imagine they might have more questions about you than us."

Devin had no idea what that was all about, but it certainly sounded like a threat to her. From the way it made

Nick go taut as a violin string, though, she decided it would be best to prevent any further such exchanges.

Besides, she was getting the impression that calling the police about this wouldn't do them any good at all. Whoever these men were, Devin was willing to bet they had very heavy duty connections, indeed. That, she presumed, was why they felt they could safely explain themselves to her.

Perhaps they could even be coaxed into saying more. But that would require tact, not bluster. "Nick, please," she said softly, although the look she gave him was as hard as ice. "I don't think the police are necessary. Neither is this hostility." She turned back to the two men. "It seems to me that these gentlemen are as anxious to find Eli as we are. Since finding him is all that's important to me, I'm just sorry we can't be of more help."

Both men smiled genuinely for the first time. "We're so glad you feel that way, Ms. Prescott," the elder said.

"Indeed," the other agreed. "To offend a musician of your caliber..." He trailed off in a shudder. "Regrettably, it was necessary to take the risk."

His gray-headed friend nodded. "All too true. In the early going, secrecy was tantamount. We're sorry for the heavy-handed methods. But we had to know if any information on the project had leaked, or if Eli had confided either his whereabouts or intentions to you." His expression was a study in remorse. "As for this encounter, our other sources had failed us and we decided a face-to-face talk was the only option left to us."

Nick opened his mouth to speak. Devin cut him off before he could say a word. "No harm done," she assured them calmly. Her mind, though, was racing furiously.

Early going? Other sources? The only option left?

"No harm at all," Devin continued as pleasantly as possible. "As long as you meant what you said." She held up the business card. "He only trashed one room at Eli's but I'm going to need a maid service at my apartment."

The gray-haired man frowned, and for a moment Devin thought she'd guessed wrong. Then he turned to the other man and said, "I told you not to use that worn-out old carpetbagger!" He turned back to Devin. "I'm deeply sorry. That particular source of ours could use some instruction in manners. He'll receive it, believe me."

His voice, full of the promise of icy retribution, made Devin's blood run cold. Somehow, she imagined they had more in mind than etiquette lessons. "Well, it's not *that* bad."

Nick was practically shaking with anger now. "You had her phone tapped, too, didn't you?" he demanded.

That was news to Devin. "You tapped my phone?"

"Also a necessity," the younger one told her. Then he looked at Nick. "Even reasonably legal. We are empowered to do a great many things in our search for Eli, including pay a Wingate employee to watch him, and to make sure his research notes on the project we commissioned were safe after he left in such a hurry."

"Take them, you mean. Just who gave you this power to run roughshod over the general public?" Devin wanted to know.

"The persons they elected to offices of power," he said smugly. "But we had hoped that as far as Ms. Prescott was concerned, the tap would be all that was required."

"But Eli didn't call me, and I couldn't get in touch with him, either," Devin said. She was gazing thoughtfully at Nick. Why hadn't he told her about the phone tap? He undoubtedly had his reasons, and she would find out what they were. Now, however, she was intent on her quarry. "If you're 'empowered' to do all this, and so well-informed, why is it my uncle is still missing?"

"As you know, Eli is brilliant, not at all an easy man to keep track of," the older man replied. "Our source at Wingate informed us of his sudden departure, and still he eluded us." Suddenly he frowned. "Most perturbing."

"So he did leave of his own accord!" Devin exclaimed. She leaned forward on the seat. "Please, you must tell me what you know about this."

He looked at his companion, who was also frowning, then back at Devin. "I don't think that would be advisable. In fact, I think it would be best if the two of you didn't involve yourselves in this matter any further."

"I *am* involved!" Devin cried, slapping the seat beside her for emphasis. "I am going to stay involved until I find out what happened to Uncle Eli. And neither you nor your sources and connections are going to stand in my way!"

Rather than angry, the pair seemed enchanted with her outburst. "Such fire!" the younger one exclaimed.

"No doubt the source of her magnificent bow work!" the elder agreed. "Will you be playing the Sibelius Concerto in D Minor again this fall?"

"No, no!" his companion maintained. "Prokofiev! I simply must hear the Prokofiev!"

For a moment Devin stared at them, and Nick put his hand on her shoulder, afraid she was about to explode. But then she shrugged his hand off and smiled. No, he decided, what she actually did was *beam* at the two men.

"Gentlemen, please!" Devin protested. "I'm an artist, not a record player. I've been working on some very fine pieces. If you come, I'm sure you'll enjoy yourselves. I might even,'' she added slyly, ''manage to get you prime seats.''

Nick didn't fully understand it, but there was no doubt that this pair of white-frocked dandies thought Devin Prescott was the best thing since sliced bread. He tended to agree, albeit for entirely different reasons. Her music was lovely, but so was she. And naturally, he liked her fire, too, but saw in it the promise not only of fine bow work, but passion, as well. At the moment, however, he wanted to kiss her because of what she was doing.

Devin was setting them up. They certainly knew it; a child could see the hook she was about to set. The thing that impressed Nick, and obviously them as well, was the smooth, almost professional way she'd gone about it.

He winked at her. Devin winked back. ''Gentlemen,'' she said. ''I'll get you those tickets and send them with my bill. But in turn I beg of you to tell me what you know of Eli.''

The men looked at one another again. This time they were chuckling. ''Very well,'' the gray-haired man agreed. ''Not because of your lovely offer, however, but in the spirit of cooperation. Eli must be found. If I divulge what we have learned, you must in turn promise to keep us informed of whatever *you* might learn about his disappearance.''

Clearly, they thought that possibility slim. Devin didn't know how she was keeping her temper in check. For Eli's sake, she supposed. When she found him she would give him the tongue-lashing of his life.

''It's a deal,'' Devin said. ''We do know that he took a shuttle flight from here to Las Vegas, but—''

''Old news,'' the younger man interrupted, dismissing it with a wave of his pale hand. ''From there he boarded another flight to Los Angeles.''

"Los Angeles!" Devin nearly had to bite her tongue. Yvette Soomes! Did the think tank know about her? They'd never hear about her from Devin's lips, that was for sure. For whatever reason, she was a million dollars worth of importance to Eli, and Devin would keep that secret.

But as rapidly as her hopes had soared, they were dashed. Eli had been doing some soaring of his own. "From Los Angeles he flew to New York, then London, then on to Switzerland," he continued. "And from there... poof! He vanished. The search continues as we speak, but so far, no trace can be found."

"That's it? That's all you have?" Devin closed her eyes for a moment. When she opened them, she was no longer in a conciliatory mood. "How do you know this project of yours didn't get him kidnapped? Or killed?"

"There are no certainties in this business, Ms. Prescott. Eli accepted that. So must you. It is vital for you to cooperate fully with us from now on," the gray-haired man told her. Once again his expression had changed, back to that grim, icy visage. "Perhaps something has happened to your uncle. Personally, I doubt it."

"Why?" Devin asked. She was willing to cherish any hope, even if it came from him.

"The timing, for one thing. And we aren't pleased with Eli's chosen destination, Ms. Prescott. Not pleased at all."

Nick had managed to contain his animosity for the two think-tank men. Barely. "I'll just bet you aren't," he said. "Eli suddenly heading for a neutral country doesn't bode well for your secret project, does it?"

They glowered at him. The elder one rapped on the smoked-glass partition and made a circular motion with his forefinger. Instantly they felt the limo slow down and make a wide arc, then rapidly return in the direction it had come. Obviously the discussion was over.

Devin had other ideas. "How dare you call Uncle Eli a traitor! He's the most honest man I've ever known!"

"He is also an idealist," the younger think-tank man returned. "As such, he has his own ideas about what is and is not proper behavior."

"I don't expect you'll understand this," Nick said, his jaw clenched. "But I feel honor bound to explain it to you, anyway. Yes, Eli is an idealist. And his idea of proper behavior, as you put it, does indeed go against the norm on occasion. But he is a great man. A decent man. The sort of scientist who puts the welfare of the planet above that of any one country, government or special-interest group. I know he must have some very good reasons for dealing with you and your think tank." Nick paused, glowering at the two men. "But in my opinion, gentlemen, what the world needs is more doers like Eli Wingate and fewer thinkers like you."

They stared at him. *Devin* stared at him. There was a curious feeling deep inside her and a very pleasant tingling along her spine. She had wondered all along whether Nick really believed in what Eli was doing, or had simply been telling her what he thought she wanted to hear.

Now she had no doubts. He *did* care. This added one more layer to Nick's already intriguing personality, and an exciting, even arousing layer it was, to her way of thinking.

"Thank you," she told him softly.

Nick smiled at her. "My pleasure."

The limo pulled to a stop. One of the goons got out of the driver's compartment and opened the rear curbside door. Nick wasted no time in getting out of the car, and

Devin slid across the seat right behind him, joining him on the sidewalk. The goon closed the rear door, then got back into the limo.

With a quiet whir, the rear side window rolled down. "It was a pleasure to meet you, Ms. Prescott. I'm sorry it had to be under such tense circumstances," the gray-haired man told Devin apologetically. Then he leaned forward and looked at them both, with eyes as dark and hard as chips of obsidian. "We'll be in touch."

The window rolled back up and the limo sped off. Devin turned to Nick. "I didn't like the sound of that," she said.

"It did have an ominous ring to it," Nick agreed.

From behind them, a strident female voice rang out from Lucinda Wingate's porch. "Get in here, you two! Right now!"

Devin groaned. How much had her grandmother seen? "As if those pompous jerks weren't enough," she muttered. "Now we're in for a *real* interrogation."

Chapter Fifteen

"What's taking you so long?" Lucinda yelled. "It's hot as blue blazes out there!"

"Let's get it over with," Devin muttered. "There's no avoiding this confrontation, not with *my* grandmother."

Lucinda was waiting on the porch, holding the glass door open for them. She was wearing white slacks with a bright orange, long-sleeved blouse, her white hair pulled back into a neat chignon.

"Come on in, young man. I have iced tea ready in the living room."

Nick followed Devin into the cool house. Polished hardwood floors ran from the entry to a hallway on the left and then continued farther to the end of the house. To his right was a living room furnished in antiques, the far wall filled with family photos.

"You two sit on the sofa."

The sofa was in the middle of the room, angled to face the front door, and opposite it were two matching chairs with an old, ornately carved table topped with a ginger jar lamp between them. In the middle of the grouping there was an oval wooden table with a tray on top holding cut crystal glasses of iced tea.

Nick sat down slowly near the middle of the rust-colored velvet sofa, worried that the spindly curving legs might break under his weight. He hated furniture like this. Devin sat on his right, leaving a good two feet of empty cushion between them.

Lucinda handed a tall crystal glass of iced tea to Devin, along with a white napkin. "Do you take anything in your tea?" she asked Nick.

"No, ma'am." He started to rise to get a glass but she waved him back down.

"Sit down, and don't worry about breaking the sofa. It's tougher than it looks. Survived through four children and five grandchildren." Lucinda handed him a glass, then looked at Devin. "Where are your manners? Introduce us."

"Sorry," Devin murmured. "Grandmother, this is Nick Lang. Nick, this is my grandmother, Lucinda Wingate."

They shook hands and then Lucinda sat down in one of the chairs opposite them, glass of tea in hand. "Now that the pleasantries are over with let's get down to business. Something's going on and I want to know what. Immediately."

Devin frowned. "But your—"

"Hush! I don't want to hear any poppycock from you, Devin. My heart is working just fine. This mollycoddling from the family is what's making me ill, not my so-called heart condition. And I'm not putting up with it any longer." She glowered at her granddaughter. "Do you understand?"

Devin nodded. "Yes, Grandmother."

"Well, then, start at the beginning." Lucinda paused and looked at Nick, wagging a finger at him. "And I expect you to fill in any pieces she leaves out, without prodding. I'll know right away," she warned him. "My granddaughter is a terrible liar. Is that understood?"

Nick kept the smile off his face. Wrathful was a good way to describe her temper. "Yes, ma'am."

"Well? Don't just sit there blinking at me like a couple of barnyard owls. Start!" Lucinda commanded. "I hate puzzles, and I don't like not knowing what's happening within my own family."

Devin began slowly, hesitant at first to burden her grandmother with the problem, but Lucinda relished the tale, prodding Nick for even more details when she felt something was being left out.

"I think it's high time the police were called in," Devin concluded after telling everything. "We should report Eli as missing."

"No!" Lucinda exclaimed, but her voice was nearly drowned out by Nick's. She looked at him approvingly. 'You and I are going to get along just fine," she said, smiling at him. "We'll get to your reasons in a moment." She set her tea glass down. "I think you should know this isn't the first time Eli has done secretive work for the government."

Devin was stunned. "I never knew that."

"You never know everything about a person," Lucinda said. "I was married fifty-five years to your grandfather and that man still managed to surprise me to the day he died. Eli is very much his father's son."

"But he's in trouble. Those strange men in the limo are after him, and we have no proof that they're working for the government," Devin insisted.

Nick leaned forward and put his empty glass on the tray, then looked at Devin. "Calling the authorities might get Eli in even deeper trouble, because we don't know what he's been doing or for whom."

"Exactly. If Eli *is* working on a delicate matter," Lucinda added, "then it's best to let him work it out by himself. He's been doing it for years, after all."

Devin was aware that the two of them were ganging up against her, and she didn't like it one bit. "You're telling me to wait and see if he shows up, just like Jay and Richard," she said angrily. "How could you?"

"Hold your tongue, Devin. I never said that," Lucinda reprimanded sharply. "I agree that something isn't right, but if the men he's working for can't find him with all their connections, then involving the local police won't help, especially if he was last spotted in Switzerland."

"I suppose that's true," Devin muttered.

Lucinda placed her hands in her lap, one finger caressing her wedding rings. "You develop a sixth sense over the years with your children—you know when something is seriously wrong." She looked at her granddaughter. "I feel that Eli is alive and well, and probably still in Switzerland. He goes there at least once a year." Lucinda smiled as Devin's eyes widened. "That's one more thing you didn't know."

"Why does he go there every year?" Devin asked.

"That I don't know. I don't like to be kept out of family business, but when it comes to personal matters, I don't believe in prying unless it's absolutely necessary. If Eli wanted me to know he would have told me."

Nick stretched his cramped legs out in front of him, the sofa too low to the floor for their length. "But I assume his other trips have always been planned in advance?"

"I have no idea," Lucinda replied. The sound of a phone ringing pierced the quietness of the room. "Excuse me for a moment."

Nick stood as Lucinda left the room. "That reminds me, I need to call and see if I have any messages. Jerry might have found out something new."

"The phone's free," Lucinda said, coming back into the room. "Go straight ahead there to the kitchen," she said, pointing to the back of the house.

Devin watched as her grandmother sat down, but she kept quiet, waiting for her to say something.

"Devin, I know you're upset. Because of Eli's influence, you've never had a very high opinion of your other uncles, and considering their recent actions, maybe it's partly deserved. But you have to remember that as much as the boys have always fought, they still love each other. I can't believe they'd physically hurt Eli."

"Maybe not physically," Devin conceded for her grandmother's sake. "But they're up to something, I can feel it. They're still furious because Eli threatened to quit three months ago over that insurance matter. They don't like to back down."

Lucinda sighed. "I'm in agreement with Eli on that, but he's not always right. Jay and Richard inherited a canny sense of business from your grandfather and I. The moves they're making are for the best of the company."

Condensation dripped down the sides of her glass to the napkin, and Devin drew a circle in it. "So why aren't they telling you about those moves?"

"Oh, I intend to find that out and more," Lucinda assured her with a smile. She looked over Devin's head as Nick came back into the room. "Is something wrong, Nick?"

"The mad trasher strikes again," Nick informed them. "My cleaning lady left a message on my machine. Said we'd have to discuss price before she'll even start on the mess."

Devin sipped her tea. "Would she clean up mine, too?"

"What?" Nick glared at her. "Don't you have a service?"

Lucinda chuckled. "That'll be the day."

"No, I'm neat by habit. And training," she added, with a nod at Lucinda. "But in this case I believe I'll make an exception. Did Jerry call?"

"No." He walked to the front door, then back to the hallway, hands thrust in his khaki slacks. If he'd been alone he would have been swearing up a storm. "This is ridiculous! Eli has never even been to my house."

"Perhaps he was looking for something else," Lucinda suggested. "We really don't know if this intruder is after the secret project, or not, now, do we?"

"She's right," Devin said. She didn't much like the way her grandmother had said *we*. But she supposed that was one reason she was so relieved to have everything out in the open. Lucinda did have a sharp mind. "Let's think this through. We know he's searched your place, mine and Eli's looking for... Well, for who knows what." Nick was still pacing back and forth but he nodded to indicate he was listening to her. "I think the only way we're going to find out what he's after is to have a chat with him."

"I'd like to have a chat with him, all right," Nick muttered. "But how do you propose we find him? Take out a classified ad?"

"Oh, he's cute, Devin!" her grandmother said.

"Just darling." She put down her glass and leaned back on the sofa, arms crossed. "No, smart guy. What I meant was, whatever he's looking for, the mad trasher is obviously making the rounds. So where's the next logical place he'll look?"

Nick shrugged. "This is your plan, not mine."

"I know!" Lucinda exclaimed proudly. "Right here! I'm Eli's closest relative and he stops by regularly." She rubbed her hands together, laughing. "It's about time I had a little excitement around this place. It's been awfully dull since your grandfather died. We'll set a trap for this mad trasher!"

"Grandmother, I really don't... You shouldn't..." Devin looked at Nick for help. No one told her grandmother what to do, but Lucinda was always more open to a man's persuasion. "Tell her, Nick. It's not safe for her to stay here."

Lucinda rose to her full height and stared down at her granddaughter with fury in her pale blue eyes. "Now you listen here, Devin! I—"

"Mrs. Wingate," Nick interrupted softly as he came between the two women. "Devin loves you and because of that she fears for your safety. I've only known you a few minutes and I'm concerned for you, too. Couldn't you stay with friends or relatives, for just a day or two?" Her stance remained unrelenting and he tried another tactic. "I'm sure whoever you choose to stay with will be delighted to have you around, as we would be if this man wasn't so mysterious. We'll tell you all about it, in vivid detail, I promise. After all, he might not even show up."

Lucinda shook her head, a tiny smile starting to show. "You're wasting your charm on me, Nick Lang. Why don't you try using it on my granddaughter for the next few days?" Her smile grew broader. "You'll both be here, correct?"

Nick glanced at Devin. She nodded. "Yes, ma'am," he said. "That way we can keep watch in shifts."

"Well, then." Lucinda sighed happily. "I think I'll pay Jay and Richard each a little visit, in turn. Raise a bit of havoc in their lives." Her smile faded and she shook her finger at them. "But when I return I expect this place spotless and the beds made. I'll hold both of you responsible if my place is trashed!"

Devin was uncomfortably aware of the mischievous sparkle in her grandmother's eyes, one she hadn't seen since her grandfather died last year. Suddenly she was less sure of her decision to stay in the house with Nick.

She wiped the idea of backing out from her mind. There was no way she'd let Lucinda know she was worried about handling Nick and the mutual attraction they shared!

"They'll be instantly suspicious," Devin noted. "What are you going to tell them?"

"What else! That my air conditioner is broken," Lucinda replied. "If it worked for you, it'll work for me." She patted a wisp of white hair into place. "After all, I'm a much better liar."

Chapter Sixteen

Lucinda packed an overnight case and left a short while later, amid a barrage of cautions, provisos and still more instructions. Nick parked his car in the garage, and locked all the doors in the house. Then Devin gave him a thorough tour of Lucinda's home.

"You sure played down your suspicions about Jay and Richard with your grandmother," Nick commented as they left the third and last bedroom.

"Not enough, I'm afraid. Grandmother knew I at least suspected them of foul play," Devin admitted. "Since her heart attack she hasn't kept as close a watch over the business, but her not knowing about something as major as the university negotiations worries me, and it makes me wonder what else my two uncles have been up to recently."

Nick followed her into the living room. "Such as?"

"I'm not sure, but I'm going to find out."

He stayed right behind her. "How? Through Lucinda?"

"No." Devin flipped on the light in the kitchen. "She can make their lives hell, but if they don't want her to know something, they just won't tell her until it's too late to change things.'' She shrugged. ''I'll come up with a way.''

Nick leaned against the counter and crossed his arms. He had nice arms, Devin observed, firm and hard without the overdeveloped structure of those goons who'd grabbed them earlier.

''Why are you so sure they're up to something that could hurt Eli or his work?'' he asked.

''I'm not *sure.* I've got a strong feeling, that's all. Over dinner I'll tell you a story about the three of them that Grandmother told me the other day. It made me think.'' In fact, it had given her a bad dream, about Eli flying through the air with rockets on his feet, while Jay and Richard cackled wildly below. ''Maybe it'll help you understand them better.''

''I'd like that.''

''When do you think our intruder will show up?'' Devin asked, heading for the refrigerator.

''Hard to tell. He's bound to get around to us eventually, maybe even sometime tonight.''

Devin frowned. ''But that doesn't fit his modus operandi or whatever it's called. So far, he's been striking in broad daylight,'' she objected.

''True. But this is not the average burglar, remember? He's been moving fast, from one place to the next in a matter of hours,'' Nick said, rapidly snapping his fingers to emphasize his point. ''I think it's time for him to change his pattern.''

Devin opened the refrigerator. ''How do you know?''

''Just part of my job,'' Nick returned casually. He peered over her shoulder at the contents of the fridge. ''So, what are you making us for dinner?''

''Oh, no, you don't!'' She shook her head. ''Just because I clean my own apartment, that doesn't make me

Little Miss Homemaker. *We* are going to make dinner together, and afterward, *we* are going to clean up the mess. Got it?''

He grinned. "Yes, ma'am."

"Would you stop calling me that?" She took a head of lettuce and plopped it into his hand. "There. See if you can make a couple of salads without maiming yourself."

"Yes, sir?"

Devin sighed. "Just chop the lettuce."

Together they cooked a meal—somehow managing not to injure each other or themselves—and while they were eating Devin told him the story of the exploding beds.

At first Nick didn't believe her, but the more he thought about it the more believable it became. He'd had his own fair share of feuds with his younger brother, but they'd never gone that far. Then again, neither of them possessed an IQ the size of Eli's. Few people did.

After cleaning up the kitchen they settled down on a cushy sofa in a small room opposite the kitchen to watch a suspense movie on television.

"This is terrible," Devin muttered an hour later.

"That blond guy might be good-looking, but he wouldn't last a minute as an undercover agent," Nick agreed. He picked up the remote control and turned off the set. A single lamp in the corner behind the sofa was turned on low, leaving the room in a cozy glow. The rest of the house was dark. "You can go to bed if you want. I'll take the first watch."

"No, that's okay. I'm too wound up to sleep."

He nodded. "Yeah, I know. So what do you want to do? Try another channel?"

"I've had enough." Devin curled her legs up beside her and faced Nick. A small, square, lemon yellow pillow sat on the sofa between them. "Tell me more about you and your security background."

"That's boring. I'd rather hear about you and your background. When did you decide to become a violinist?"

"Decide?" She laughed. "I don't think there was much of a decision involved. It was more like fate," Devin told him. "When I was very young, Uncle Eli took me to hear the symphony play *Peter and the Wolf*. It's something of a standard introductory piece for children that—"

"I know it," Nick interjected. "I heard it when I was young, too. The imagery is so clear. From then on, I never listened to classical music the same way."

Devin smiled. This man continually surprised her. "That's the idea," she said. "While most of the other kids fidgeted in their seats, I just sat there, totally absorbed. The music of the violin seemed especially vibrant to me, as if it were the voice of the orchestra. Eli noticed my keen interest and bought my first, scaled-down instrument."

"And voilà!" Nick waved a hand in the air. "You took to it like a duck to water and a star was born!"

"Hardly," Devin said, laughing. "I was not a child prodigy, by any means. I had to work hard, but the violin slowly became *my* voice, too, in a way. Through it I could communicate my inner feelings, my moods. For me that connection and communication are what make me a musician."

"But not a star?"

"Not really. Well-known in certain circles, yes. But to become a major force in classical music requires a drive and all-consuming dedication I simply don't have," Devin explained. "It also requires more than talent.

There has to be a spark, a genius. Like Eli has in his field."

Nick was nodding thoughtfully. "I see. But if you're not completely dedicated to your music, what else is there to your life? You're not married, no kids...."

"My life is very full!" Devin objected.

"Hey! No offense. I was just asking."

Devin cursed herself for overreacting. But he was getting too close to a sore point of hers. Her mother and Lucinda were constantly pestering her about boyfriends and the ticking of her biological clock. She didn't need anyone else putting their two cents in, especially Nick.

"How about you?" Devin asked. "You didn't make it sound as if your life is one big scintillating experience after another."

Nick laughed. "No, it's not." Not anymore, at any rate, and that's just the way he liked it. Most of the time. He was getting a pretty big kick out of this mystery with Eli. He was also getting a kick out of Devin. It put him in an expansive mood. "I'm a workaholic, something of a loner and not all that popular with my family."

"Oh?"

"I was a bad boy, a rebellious teenager and then turned into what you might call the black sheep," Nick told her. "My education was sporadic, separated by stretches of laboring at the various businesses under my family's control." He laughed again. "In the end, that's what made me so adept at judging investment potential. I've worked for all sorts of firms, so I know a sound structure when I see it."

Devin's interest was piqued. "That's not boring at all! How on earth did a 'bad boy' get interested in security consulting?" she asked.

He cleared his throat. His expansive mood was getting him into trouble, and Devin was getting just a bit too close to the truth. As much as he liked her, there were still parts of himself he wasn't willing to share—perhaps never would be, no matter what happened between them.

But he did want something to happen. And he supposed he owed her the bare bones, at least. "That came as a result of one of those sporadic educational episodes," Nick replied. "I was back East, working for an electronics firm in New Jersey. The opportunity presented itself to attend a sort of security technician's trade school, and being the impulsive young man that I was, I jumped in with both feet."

"What sort of trade school?"

"Oh, just an informal kind of thing," Nick replied, dismissing its importance with a wave of his hand. "But I turned out to be good at the work. A tiny portion of that spark of genius you mentioned, maybe. Anyway, I pursued it independently for a while, but was eventually forced to realize that was too dangerous."

"Dangerous?" Devin repeated, arching her eyebrows.

"Uh, I mean risky," Nick said. "You know what I mean. In your line of work, you're at risk when you play a solo, right? The rest of the orchestra isn't playing to cover your mistakes. What I was doing was like that—no one to cover my back. So I convinced my family to form a security division within the company. My father doesn't like it at all, partly because I proved him wrong and made a success of both the division and myself."

Devin was gazing at him, her brows knit into a frown. There was something about his story that smacked of evasion. Not out-and-out lies, really. It was more like a double meaning.

"About this trade school," she said. "What—"

"I've just realized how much we have in common," Nick interrupted. "Eli gave you your first violin, so you owe a part of your success to him. I owe him part of mine, as well."

Apparently Nick had no intention of answering her question, at least not now. She sighed. Still, he had just said something every bit as intriguing. "What did Eli do for you? Give you your first lock to pick?"

He chuckled. "No. He was the one who convinced me to set up a security consulting division at Lang. Probably saved my life," Nick said. Then he added quickly, "In a manner of speaking, I mean. Being self-employed may be the American dream, but it sure is a hard row to hoe."

"Uh-huh." Devin continued to gaze at him doubtfully. "So that's another reason you were so adamant about helping me search for him. You feel you owe him a debt."

"I do owe him. More than I can say," Nick corrected. "But there's more to it than that. I believe in him."

"That's obvious." She smiled, remembering the way he had stood up for Eli against the think-tank men. "Thank you again for that speech you made to those two guys. It was exactly what I was thinking, but was too mad to put into words."

"I know. And again, you're entirely welcome." Nick took the pillow that was on the sofa between them and set it aside so he could move closer to her. "That's another thing we have in common. Our respect for Eli's work."

Devin nodded. His closeness made the temperature in the room seem to rise. "I think there really is something wrong with Grandmother's air conditioner."

She started to get up off the couch. Nick gently took her hand and prevented her from getting to her feet. "I just thought of something else," he said softly.

"Excuse me?" Devin asked.

"Something else we have in common. We both have full lives. Full lives with great big holes in the middle."

It was very warm now. Nick was even closer. There was a warning voice in Devin's mind, but it was rather dim, some nonsense about not really knowing this man—and more to the point, not knowing what he had been. But how was she to find out about him if she didn't allow him closer? She *wanted* him closer.

"I don't know what you mean," Devin murmured, her voice scarcely above a whisper. "My life doesn't have any holes."

"Sure it does. Let me show you."

Nick leaned toward her, his lips brushing hers gently. When he met no resistance he lightly kissed her again. She sighed and pulled away from him a fraction.

"I didn't say you could do that," she said, but in a lazy voice she almost didn't recognize as her own.

He nibbled softly at her neck. "I didn't ask."

Devin slid her hand around his head, her mouth opening beneath the onslaught of his tongue as they greedily drank of each other. As he put more weight on her she fell back into the cushions, Nick following her down to lie on top of her as they kissed again and again.

Breathing heavily, he leaned up on one elbow and pulled on her silky blouse with his free hand, parting it from her slacks, eager to touch her soft skin. Devin unbuttoned his shirt with trembling hands, wanting to feel the warmth of his skin beneath her fingers. She pushed his shirt aside, her hands roaming over the hard muscles of his chest.

Suddenly Nick became perfectly still.

Devin looked into his eyes, bewildered. "What—"

He gently clasped his hand over her mouth and whispered in her ear, his breathing uneven. "I heard a noise coming from the living room." Devin became a frozen statue beneath him. "Please, stay here."

Nick eased himself down to the floor, then crawled on all fours to the end of the couch. When Devin touched him lightly on the shoulder he almost had heart failure.

"What?"

Her hot breath caressed his ear as she spoke. "Remember, the first bedroom on the right is her home office. There's a safe in the floor behind the desk."

"Right. Now stay here."

Nick stood, letting his eyes adjust to the darkness of the room before he ventured any farther. Once out of the room he kept his back against the wall, moving slowly toward the living room. The long room was dark, the few shadows he could see not moving at all.

At the edge of the hallway he peered around the corner. He could just barely see the figure outlined in black moving silently forward. The silhouette stopped outside the first bedroom on the left and slipped inside.

Quietly Nick moved to a position outside the closed bedroom door, listening for noises. The guy was good, his movements as quiet as a feather landing on the floor. He'd also had more practice of late than Nick, which meant Nick would have to rely on timing and luck.

He waited patiently until he felt the slight breeze caused by the door opening. As the man came out of the room Nick stepped forward and punched him hard in the solar plexus, hoping to knock the wind out of him.

The black figure bent over a tiny bit, but still had enough fight left in him to make a charge at Nick, his full weight knocking them both backward into the wall. They rolled to the floor, scuffling for the upper hand.

Suddenly a brilliant flash of light blinded both of them momentarily, and they fell apart. The other man was older, and Nick's eyes recovered first, giving him a tiny edge. He seized it, landing another solid blow to the intruder's solar plexus. This one did the trick. He rolled to his side, gasping. Nick jumped up to find Devin at the entrance to the hallway, a huge butcher knife in one hand, a big flashlight in the other.

"Thanks for not doing as you were told," Nick said, his eyes never leaving the man on the floor. "I'll take the knife. Can you find some rope and turn on more lights?"

"Yes," Devin replied, turning on the hall light.

The intruder was recovering. He got to his knees, his eyes focusing on Nick. Nick deftly flipped the butcher knife around so he was holding it by the blade, and raised it to right above his shoulder in good throwing position.

The man peered at his captor through the slits in his black ski mask. "Take it easy, Nicky! You wouldn't stab an old comrade in arms, would you?"

Chapter Seventeen

"Take off that mask," Nick ordered. The other man obliged. Nick couldn't believe his eyes. "Frank Delano?"

"The very same, Nicky." He winced. "Do you mind if I get up? My knees are killing me."

It had been quite a few years since Nick had last seen this man. He would have preferred it to have been a hundred more. "All right," Nick said. "But do it slowly."

"There's no other way I *can* do it," Frank told him, getting painfully to his feet. "Ouch! It's a terrible thing to get old, Nicky. Especially in our profession."

Nick lowered the knife and flipped it around again, grasping the wooden handle. He then moved closer to the other man, holding it up so that the hallway light glinted off the blade. "Your profession, Frank. I'm a security consultant. We're on opposite sides of the fence now. If you want to get any older, you'll keep your mouth shut about the past, especially in front of the lady."

"Oh, I get it," Frank said, looking pointedly at Nick's open shirt. He winked. "Mum's the word, Nicky."

"Grab some sky. And stop calling me Nicky!"

Frank held his hands up. "Sure! Anything you say!"

"That's right, Frank. Anything I say." Nick motioned with the knife. "Move into the living room."

Frank did as ordered, the wicked glint off the thin blade making compliance a given. Frank Delano and Nick Lang had been more rivals than friends, and even that relationship had ended long ago. He couldn't be sure what the guy might do.

"Could've knocked me over with a feather when I found out you were the guy squiring Eli Wingate's niece around," Frank said. "Funny. We kept crossing paths but I never saw your face."

"I didn't see yours, either. If I had, I would have told the police," Nick informed him. "I still might if you don't tell me the sort of things I want to hear."

"Brother! You *have* changed."

"Sit down in that chair," Nick ordered.

"Sure thing. Just watch the knife, will you?"

He sat in the spindly-legged chair with matching frail arms, his muscles protesting at the abuse he'd just given them. Maybe it was time to change professions. The way Nick was acting, he was starting to think he'd be lucky to get out of this embarrassing situation alive.

"Sorry about your apartment," Frank said. "But I just had to check it out. I mean, knowing you like I do."

Just then Devin entered the room carrying a coil of white rope on her forearm. She stopped dead in her tracks, eyes wide and staring at the two men. "He *knows* you?" she asked Nick incredulously.

"He thinks he does," Nick replied with a warning glance at Frank. "Devin Prescott, meet Franklin Delano, otherwise known as the mad trasher."

He gave her a winning smile. "Just call me Frank."

Devin was totally bewildered. "But how—"

"We sort of went to that same trade school I told you about," Nick interjected. "I was a freshman, Frank was an alumnus. He'd been in the business for years and years. He was something of a role model for me, until I found out he was using his skills for evil purposes."

"You mean he's a thief?" she asked.

"I beg your pardon," Frank objected. "I, madam, am no common thief. I'm an industrial spy!"

"Shut up, Frank," Nick said. "Hand me that rope, Devin. This guy's too tricky to leave loose."

Frank was clearly offended. "Come on, Nicky...I mean Nick. I'll behave. Heck, I can barely run, anyway." He looked at Devin for sympathy. "It's the knees, you know. Arthritis. Happens to the best of us."

Devin was completely out of her depth. Spy or thief, Frank Delano was hardly the sort of man she met every night. Looking at him, it was hard to believe he was the one who had been doing all this breaking and entering, yet there he sat, living proof. She was mad, curious and frightened, all at the same time. Frightened won; she handed Nick the rope.

While Nick tied him up, Devin walked over and sat on the edge of the sofa across from the man. He was older than she'd expected, probably middle forties. She supposed he was fairly handsome, in a rough-hewn sort of way. His brown hair was sticking out all over from the ski mask he'd been wearing. From the look of his pointed, hawkish nose, it had been broken at least once. While she studied him, he studied her, as well, with interested hazel eyes.

"Who are you working for?" Devin asked.

Frank laughed. "You really are new at this, aren't you?" He looked at Nick, who put the finishing touches on a knot and stood up to face him. "Tell her how it goes, Nick. I don't talk for free. Give and take, right?"

"Right," Nick said. "You give us what we want, we take it, and maybe you'll walk out of here in one piece. Answer the lady, Frank. Who's your employer?"

Some of Frank's easygoing manner disappeared. "Hey. I can't do that. They'd kill me."

That was all the confirmation Devin needed. "I think they have that in mind already," she told him. "We had a little chat with two men from C Group earlier today. They don't approve of the way you've been performing your searches."

Frank was no longer smiling. There was only one way she would know about C Group. "They contacted you?"

"That's a nice way of putting it," Nick replied. Once again, Devin had a plan, and he thought he knew what it was. If it worked, everything would be much simpler. "And Devin isn't kidding about the threat. They said something about regretting hiring you, and about giving you some lessons in manners for messing up their favorite violinist's home."

"Damn!" Frank squirmed in his chair. "Let me go! Those guys have more power than the electric company. I've got to find a rock to hide under, Nicky, but quick!"

"Call me Nicky one more time and I'll pack you in a box and ship you to them myself," Nick said.

"Come on, Nick. This is no joke."

Nick shrugged. "You chose the profession, not me."

Frank gnawed at his lower lip. He didn't scare easily, but his bones didn't heal like they used to, either. Worse, C Group could also fix it so he would have great difficulty getting the only sort of work he was trained to do. If he did retire, he'd rather it be his decision, not theirs.

"I'm not the only one in trouble, you know," Frank said. "C Group has a lot of clout and the ego to use it. If they want something from you two, you'd better give it to them or climb under that rock with me."

Devin didn't like the sound of that. But she had made up her mind to stay with this, no matter what. "All they want from us is help finding Eli Wingate. Since I'm his niece, and it's to their advantage to stay on Eli's good side, I doubt Nick or I are in much danger. You, on the other hand, have fouled up," she said, pointing to the ropes. "Which brings to mind a solution to your dilemma, Mr. Delano."

Frank looked at her warily. "What's that?"

"Get on *my* good side," Devin replied. "All I want is to find my uncle, and I'll do anything necessary to achieve that goal. It happens to be C Group's goal, as well. Cooperate with us, and everybody will be happy."

Nick grinned. It did his heart good to see his one-time rival in this situation. "She has a point there, Frank."

He was scowling, deep in thought. She did have a point. There was also the possibility he could make this a two-way street. The way things were going, a bit of extra cash might come in handy about now. Besides, it was the principle of the thing. Frank wanted those research notes so badly he could taste it; Devin Prescott might know where they were.

It was cooperation time.

His smile returned. "You've got a deal."

"Good," Devin said. "First of all, what are all these break-ins about? What are you after?" Devin asked.

"I was after anything and everything," he admitted with a shrug. "Clues as to where your uncle had gone and why, mainly." Now came the tricky part. "I was also looking for his research notes."

"Which ones?" Devin asked.

Frank shrugged again. "I'm not a scientist, lady. But it's evidently the rest of a formulation. There's a piece of paper in my turtleneck pocket with the particulars I'm looking for written out. It's too complicated to memorize."

Nick leaned over and plucked a narrow white strip of paper out of Frank's pocket. He looked at it, then at Devin. "Beats me."

Devin reached for the paper and studied it. "I hate these things, all symbols and numbers." She sat on the sofa, still puzzled. "Wait a minute. You said the *rest* of a formulation. It doesn't sound like Eli to give them part of his notes, but if he did, I find it difficult to believe they'd let anyone wander around with that much information about a secret project."

"Very difficult to believe," Nick agreed, glaring suspiciously at Frank. "You're playing both ends against the middle again, aren't you?"

Frank cleared his throat nervously. The woman was sharper than he'd thought. And he should have known that Nick would remember his methods. "Okay. So I'm working for two employers at the same time," he admitted. "One wants Eli Wingate, the other wants his notes. It's a living."

"A living that can get you killed," Nick said dryly.

Devin wasn't satisfied. "But not even the people at Wingate know what Eli's secret project is. Why would anybody pay you to steal something if they weren't sure it was worth it?"

"What's this secret project jazz?" Frank asked. "I was told the formulation was for a product of some kind. Worth some bucks, too, judging by how much I'll get paid for it."

Nick groaned. "Oh, no. Not *another* wrinkle. We'll never figure this mess out!"

Devin was more sanguine. "Remember, Nick. One piece at a time." She looked eagerly at Frank. "Who is this other employer of yours?"

"I don't know."

"You have to know!" Devin exclaimed.

"I'm not a doctor, lady. My clients don't come to my office for face-to-face consultation," Frank told her. "See, they get word to me that they need something, and if I think I can acquire it, I get back to them about how much it'll cost. If they go for the deal, some money finds its way to me. I get the stuff and, in return for some more money, the stuff finds its way to them. It's safer for both of us."

"Oh," Devin said, sighing. Maybe Nick was right, after all. "What a mess! I know Eli hasn't come up with anything new recently, which means that whatever this product is, it has to be old stuff. Why would your employer be interested in it now?"

"If the product was patented, as most of Eli's work is, then it's possible the patent is about to expire," Nick suggested. "That leaves an open market. With the formula in hand, they can then whip up their own generic version of whatever it is without doing much research."

Frank chuckled. "That's one of the first things they teach you at trade school, right, Nick?"

Nick ignored him. His attention was on Devin, who in turn was gazing at their captive spy. Nick could almost see the wheels turning in her head. What now?

"How would you like to put your considerable skills to a noble use for a change, Mr. Delano?" she asked.

He looked at her warily. "What do you have in mind?"

"I assume you've already been inside Wingate?"

"Yeah," he replied. "But I didn't find anything."

"Neither did we." She smiled. "Perhaps we didn't look in the right place. The offices of Eli's brothers, Jay and Richard, could hold the key to where he went and why. Since I think they're up to something, however, I want you to get us into their offices without their knowledge. Tonight."

Frank arched his eyebrows. "That's crazy!"

"I think it's a great idea," Nick said.

He was all for it. He knew that look in Devin's eyes by now. She was determined to find out what secrets those offices held. By getting Frank to do the dirty work, he wouldn't have to reveal—or explain—his own expertise in such things.

Frank didn't share their enthusiasm. "Look. I've checked it out, and in some ways it's riskier getting into those offices than it was the lab. What if we get caught?"

"I'll vouch for you," Devin promised. "I am a member of the family, after all."

Nick smiled. She wasn't that bad a liar. Devin looked and sounded quite convincing to him, even though she was promising something she couldn't deliver. "I will, too," he said. "I'm a major investor in the company."

"What's in it for me?" Frank asked.

"Your freedom. You did break into my grandmother's house," Devin reminded him. "And we could still turn you over to the police."

"Might be a better deal for me all around if you did," Frank said. "I don't have a record, so with luck and a good lawyer I can probably get off with just probation. Prison overcrowding being what it is."

Devin gritted her teeth. "What do you want?"

"The research notes." Frank couldn't believe he was actually doing this. Those darn things were going to be his undoing yet. "If we find them, you hand 'em over to me."

Nick motioned to Devin, and the pair went to the far corner of the living room where they could talk privately and still keep an eye on their captive.

"I say we go for it," Nick said quietly. "We'll have to watch him closely, in case he decides to help himself to whatever he can grab. But C Group evidently has the notes on the government project, so that's safe. Besides, from what I've seen, I don't think Eli's notes alone would do anybody much good."

"I don't care one way or the other," Devin told him. "I only want to find Eli. If it means making a deal with a thief, so be it." Her attitude amazed her. But she had to know what was going on. She glanced at Frank. "The question is, can we trust him not to abandon us if we hit a rough spot?"

"As long as he thinks he's still on the trail of those notes, yes. It shouldn't be too hard to string him along. Let him look. For all we know, Jay and Richard do have what he's after."

Devin felt a surge of excitement. "Let's do it." She turned and went back to where Frank sat. "Okay, Mr. Delano. You've got a deal."

"Please call me Frank, Devin," he said with a grin. "Partners in crime should be on a first-name basis. Now, if you'll untie me, we'll get this show on the road."

Chapter Eighteen

Fence climbing had never been one of Devin's favorite childhood pastimes. The fact that she'd had little practice made the nine-foot chain-link one that surrounded Wingate look especially daunting. But at least the metal was cool beneath her fingers as she climbed over the top, the nighttime desert temperatures having dropped to the low seventies.

Devin scampered down the other side, hitting the ground seconds after Nick and before Frank, who, dressed all in black like the rest of them, seemed to be moving very slowly. A sliver of a moon illuminated the three of them as they ran across the dusty ground, dodging thorny cacti and the eerie branches of Joshua trees as they headed for the closest edge of the Wingate building off in the distance.

Once at the side, all three stopped, panting for breath. "How do you go in?" Nick asked. He and Devin had decided it would be unwise to show Frank the secret entrance.

Frank took a last deep breath and blew it out before answering. "Through the front doors."

"Idiots," Nick muttered. "They should have one of those surveillance cameras in the lobby."

"That's how I'd plan it," Frank agreed. "But lucky for us they don't. It's easier to approach the entrance by going around the back side. Ready?"

Frank had obviously been exaggerating the extent of his health problems, because she hadn't regained her breath when he took off jogging again. Apparently her regular workouts weren't designed to deal with this kind of activity.

"Go ahead," Nick told her. "I'll follow you."

"Okay." She nodded and trotted off after Frank. She was wearing a black turtleneck and pants she'd found in her grandmother's closet. The clothes were baggy on her slender frame, but had saved them valuable time. Frank had told them they had to get there before the hour, and since he wasn't familiar with the security personnel patterns after midnight, they had been forced to move quickly.

They stayed close to the building, running along the back then up the side to the front. As with the rest of Wingate, the landscaping near the main entrance was all natural, but here the rocks and few puny cacti weren't big enough for any of them to hide behind.

Recessed lighting in the building overhang was dim and angled out toward the rocks, leaving a narrow path of darkness for the intruders to move in as they approached the glass-fronted entry. Lights from inside the building cast a golden glow outward onto the pink cement sidewalk, which ran the entire length of the entryway.

Frank stopped just before he reached the windows. Using the building for cover, he took a quick look inside at the lobby, then leaned back against the still-warm stucco and checked his watch. The luminous green dial flashed the time—ten-fifty.

"What are we waiting for?" Nick whispered irritably over Devin's shoulder. "Christmas?"

"The guard in the lobby takes a break every hour. In about three minutes he'll be leaving and will be gone for, at the most, five minutes."

"No one relieves him?" Nick asked.

Frank shrugged. "Nope. The door lock is double keyed, so they assume no one could get in or out in five minutes." He turned and looked into the lobby again. "Break time," Frank whispered. "You two stay here until I get the door unlocked. Whistle if you see any guards."

Frank took off. Nick leaned closer to Devin and spoke softly in her ear. "I can't whistle."

"Then you're lucky I'm here," Devin told him, keeping her eyes on the action. Frank was kneeling at the front door, fiddling with the lock.

"Come on," Nick muttered. "My grandmother could pick that lock faster."

"Quiet, or go do it yourself."

Nick was tempted to—he had the tools hidden in his pocket. It was one of the reasons he'd insisted on stopping at his place to change clothes. Everything in his house had been turned upside down, but Frank hadn't found his hiding place in the false-bottomed dresser drawer. Good thing, because it seemed as if Nick might have to jump in and help him, no matter how it looked to Devin.

Finally Frank pulled the glass-front door open and motioned them to join him. "Stay close to me," he whispered once they were all inside. "There are pressure alarm plates in the first corridor, and I know the pattern."

They quickly crossed the empty lobby in single file and slipped through an unlocked door without incident. The hallway was pitch-black, except for the green-and-white exit signs over the top of the doors ahead and behind them. After passing through two more doors Devin knew that this plushly carpeted hallway led to the executive offices. In their hasty planning session, Frank had informed them that the doors would be locked, as would both the inner and the outer office doors.

"Now comes the fun part," Frank whispered tersely. "In the labs there's a routine, but here the guards walk through at random. Getting through all the locks will be time-consuming, so keep your ears open."

Frank pulled a pen-sized flashlight out of his pocket and turned it on. He pointed it at the closed door up ahead as he walked past the three offices in this section and knelt in front of it, Devin and Nick right behind him.

He cursed quietly. "We're in trouble."

Nick turned on a similar light and pointed it over his shoulder at the doorknob. "What's the problem?"

"The locks have all been changed recently," Frank muttered, twisting a sliver of metal around as he poked and jabbed at the lock's innards. "Newer, harder to pick."

Mentally, Nick began counting the seconds, trying to give Frank time, but when he reached thirty he knew the risk was too great. Picking locks required a certain touch and Frank had either lost it or was having a particularly bad night. Alarms had been Frank's forte, anyway. Nick handed his flashlight to Devin and knelt beside Frank.

"Give me that." He pushed Frank's hand aside and took possession of the silver needle. A quick twist one way and then the other and the cylinder turned. He pushed the door open and ushered the other two past him, then closed it behind him. "Maybe you'd better let me handle this."

"I softened it up for you." Frank grabbed his lock pick back. "No more pressure plates now," he added, heading for the next door.

As with the front door, this one needed to be locked again so as not to alert the guards. Since they were double keyed, Nick had to use his own pick. But now it was a simple matter of turning the cylinder until it clicked, and the job was accomplished quickly. He then turned to go after Frank, but Devin was still there, standing in his way.

"You certainly look like a master of that trade, Nick."

He smiled, his teeth white in the darkened corridor. "What can I say? It was a good school."

"Uh-huh."

Scowling, she followed him down the hall toward Frank. Now wasn't the time or place to ask questions, but question him she would. He had better have some pretty good answers, too, great body or not. Trade school, indeed!

By the time they reached him Frank had already picked the next lock. He grinned smugly at Nick and started to push the door open, but just then they heard a noise on the other side. Someone was whistling. Frank pulled the door shut softly, a stricken look on his face.

Devin paled, too. A guard was coming right at them!

"Lock it," Nick whispered, then turned and headed for the nearest office, pushing Devin ahead of him. The office door was locked, too, but it was a different type entirely and he had it open in an instant. "Inside."

She obeyed the curt command, and in a moment Frank stumbled in behind her, followed by Nick. He eased the door shut, pushing the button on the round knob to lock it again.

The office was without windows and completely black. They couldn't even see each other, but they could hear the guard as he entered the corridor and shut the door behind him.

Keys jingled. Devin saw the beam of a flashlight beneath the door near her feet and the doorknob rattled. With her blood pressure skyrocketing, she held her breath, only releasing it when she heard the guard rattling another knob farther down the hall.

"You said no pattern at all?" Nick asked softly.

"Circular," Frank replied. "Usually. But we still won't know when."

"Then we'll have to move faster, won't we, Frank?" he said sarcastically. "You ever think of retiring?"

Frank sighed. "Yeah. But there's life in the old dog yet, Nicky. You'll see."

"I'd better."

Devin's chest was heaving at their near escape. She noticed that neither of the men was affected, their quiet voices and breathing patterns perfectly normal, as if they were keeping a casual secret. Frank's nonchalance she understood, but Nick was another story. A story she really wanted to hear. At least, she thought she did.

Knowing about locks and alarms didn't explain his knowledgeable facility with them. Being a security consultant wouldn't give him the cool head and icy nervous system he had just displayed. Those things took experience, and the possible ways Nick might have gotten it worried Devin.

Nick eased the office door open. "Okay. Let's go."

Frank was warming up. He defeated the lock in short order and they all filed into the executive wing. In keeping with Wingate's capricious security methods, there were no cameras here, either, so while Frank relocked the door, Nick hurried over and picked the one on Jay's outer office door. To Devin it seemed as if they were having some sort of bizarre duel.

When they reached the inner office door, however, the duel came to an abrupt halt. This time Nick did all the cursing. Then he said, "Me and my big mouth."

Odd methods aside, the Wingate security department had been busy, just as he'd advised. Jay's door was no longer guarded by an easily picked lock, or even an improved version like the others. They now faced an electronic keypad similar to the one at the entrance to the secure labs.

"You're responsible for this?" Frank asked.

"I told them to check all their systems," Nick replied. Frank glowered at him. "That was stupid!"

"Hey! I didn't know we'd have to break in here then!"

They were standing nose to nose, fists clenched. Devin pulled them apart. "Hush!" she whispered vehemently. "Maybe if you two experts put your heads together instead of trying to get one up on each other, you can figure a way. I have to get into that office!"

"I didn't bring a black box," Frank said. "You?"

"Yes, but just a regular bypass. I didn't think we'd run into anything this sophisticated." Nick took his light and bent to inspect the device. He cursed again. "Wingate! Overkill in the weirdest places. It's the model two thousand. I have a feeling they've changed all the codes, but it's worth giving Myrtle's a try." He punched in the code. Nothing happened. "So much for that idea."

"Why don't you just defeat it?" Devin asked Frank. "If you could get past mine and Eli's, surely you can get past this little thing."

"First of all, C Group gave me inside info. Your uncle had taken the idea to them for refinements," he informed her. "Secondly, this little thing is state-of-the-art and top of the line. If I'd known it was here, I could have been ready for it. But I didn't. Sorry, Devin."

"Some spy you turned out to be!" She turned to Nick. "Well, Mr. security expert?"

Nick was not one bit happy with this situation. He was already in for the third degree from Devin later for what she had seen him do so far. His facade was wearing thin.

But she had to know the options facing them, because it would ultimately be her decision to leave empty-handed or try a risky break-in. "I can run a bypass on it, but with the tools I have it would take a while. I'd have to partially dismantle the lock. If a guard comes by, I wouldn't have time to put it together again. If he sees it, we're sunk."

Her eyes widened. Nick would have to be thoroughly acquainted with the procedure to make such an assessment. He was experienced, all right. But was he experienced in choosing locks and security equipment, or getting past them?

As suspicious as she was, however, at the moment she was also very glad he knew what he was doing. "Can't we just start punching in codes? Maybe we'll get lucky."

"We could, on any other model, although the odds are something akin to winning a million in the lottery," he informed her. "But this particular model has a limiter in the circuitry," Nick told her. "You can only punch in three wrong codes before it sounds an alarm."

She hadn't come this far to be turned back by some electronic gizmo. "So we have one more chance, right?"

"Technically, two," he replied. "As long as the second one is right, that is. But the possible permutations—"

"I know," she interrupted. "That's why I'm not going to choose at random. Step aside, boys." They both did so. Devin approached the lock. "Five digits, right?"

"Right," Nick said.

The keypad, she had noticed, was like that on a push-button phone, with both numbers and letters printed on it. She was counting on her knowledge of Jay to get them inside.

"Jay wouldn't want to be bothered learning a number sequence," she said, more to herself than the two men. "He'd use the letters to form a word he could easily remember."

Nick grinned. "I get it. Something important to him."

"We both know what that is." Devin lifted her finger, hesitated, then quickly punched in a code. "M-O-N-E-Y."

Nothing happened.

Nick patted her on the shoulder. "It's a good idea, Devin," he said sympathetically. "I'll bet you're right. You just ran out of chances, that's all."

"No, I didn't. I have one more."

"But it has to be correct!" Frank exclaimed. "May I remind you that there are three locked doors between us and the outside, not to mention the guards. If the alarm goes off, we haven't a prayer!"

Devin lifted her hand again, forefinger extended. "But I know what it is now," she assured them.

"You can't be sure, Devin," Nick objected. "Let me try a bypass." He frowned at the determination on her face. Frank was already heading for the outer office door. Her hand moved forward. "No, Devin! Don't!"

It was too late. "P-O-W-E-R."

There was a soft *clunk*. Devin looked at Nick, stuck her tongue out at him, then turned the knob and sauntered into Jay's office.

Nick leaned against the wall with a heavy sigh. Frank joined him. His face was ashen. "Are you sure you want to get involved with that woman?" Frank asked him. "She's nuts!"

"Two days ago she reminded me of a schoolteacher," Nick muttered. "Now she reminds me of me in the old days."

"That's a scary thought."

Devin poked her head through the doorway. "Would you guys get in here? I could use some help!"

The file cabinets were no match for the combined efforts of Nick and Frank. Soon they were all perusing the contents in the safety of Jay's private office, behind a door probably even the guards couldn't get past. Nick kept an eye on Frank the whole time, making sure he didn't find something else he thought he could sell.

Devin turned over a thin stack of papers and flipped up the last page. "Look at this. The university agreement has been signed." She held the small light Nick had given her on the signatures. "It's dated today."

"It was on the news tonight," Frank said from across the room. He was going through the file cabinets, searching for the one little piece of the formulation that stood between him and victory. "It pays to keep up, you know."

"We were busy," Nick said, with a sly wink at Devin.

She felt a flutter in the pit of her stomach, but looked away. If he thought that was going to happen again before she got an explanation, he had another think coming! Of course, if it was a good explanation . . .

Devin went back to work. They spent a little longer in Jay's office, then tidied up and left, locking his office doors on the way out. With some trepidation, they then went down the hall to Richard's.

Although she was fairly certain now that it would be Richard who would pick money as a code word, much to Devin's relief she didn't have to test her theory. He was going to get a fancy lock too, but the workmen hadn't gotten around to installing it yet. It lay in a box beside his inner office door. The door was locked, but with these two, it was no trouble.

They continued their search. A few minutes later Frank was starting to get a bit frantic. Devin was just disgusted. "Those low-life scum," she muttered from her seat behind Richard's desk.

Nick leaned over her shoulder. "What's wrong?"

"They've hired a scientist to take Eli's place. He starts work next month." She looked up at Nick. "No wonder they didn't want us to launch a full-scale search. They've used the time to replace him!"

"Maybe Eli knows about it."

"If he knew, he'd have said something," Devin insisted.

Nick sat on the edge of the desk, his flashlight clenched between his teeth as he picked up the employment contract. It spelled out quite clearly what the new scientist's duties would be, and they included his being appointed head of what was now Eli's department.

"It's been in the works for a while, that's for sure," Nick said, putting the papers down on the desk. "You don't hire a scientist with this guy's credentials overnight. It takes months of planning."

"How about three months?" Devin asked. "That's about the time Eli threatened to quit. It's also when they took out that huge life insurance policy on his life."

"What's that?" Frank asked from across the room. "You think his brothers might have done him in?"

Nick stood. "It's a possibility. Their relationships are volatile at best. When he took off, Eli might have been running from them—or from someone they hired."

"Interesting," Frank muttered. Maybe he'd be able to salvage something from this, after all. If he put that bit of news and everything else he'd learned tonight in the right ears, then just maybe C Group would lay off him. Heck, they might even give him a bonus.

That would be nice, since he certainly wasn't going to get paid by his other employer without those notes.

Devin saw his dejected expression. "No luck, Frank?"

"No." He closed the file cabinet with his foot. "We've been in here almost an hour. Unless you have somewhere else you want to look—for another hour while we wait for the guard to take a break—I'm ready to call it quits."

"We have enough to force a confrontation with Jay and Richard," Devin said. She stood. "Let's clean up and get out of here."

"Fast," Nick agreed.

They retraced their steps, leaving through the front door when the guard took his five-minute break. The run across the desert seemed longer, the fence even higher than before. Devin was more weary than she could remember being in her life, the mixture of physical and emotional stress having taken its toll.

They were on their way back to Lucinda's place before anyone felt like speaking. Nick and Frank were in the front seat, with Frank at the wheel. Nick was still keeping an eye on him. Devin had opted to stretch out in the back seat.

"This other employer of yours. It wouldn't by any chance be a woman, would it?" Nick asked.

Frank glanced at him. "Yeah. How'd you know?"

Devin sat bolt upright in the back seat. "Is she blond, with a white streak?"

"I told you, Devin. I rarely meet my clients face-to-face and I never ask for names," Frank replied. "In this case, I call a message service, she calls me back. For all I know she may be a go-between. She sure got ticked off when I'd report a failure, though." He scowled. "I was really looking forward to taking her money."

Devin knew what Frank was. There was no reason on earth for her to feel sorry for him. In a way, though, she did. She had the suspicion that Nick could have gotten them into Wingate without him, but not without even more risk, and that counted for something in her book.

She at least owed him the truth. "I should tell you, Frank, that C Group had some of Eli's papers taken. They were supposed to be for the secret project, but who can tell what their hireling really grabbed."

"Great," he muttered. The way things were going, the deal with C Group was blown, and if they had the notes on that formulation, then that deal was kaput as well.

"It's also entirely possible the notes you're looking for don't exist at all," Devin added.

"What!"

"It's the way Eli works. Part here, part there, and some key ingredient or operation only in his head," she explained. "So you probably wouldn't have been able to get the entire formulation for her, anyway."

"Blast her!" Frank was beginning to think the woman had set him up, maybe as some sort of revenge or something from his past dealings. "I knew the deal was fishy!"

His animosity gave Nick an idea. Of course, Frank was still Frank; he wouldn't do it for nothing. "I've got another proposition for you," Nick told him.

Frank shook his head. "No way. I'm ready to throw in the towel on this mess."

"There'd be money in it for you this time," Nick continued. "And a touch of revenge, as well."

"You do know my weak spots, Nicky." He grinned. "I'll probably regret this, but okay. What's the deal?"

Nick was grinning, too. "How would you like to find out who this lady is for us?"

"That's a great idea!" Devin exclaimed, leaning forward between the two bucket seats. She smiled slyly. "Why, we could even get Jay and Richard to pay for it, Frank. After all, it's Wingate's product she wanted to steal."

Frank liked the idea, too. "Not bad! Money, revenge and poetic justice, all rolled into one job. How fast do you need the information?" he asked.

"It would put another weapon in our arsenal for the confrontation with Jay and Richard," Devin said.

"And just the ticket to get us an appointment with them, too," Nick agreed. "Think you can do it, Frank?"

"I'll start digging right after I drop you two off at grandma's," Frank said with a smile. "You know me, Nicky. I'm very fond of working at night."

Chapter Nineteen

A rattling noise pierced through Devin's sleep-clouded mind and she shot straight up in bed, blinking as she opened her eyes in the sunny room. A man was standing beside her bed, his white shirt hanging open over black slacks.

She closed her eyes tight, but when she opened them again, he was still there. No, it wasn't a bad dream, it was Nick, and he was smiling down at her. He had a tray in his hands. The coffee smelled wonderful.

"Dammit, you scared me!" she exclaimed.

"Sorry. You were really out."

"How'd you get into the house?" Devin asked grumpily, using her fingers to comb her hair back out of her eyes. He had opened the curtains, and the sunlight filled the bedroom, making her squint up at him.

Nick laughed softly. Her flower-print nightgown had a low neckline that showed plenty of creamy skin. That sight made it hard for him to keep his eyes on her face. "I slept here last night, remember?"

"Oh." She yawned. "I do now."

They'd been exhausted, and she hadn't seen any reason for him to drive all the way home to a ransacked house when there were four empty bedrooms at Lucinda's. Also, the limo guys might have decided to pay another visit, and having help on hand seemed like a good idea.

At least, it had last night. Now Devin wasn't so sure. Waking up to a handsome man bringing her coffee in bed was not an experience she had all that often. She rather liked it. That could spell trouble.

Nick set the tray down on the bedside table. "How do you like your coffee?"

"Black." Devin scooted across the bed away from him and slipped out the other side, leaving the room without another word.

She went into the bathroom across the hall, locking the door behind her. Time was what she needed, the time and distance to think rationally. After brushing her teeth and washing her face, she ran a brush through her auburn hair, still debating whether she was going back into the bedroom.

Silly. Of course she would; her clothes were in there. But so was Nick. Devin looked in the mirror, feeling quite peculiar. For some reason the person she saw reflected there didn't seem like her. If this new Devin went into that bedroom, she knew quite well what might happen.

From the very beginning she'd been attracted to Nick, and their time together had made those feelings stronger. She liked him, maybe too much, because she was falling for him hard, falling in love. But she didn't know how he felt, if his feelings even went past simple desire.

And she'd never find out in the bathroom. The direct approach worked best for most things—why wouldn't it work for this?

Nick watched as Devin walked back into the room, enjoying the way the sunshine let him see through her thin nylon gown for a brief moment. Her legs were shapely, as strong as her calves, and the desire to caress them was more overpowering than ever.

He was sitting on the far side of the bed, his back against the headboard, bare feet on top of the peach-colored sheets crumpled just as she'd left them, the matching fluffy comforter sliding sideways to the floor. Nick leaned over and poured steaming black coffee into a delicate china cup, then held it out to her across the middle of the bed.

Devin tucked a strand of hair behind her ear. She had two choices. Crawl up on the queen-size bed or walk around to where he sat to get the coffee. Was it that tough a choice? Deep down she knew what she wanted, didn't she?

Yes. She wanted an explanation. She wanted to know who he really was, or, more importantly, what he had been. Why couldn't they talk while having coffee?

Nick was surprised when she climbed onto the bed. His loins ached as she sat down and carefully moved across it so she wouldn't spill the hot liquid. She stopped an arm's length away from him and sat gracefully back on her feet before taking the cup from his hand.

"Thank you," she said.

Devin was close enough that he could just extend his hand and touch her knee, but he didn't. Not yet. Instead he smiled. "I hated to wake you up, but it's after eleven. Like I said, you were really out."

"I never sleep that late!"

"You've done plenty of things since you met me that you'd never experienced before," Nick reminded her.

That was true. Until Nick had come into her life her daily routine had rarely changed, and she'd liked it that way. If she took the next step her life would never be the same. Nick was spontaneous, ready to alter plans at the last moment, the total opposite of her.

What was wrong with her? Why couldn't she just ask him who he was, how he really felt? Be direct and to the point like she was with everything else?

Nick took the coffee cup from her hand and set it on the bedside table, then turned to face her, surprised to find himself nervous. Her nightgown was slipping off one lovely white shoulder, the drooping neckline revealing the valley between her breasts. With one finger he traced the delicate curve of her collarbone, then slowly he drifted down to the edge of her gown, following the line of it from across her arm to the swell of her breast.

"Is this a yes?" he asked, removing his hand.

The brief touch of his fingers ignited the fire that had been simmering deep inside her, and left her begging for more. All thoughts of logic disappeared as the warmth of his touch continued to radiate heat and tingling sensations through her even after it had been removed.

Was she about to go to bed with a thief? She could ask, but knew the answer wouldn't matter anymore. He had already stolen her heart.

"Yes," she told him in a whisper.

Devin put her hands on his waist, then slid them upward over his chest to push the white shirt off his shoulders. He shrugged out of it, his pants quickly following it to the floor. She rose up on her knees and Nick joined her, his mouth covering hers as her hands slid around his waist to pull him even closer.

They kissed each other greedily, lips and hands wandering at will. Eventually they fell back to the bed, letting their desire for each other consume them and take them soaring upward until they reached a shattering pinnacle; then slowly they drifted back down to a fluffy bed of clouds, only to have their desire consume them again.

Quite some time later, as they lay entwined in each other's arms, Devin sighed and murmured, "Thank you, Nick."

Nick smiled at her. "My pleasure."

She laughed, then kissed him lightly on the chin and sat up, gazing into his eyes. "Mine too. But I mean thank you for caring."

"You're easy to care for," he told her softly.

"No I'm not. Neither is Eli. And you know it."

"There have been moments," Nick agreed. He tenderly stroked her cheek. "But you're worth it."

She couldn't stop the tears welling up in her eyes. No one had ever made her feel so loved, wanted or cherished. And she needed that desperately.

Loud rumblings from Nick's stomach startled them both. Devin laughed as she slipped away from his grasp and out of bed, feeling better than she ever had in her life. "What's for lunch?"

"*You,* if you don't hurry up and get dressed."

EVENTUALLY, THEY DID manage to get around to making a late lunch. They were cleaning up the dishes when the doorbell rang.

"I'll get it," Nick told her, tossing a dish towel at her. She was wearing navy blue slacks and a white-and-blue sleeveless sweater. She looked almost as great as she had an hour ago. Almost, but not quite.

Devin dodged the damp cloth and followed him into the living room. "You might need help." She smiled.

Nick finished buttoning his white shirt, then looked through the peephole before opening the front door. "That was quick work."

"I've still got a few tricks up my sleeve." Frank walked past him into the house. "Man, it's hot out there."

"It's summertime, and this is desert country," Nick told him. Frank had on a nicely tailored, lightweight tan suit. Nick was instantly suspicious. He'd never seen the man in a suit before. "Well? Do you know who's paying you?"

"Yep." Frank walked over to the sofa and sat down, crossing his legs. "And no, Devin, she's not a blonde."

Devin was clearly disappointed. "What's her name?"

"Look, guys, it's been fun," Frank said. "And I really do hope your uncle Eli's okay, Devin. But I'm not in this for my health."

"You'll get paid," Devin assured him.

"Yes, I will." He smiled pleasantly. "And that's when you'll get the name."

Devin started toward him with clenched fists, but Nick stood in her way. "Think about it," he said. "After all he's heard from us about Jay and Richard, he knows he can't trust them."

"He can trust us!"

"Can I?" Frank asked. "If those two won't pay my price, and you had the name, you'd tell them if it worked in your favor, wouldn't you?"

She scowled at him for a moment, then sighed and slowly nodded her head. "Yes. I guess I would."

"I rest my case," Frank said with a shrug. "Now, shall we adjourn to Wingate?"

AN HOUR LATER THE THREE of them were in a conference room at Wingate, sitting behind a long oval table facing the door. Devin was in the middle chair with Nick to her left and Frank on her right, all waiting for Jay and Richard to get out of another meeting.

Nick had dropped Devin off at her place, then had gone to his own house to change into a light-colored suit before returning to pick her up. She was now wearing a coffee-ice-cream-colored dress with white piping around the pocket and sleeves. Large two-toned earrings of the same color hung from her ears and matched the V-shaped necklace around her slender throat. She looked cool, reasonably calm and utterly delicious.

Devin rocked in the plushly padded swivel chair, wondering just how long her uncles were going to keep them waiting. As she'd thought, they hadn't wanted this meeting, so Devin had been forced into using one of their tactics. She told them just enough to whet their appetites, leaving them hungry for more. It had worked, thus clearing their way inside without a hitch.

"Looks different in the light," Frank commented.

"Most things do," Devin said as the door opened.

Jay strode into the room, Richard right on his heels. Both of them were wearing conservative tan suits, white shirts and boring ties. "Make this quick, Devin," Jay ordered. "I don't like being coerced."

"But it's all right for you to do it to others," she shot right back.

"You're wasting time. Exactly why are you and your friends here?" Jay asked. He made the word *friends* sound like an epithet, and he was looking warily at Nick.

Devin ignored Jay's question and stuck to her own agenda. She looked pointedly at Richard, who was standing near the head of the table. She'd given his secretary a copy of the incomplete formulation Frank's mysterious employer had provided, to have someone who worked with Eli verify its potential. By the worried expression on Richard's face, Devin imagined it was worth quite a bit.

"Did it check out?" she asked.

"Yes. What do you want?"

"For me, nothing," Devin replied. "But Frank here has other ideas. I'll let you judge his worth for your-selves."

Frank leaned back in his chair. "The name of the person who hired me to appropriate the other part of your formula is for sale, gentlemen. Cash only."

"How much?" Richard asked.

He winced when Frank mentioned a high five-figure sum, but he couldn't be any more shocked at the price than Devin was. She glanced at Nick, but he only shrugged.

Devin listened and watched as her uncles and Frank negotiated a final figure midway between what each wanted. As weird as it seemed to her, both sides acted satisfied with the price. To them, it was simply business.

Jay sat down in a chair opposite Frank. "Who hired you?"

"First the cash, then the name," Frank told them.

Richard left the room without a word. No one spoke until he came back with a square maroon bank bag. He tossed it across the table at Frank. "Talk."

Grinning smugly, Frank unzipped the bag and quickly checked the contents. Satisfied, he folded his hands over it on his lap. "Her name is Annette Jones. She works for a close rival of yours, Biosphere."

"Damn!" Jay hit the table with his fist. "Those up-start thieves! They wanted to beat us to the patent."

Richard sat down, looking slightly stunned. "That formulation is something Eli has been working on for a long time, and according to the lab assistants, it still isn't perfected. When—and if—it is, the profit potential will be solid, but not enormous. Hardly worth the risk of using an industrial spy." He looked at Frank. Again, it amazed Devin how businesslike they both were. "I don't suppose you know why she wanted that particular one?"

"I do, and I should probably charge for that, too." He patted the bank bag in his lap. "But what the heck. I'm in a generous mood. Annette Jones had two reasons for wanting that particular product," Frank said. "Scientists who don't produce viable results don't advance or keep their jobs. According to lab scuttlebutt, Ms. Jones hasn't been producing and her job is on the line."

"And the second reason?" Richard asked.

"Years ago, when she and your brother Eli worked for another company, he turned her in for falsifying data, and she was fired when his accusations were proven correct. For a scientist that's almost certain doom."

Jay nodded. "Eli did the right thing."

It was obvious Jay and Richard considered the money they'd given Frank well spent. What galled Devin was that neither appeared concerned that Eli was still missing.

"It's a shame no one will ever say the same about you two!" Devin exclaimed, no longer able to keep quiet.

Jay looked at her. "What are you talking about?"

Before she could open her mouth, the conference-room door banged open and Lucinda Wingate stepped in. Jay's face went pale and he jumped up from his chair.

"Mother!" he cried.

"So you do remember me." Lucinda glared at them. "As I wasn't invited, I've been listening at the door, and from what I've heard so far you all deserve a good spanking!"

Chapter Twenty

Jay was smiling, but it looked forced. "I thought you were resting today?" He looked accusingly at Devin. "How dare you subject my mother to this much stress!"

"Oh, shut up, Jay," Lucinda told him sharply. "Devin didn't call me. I happen to have many *friends* here at Wingate who feel obligated to keep me informed."

Lucinda walked over to the chair at the head of the table and stood beside it. She looked quite regal in a lilac silk dress, a thick rope of pearls around her throat. Richard held the chair out for her and she sat down, her grace belying her years.

"Everyone sit down." Lucinda glanced at Nick. "How's my house, young man?"

Nick winked at her. "Spotless."

"It had better be," she returned, a twinkle in her pale blue eyes. She looked at Frank. "And you must be the man who called me. Mr. Delano, wasn't it?"

"Frank Delano, ma'am," he said, standing to give her a slight bow. "I'm . . . I'm an associate of Nick's."

"I see."

Lucinda glanced at Nick again, a question clearly on the tip of her tongue. He breathed a silent sigh of relief when she left it unasked and returned her attention to

Frank. But Nick had a question of his own. What was Frank up to now?

"You're remarkably well-informed, Mr. Delano," she said. "I don't suppose you'd care to tell me how you got that way?"

Frank cleared his throat. "Without going into details, you have some serious security problems here at Wingate," he replied. "But they're nothing that can't be solved. With expert advice and continuing supervision, of course."

"Of course." She smiled pleasantly. "I'd appreciate it if you would please wait outside for a few minutes now. Family business, you understand. But don't leave. I have a certain matter I wish to discuss with you."

"Certainly, Mrs. Wingate," Frank said.

Right after he left, the door flew open again and Myrtle rushed into the room, a stenographer's pad in her hand. "Am I late?" she asked, huffing and puffing.

"Not at all. I appreciate your coming on such short notice," Lucinda replied. "Please, have a seat at the other end of the table." She looked at the others. "Myrtle will be taking down the minutes of this meeting for me. You may continue now, Devin."

Devin waited until Myrtle was seated and her notebook was open. "I think Jay and Richard should explain why they're ousting Eli from the company," she began. "Behind his back."

All eyes turned to Jay and Richard, who were sitting side by side now. Richard in turn looked at his brother. Jay didn't seem at all perturbed by the scrutiny.

"Explain yourselves," Lucinda ordered brusquely.

"We've had it with Eli's continued interference in the way we run our company," Jay replied firmly. "His actions have become detrimental to the success of Wingate. He's forced us into taking action on the situation."

"So you planned a little vacation for him, right?" Devin asked. "Maybe one he'll never come back from?"

Richard jumped up. "Of course not!"

"Try to contain that absurd imagination of yours, Devin. While Eli's sudden departure has been quite convenient," Jay informed them, "we certainly didn't orchestrate it. We merely took advantage of it."

Richard sat back down. "Taking off has always been one of Eli's quirks, and an annoying one, at that."

"What exactly have you planned?" Lucinda asked.

Jay leaned back in his chair. "We've hired Nathan Cox, a noted scientist in the same field, to replace Eli. He takes over as department head next Monday. The papers are signed. No one can stop us now."

Nick put his hand on Devin's to stop her from speaking. They both knew the contract wasn't supposed to start until next month, but if they personally revealed that information, they might have to reveal a whole lot more. It was better to let everybody think that Frank had told them all they knew about what was going on. But how much had he told Lucinda?

"Oh, really?" Lucinda asked softly.

Richard cleared his throat. "I'm sure Eli will have no trouble finding another job."

"We'll give him excellent references," Jay added.

"You two still have so much to learn." Lucinda was shaking her head, her disappointment visible as she looked at Jay and Richard. "This isn't just *your* company." She sighed loudly. "As you two well know, I have always had little tolerance for corporate skulduggery, as do most of my friends," she reminded them. "Friends who also just happen to be stockholders in this company."

Jay crossed his arms defensively. "Precisely what are you trying to say, Mother?"

"You need it spelled out?" Lucinda asked. "Then spell it out I shall." Her face hardened. "I have the connections to oust you two from this company without so much as a golden parachute. Sons or not, I'll do it if I must. Is that plain enough for you two?"

"If Eli leaves," Nick added, "then Lang will also pull its investment. Since others followed us in, I'm sure they'll follow us out, as well."

Richard was shocked, but Jay revealed nothing, his voice smooth when he spoke. "You had both better consider all the ramifications. Breaking Cox's contract will be expensive."

"You two have underestimated your brother Eli so many times I've lost count," Lucinda said. "And once again, in trying to outmaneuver or hurt him, you've ended up playing right into his hands."

At last Jay looked concerned. "How?"

"Eli doesn't like being a department head," Devin couldn't resist inserting. "The responsibilities take too much time from his beloved research."

"Quite right, Devin," Lucinda agreed. "Eli will be thrilled to step down from the position. He'd had it in mind for some time, in fact."

"You're saying this will make him happy?" Richard asked.

Lucinda smiled. "Oh, very. He and Nathan Cox attended graduate school at the same time and Eli has always wanted to work with him. I remember him telling me once, years ago, that their minds complemented each other." She chuckled. "It looks as if you've been blown out of your beds again, boys. I suppose I must pick you up and dust you off, mustn't I?''

"What's your deal?" Jay asked.

Her expression turned hard once more. "I expect you two to quit rocking the boat," Lucinda ordered, pointing a finger at them. "From now on, you will keep your personal feelings about your brother out of company business."

"We already do!" Jay objected. "But Eli—"

"Hush!" she interrupted. "That's a lie and you know it. I'm well aware of what started this latest round of bickering. It was obvious you didn't like the way he stood up to you publicly over the medical benefits. But that time he was right, and you should have had the grace to admit it."

Richard glared at his mother. "Do you know what that's costing us? No one gives benefits like that anymore."

"*We* do, and we will continue to do so," Lucinda said. "It's an added incentive to get and keep good, productive employees, who make us even more money."

Jay stood. "Very well, Mother. We agree to your terms. Now, if you'll excuse us, I have another meeting."

"Sit down!" Lucinda ordered. "I'm not finished."

Jay sank slowly back into his chair, his rage barely held in check. "What else?"

Lucinda looked at Nick. "As a security consultant," she began, enjoying the way this information startled Jay and Richard, "I imagine you make recommendations on security personnel from time to time, don't you, Nick?"

He nodded. "Yes, ma'am."

"And what is your assessment of Mr. Delano?"

Nick arched his eyebrows. "Well, he's certainly an expert on security systems," he replied uneasily. "But I must tell you that in the past—"

Lucinda held up a hand to interrupt him. "The past is just that, Nick. The past." She smiled. "You can stop looking so uncomfortable. I had a chat with an old friend of yours this morning. Nice man. Unusually jovial for an accountant. Anyway, like him—and Eli—I'm a great believer in the ability of people to change for the better."

Nick was at a loss for words. Devin wasn't. "Somebody better tell me what this is all about," she demanded, her fiery glare directed right at him.

"Devin!" her grandmother scolded. "Stop being so pushy. I'm sure he'll tell you when he's ready and not before. And don't slouch!"

She straightened instinctively. "Yes, Grandmother."

"That's better," Lucinda said. "Now, I'm sure you two have better things to do. You're both welcome to use my home until your places get straightened up."

"Thank you," Nick said.

Lucinda picked up the phone to her right and punched a button. "Send Mr. Delano in now, please."

Clearly, they had been dismissed. Devin stood, as did Nick, and he followed her out the door, passing Frank on his way in. He had a big smile on his face.

"Not a very good door. You can hear right through it," Frank said. "You know, my knees have stopped hurting. I think this climate is going to be good for me after all."

He gave them the thumbs-up sign, then went to join Lucinda and her sons. Nick chuckled as he closed the door. He had the feeling security at Wingate was about to improve greatly. Frank could no doubt wheedle himself into a nice job, and Nick had every intention of being around to make sure he did it properly.

"Come on, Devin. Your grandmother was very polite but she was not giving us a choice. Let's go."

She grabbed the sleeve of his coat. "I don't care what Grandmother said. I want an explanation about that 'the past is past' stuff, Nick."

"I promise to give you one, but not here."

"Good."

They walked out into the corridor, among a group of employees who were just getting off work. The halls were alive with myriad conversations, both technical and social.

"We still don't know where Eli is," Devin said.

Nick couldn't resist hugging her as they walked along. "But we have made sure that he has a place to return to."

"If he returns." She sighed. "I'd still like to know who C Group paid to spy on him. And we still don't know why he's leaving Yvette Soomes a million. We have to keep digging, Nick."

"We will," he assured her.

In the lobby, office workers blended with lab technicians as they all trooped out the front doors. Devin noticed that one of the people in the group ahead of them was the leggy blond woman, Natalie. Without her lab coat on she could subject every man within range to the full effect of those tan legs and shapely hips. She was, in a word, stunning.

Devin felt a stab of jealousy and looked up at Nick. Lucky for him, he was gazing out across the parking lot, frowning at all the cars pulling away.

"A lot of traffic," he said.

"Hmm," Devin hummed, barely listening to him.

She had returned her attention to Natalie. From the very first time they had almost literally run into her, something about the woman had bothered Devin. Nick had noticed something about her, too, she recalled. It had been one of the first indications that their minds ran along similar tracks. How long ago that seemed now!

But what was it about Natalie? Of course, she was a total knockout, but that wasn't the problem. Devin had always been fairly confident of her own, admittedly less spectacular looks—on her good days, that is. And she was accustomed to being around pretty women. There were quite a few in classical music circles. Then, too, it was not at all unusual to find Uncle Eli in the company of a real beauty.

"Oh!" Devin stopped in her tracks so suddenly that someone bumped into the back of her and Nick.

"I'm so sorry," a young man apologized.

"My fault." Devin stepped out of the flow of people leaving work and grabbed Nick's arm. "It was Natalie!"

"Natalie who?" Nick asked, bewildered. Then he remembered. "You mean that gorgeous blonde from the lab?"

Devin was so excited she didn't even comment on his choice of adjectives. "Yes! Something about her bugged me, but I just couldn't put my finger on it before. That was her voice on Eli's answering machine, Nick. Remember, the one who was so mad about being stood up?"

"Now I really am worried," Nick said. "I can't believe Eli would have stood her up unless his life depended on it."

"Very funny," Devin returned, jabbing him in the side with her elbow. "Just help me find her, will you? She was right ahead of us a moment ago."

Nick stood on tiptoe as he searched through the crowd. "I think I see her." He pointed at the parking lot. "She's getting into a shiny blue car."

He took off, running between two parked cars in the visitors' section and down two rows, Devin not far behind. Nick thumped on the trunk of the blue car as it began backing out. The noise made the woman slam on her brakes. People turned and stared.

The blonde jumped out of the car. "I didn't see you back there! Are you all right?"

"I'm fine," Nick said.

Devin caught up with them. "Why have you been leaving threatening messages on Eli's machine?"

Natalie frowned and took a step back, ready to jump back into her car. "I don't know what you're talking about."

"You can either talk to us, or security," Devin told her.

Her hand stayed on the door handle. "Keep your voice down," Natalie demanded. "I work with these people." She smiled and waved as two men walked past the car. "What do you want from me?"

"As if you didn't know. Where is Eli?" she demanded. "What have you done to him?"

"Whoa, wait a minute!" Natalie said. "I don't know what's going on, but I haven't done anything to Eli."

Devin looked as if she was about to strangle the other woman. Nick put his hand on her shoulder. "Have you been misplacing Eli's papers?" he asked. "Erasing his tapes?"

Natalie grinned at him. "So what if I have?"

"You're the C Group spy!" Devin exclaimed.

"C Group?" Natalie asked, baffled. "Look, I really don't have the slightest idea what you're talking about. Eli and I . . . well, let's just say I'm not accustomed to being rejected, okay? I got mad, and decided to freak him out a little. I moved his papers around, made him think stuff was disappearing. It was childish, I know. But it was fun."

"Fun!" Devin started to take a step toward her. Nick held her back. "How dare you!"

"Hey, I didn't destroy anything, nor would I, ever," she told them seriously. "Eli's work is too important."

Devin frowned. "But you did erase the tape?"

"Yes," Natalie admitted. "I'd had it with him. He'd stood me up one time too many, so in a fit of pique I went into his office and erased part of the tape on his desk. It's no big deal. Between his paper copies and the computer he can reconstruct it," she said defiantly. "I just wanted to tick him off, that's all. He always has time for work."

It was stupid enough to be the truth. "Do you know where he is right now?" Devin asked.

"On vacation somewhere." Natalie shrugged. "He didn't confide in me. Or invite me to go with him, either," she said, her pert nose in the air. "Now, is there anything else? I have a dinner date to get ready for." She winked at Nick.

"You're free to go," Devin said, then added in a quiet mutter, "And I hope you choke!"

They watched her leave, then walked to Nick's car and got inside. Nick joined the flow of exiting traffic. "Maybe Eli really is just on a vacation. When you break this down piece by piece it certainly seems that whatever Eli is doing, he's been doing it on his own from the start."

"But he could still be in trouble," Devin said. "Don't forget that C Group is after him. Maybe their project is something so hideous that Eli feels compelled to hide it, or try and reveal it to the world.''

Eli was an idealist, and he'd do something like that, if he felt he must. ''If that's the case, then we won't be able to stop him,'' Nick said quietly. The look of sadness on Devin's face moved him. ''We'll keep looking.''

''You really do care,'' Devin murmured.

''Yes, I do,'' Nick said, stopping at a red light. He caressed the curve of her cheek with his finger. ''I care about what happens to both of you.''

Devin stared at him, moved by his words. ''I—'' The car behind them started honking its horn. ''You'd better move before he rear-ends us.''

''Where are we going?'' Nick asked.

Devin toyed with her seat belt. The magic moment was gone, ruined by some impatient jerk. ''Let's go back to Eli's place.'' She sighed. ''I know. We've been through it and Frank's been through it, but we have to keep trying and it's the only thing I can think of to do.''

A short time later Devin was sitting at Eli's diningroom table, the old shoe box in front of her filled with papers and envelopes now yellowed with age.

Nick set a stack of four shoe boxes on the dining-room table and sat down. ''This is the last of his canceled checks.''

They worked in companionable silence, going through each one. ''Find anything?'' Devin asked when they had finished.

Nick replaced the lid to the last shoe box. ''No, but there is one more possibility. Not a pleasant one, either.''

She'd thought of it, too, but had been putting it off. ''The letter addressed to me that we found in his file cabinet, along with his last will and testament," she said. "It's not supposed to be opened until his death."

"That's right. It's your decision as to whether it's time to open it," Nick told her. "Could be grim."

"I know. But opening it doesn't mean I'm giving up on him, and it has to be done."

Devin stood and left the room with the box of personal letters. After gathering up the other boxes, Nick returned them to the top shelf of a bedroom closet. He found Devin coming out of the messy office, the dreaded envelope in her hands.

"We've been through everything else. I don't know what else to do." She looked up at Nick beseechingly, wanting his understanding, needing his support.

He cupped her cheek in his hand. "I don't either, Devin."

"I'm glad you're here." She kissed the palm of his hand, then turned away, going back to the kitchen. With a knife, Devin slit open the top of the envelope and pulled out a single sheet of paper. Nervously she sat on one of the stools and unfolded the white paper. "Well. Here goes."

Nick watched as she slowly read it, her eyes getting bigger line by line. Disbelief and confusion chased the sadness from her face. When she was finished she held the paper out to him. He took it from her trembling hand.

"I can't believe I never knew," Devin said, stunned.

Nick quickly scanned the scrawling black writing. He, too, was astonished. "What do you want to do?"

"I need to talk to Yvette Soomes. In person."

"Definitely. I'll make some phone calls. We should be able to fly out there tonight if I can borrow the plane."

Devin stood, shaky on her feet. "Good Lord! How could Eli have kept something like this a secret from the whole family for all these years?"

Chapter Twenty-One

The temperature in California was cool and pleasant this late in the evening. They found Yvette Soomes listed in the local phone book, and a convenience-store clerk gave them directions on how to get there. She lived in a newer subdivision of sand-colored townhomes not far from NHS, the address clearly marked in turquoise over each garage.

Devin rang the doorbell, still unable to believe what had been in that letter. Thirty years ago Yvette Soomes had given birth to Eli's baby, then relinquished all rights to the child. Something was obviously wrong with Eli's daughter because Devin was to be named guardian should he die without making other arrangements. It was a sad tale indeed, but why all the mystery? She had thought they were close. Why had Eli never confided in her?

Nick squeezed her shoulder briefly in reassurance as the porch light came on. A moment later the door opened and Yvette was facing them, dressed in a powder blue jogging suit and running shoes.

"I have nothing more to say to you," Yvette said, then started to shut the door in their faces.

Nick caught the door with the palm of his hand before it finished closing. "Please, hear us out. Eli may need help, and there's nowhere left for us to turn."

"No. Either you leave or I'm calling the police," Yvette warned through the foot-wide opening.

The woman was clearly upset by their reappearance on her doorstep. "I know you must have a reason for the way you're acting, but couldn't you put it aside? Eli has been missing for a week," Devin said quietly.

Yvette opened her mouth, then closed it. Finally she spoke. "I haven't seen him. Nor do I wish to." She started to close the door again.

"Will you at least read this?" Devin shoved a piece of paper at her through the opening. "Please?"

Reluctantly Yvette took the note and unfolded it, the door swinging backward as she read it. By the time she was finished, tears were trickling down her face.

Yvette turned and walked over to the couch as if in a daze. She sat down, still staring at the paper in her hand, though it was evident she wasn't really looking at it. Her eyes were unfocused, her thoughts in the past. Devin followed her while Nick closed the door. The ice queen was crumbling.

Tears dripped onto the paper, the ink spreading out into black pools. "I . . . I convinced myself she was dead. Part of me still believes it. Now the two of you show up and give me this and . . ." She trailed off, struggling for some semblance of her former control.

Devin sat beside her on the couch, but didn't touch her or say a word as she waited for Yvette to continue. Nick stood behind the couch, unsure of just what to do.

"We were so in love," Yvette murmured, seemingly lost in the past.

"You and Eli?" Devin questioned softly.

Yvette nodded. "At twenty-six he was a dashing visiting professor, and I, a seventeen-year-old college freshman, in Switzerland and away from home for the first time." Her smile was sad, bittersweet. "It all started out so innocently, a fascination of the minds, but it quickly grew into something very different. He was brilliant, gifted and very sexy with his premature white hair and pale blue eyes."

Eli's letter to Devin floated to the floor and Yvette used both hands to wipe the tears from her cheeks. Devin heard her sigh softly before she continued.

"In class he taught me microbiology, and away from class he taught me all about love. We had to meet secretly and when I found out I was pregnant, we were both ecstatic. He was so proud, he wanted to tell everyone, but we couldn't."

Devin didn't want her to stop reminiscing. "Why?"

"Student-teacher relationships were forbidden at that school, and of course my age was a problem. I would have been expelled, and he'd have been fired from his position. I convinced him that his career could be irreparably damaged, his research destroyed if we told everyone."

"Is that why no one knows about this?"

Yvette nodded. "Very few people knew I was pregnant, and no one knew who the father was. At my dorm most assumed I was just getting fat because I ate so much, and I was too happy to care." New tears rolled down her face. "We had everything planned. His teaching contract was up in May and the baby due in late June. He already had a good paying job that started in September, so by August we'd be back in the States. That way I would have time to enroll in school for the fall semester." She managed a small smile. "He was adamant that I continue with my education."

"What went wrong?" Devin asked.

"Everything," she said quietly, her tears flowing faster as she talked. "It wasn't fair, we didn't do anything to deserve what happened to our baby."

Devin touched her shoulder. "What happened?"

"There was nothing anyone could do. She was born severely handicapped."

Nick sat beside Devin and placed his hand on her knee, squeezing it gently. He could see that forcing this confrontation was taking its toll on Devin, too.

"It wasn't fair!" Yvette cried, burying her face in her hands. Sobs racked her body, her icy reserve gone as all her boxed-up feelings came bubbling to the surface for escape. "Why us? Why?"

"Shh," Devin comforted, putting an arm around her quivering shoulders.

Nick got up and returned a moment later with a box of tissues. Her anguish was too great for useless words of comfort, so they let her cry, Devin rocking her gently until the anger and remorse inside Yvette finally subsided.

"Thank you," Yvette mumbled, accepting some tissues.

"What happened?" Devin asked again.

Yvette took a deep, shuddering breath. She was looking straight ahead, shaking her head slowly. "I abandoned her. At seventeen I was so full of rage, of resentment against Mother Nature, that I disavowed all responsibility for the child. For a long time, all through college and graduate school, I completely blocked out what had happened." She looked to Devin for understanding. "It was the only way I could survive."

Her eyes became watery again and Devin handed her more tissues. "Go on," she encouraged.

"Eli—" Her voice broke when she said his name, and she took another deep, shuddering breath before continuing. "He took charge. It became his sole responsibility to look after the welfare of the child. I ran away, refused to deal with the situation. Don't you see?" she asked.

Devin started to reassure her, but Yvette hadn't really expected an answer. She wiped her eyes and continued to let the story pour out of her. Perhaps for the first time.

"I *couldn't* deal with it," she told them. "Before it happened my life had been storybook perfect. Absolutely nothing prepared me for what might and did occur. Life!" Yvette wrung her hands, and they could see the anger that lay beneath her sadness. "I told no one, I was too ashamed, too distraught. The few who knew about the baby were told she had died at birth. And so the years went by."

Her anguish was heart wrenching. Yvette had been all alone, facing guilt, denial and a devastating loss, of both her baby *and* Eli. At seventeen, Devin didn't know how she would have handled the situation herself.

Yvette suddenly looked at them, her eyes reddened from tears and full of need. "You have to understand," she pleaded. "This happened over thirty years ago. It was a very delicate situation. Things would be different now."

"What things?" Devin asked, confused.

She wiped her eyes again. Some of her former calm was returning. "Eli knew what some ignorant people would say about a scientist who worked with genetically altered bacteria fathering a severely handicapped child. To spare himself and our daughter further cruelty, he, too, hid the facts. He took her to a very private Swiss sanitarium, not far from the hospital where she was born.''

''It sounds as if he did the right thing,'' Devin said.

She looked at Nick and he nodded. They both knew there were other reasons Eli might have gone to Switzerland. In a way, Devin almost hoped one of them was the truth. If there was an emergency with his daughter, it was very severe; otherwise he would have contacted someone by now.

''In my heart I can't believe that. I still can't accept that she was born totally oblivious to the outside world, that she'll never even recognize her own mother or father.'' Yvette averted her gaze, ashamed. ''I've only seen her once.''

Devin patted her on the back. ''You can't change the past,'' she said softly. ''But you *can* change the future.''

''I know that.'' She looked up at Devin. ''Those blue eyes. I nearly broke down when you came to see me at the lab. Are you his daughter?'' Yvette asked.

''No, his niece,'' Devin replied. ''But he's been like a father to me. My real father died when I was two. Eli's always been there for me.''

A fresh set of tears trickled down Yvette's face. ''He'd have been there for me, as well, if I'd let him.''

Devin let her cry, let her find solace in the tears she'd refused to shed over the years.

''I'm all right,'' she said a few minutes later. ''Thank you for your kindness.'' The tissues in her hand were twisted and frayed. ''What did you say about Eli being missing for a week?''

Devin told her only a few of the facts, just enough to get her cooperation. ''Eli was last spotted in Switzerland.''

''Oh, no!'' Yvette gasped. ''Eli's . . . *our* daughter!''

"We can't be sure," Devin said. "But it is possible something happened, an emergency of some kind. Will you give me the name of the sanitarium?"

They could contact Eli's attorney and try to get the information that way, but it would be slow going, and in the process open up a whole new can of worms.

Yvette left the room and returned a few minutes later with a business card. On it she'd written the address and phone number of the sanitarium. "Are you flying over?"

Devin took the card and stood. "I'll call first."

"It won't do you any good." Yvette wrapped her arms around her waist. "Occasionally the guilt would bring old memories to the surface. So I tried a few times to get information over the phone, but they wouldn't tell me a thing. It's a private hospital, and in Switzerland a private matter stays private."

"Then I'm going on the next flight out," Devin said. "If something did happen, Eli's going to need my support."

Fresh tears rolled down Yvette's red-splotched face. "I'd like to go with you, if I may."

"Eli may not be there," Devin said gently.

"I'm not going just to see him. That hospital has the only medicine for the sort of wounds I have. I think it's time I tried to heal them."

Devin hugged her. "I'd like the company," she told her, and she meant it, too. This wouldn't be an easy trip.

"I need to return the borrowed plane to Phoenix," Nick said, standing up. "You can fly back with us, then we'll catch a commercial flight from there. Are there arrangements you need to make before we go?"

Yvette nodded, and walked out of the room, tears streaming down her face.

"You don't have to come with us," Devin told him.

Nick pulled her into his arms. "I know, but I want to, and I'm not about to let you go without me." He held her face between his hands and kissed her lightly on the mouth. "Devin, please don't get your hopes up," he whispered. "Eli may not be there."

"I know that, but if he's not I'll just keep looking." She kissed him and they didn't draw apart until a noise in the other room reminded them of where they were.

"I'd better call Jerry." Nick glanced at the wall clock and shook his head. "No, this late it'll have to be Myrtle," he amended. "She can start trying to find us seats to Switzerland."

The flight back to Phoenix was uneventful and quiet. Since neither Devin's nor Nick's place was habitable, they took Yvette to Myrtle's house to stay until everything could be arranged for their flight out, knowing that Myrtle would accept her without question.

Devin had briefly considered taking her to Lucinda's, but that would require far too many explanations. It didn't seem right that she be the one to tell her grandmother about Eli's secret child. The story was his to tell, if he chose to do so.

But she did want to update her grandmother on the situation, and did so from her apartment after Nick headed for his own to pack.

"I know it's late, Grandmother, but I wanted to let you know that Nick and I are leaving for Switzerland in the morning," Devin said. She had the phone receiver cradled under her chin as she sorted through the clothes thrown all over her bedroom, trying to find things to take with her.

"Why, Devin, that's wonderful news!" Lucinda told her. "You two should take some time to have a vacation, get to know each other better."

"Grandmother, I'm not going there to have a good time. Eli may be there, remember."

Lucinda sighed. "You worry too much, and always have. I suppose losing your own father when you were so young made you that way. But Devin, you're not getting any younger and your childbearing years are shortening all the time. It's something to think about while you still *have* a handsome man around."

Devin was tempted to remind her she was only thirty-one, but it wouldn't have done any good. Lucinda had had four children by that time. "I'll call you when I get back," Devin promised.

"I hope you have good news for me, too. Don't worry about calling your mother. We're having lunch tomorrow—I'll tell her everything." Devin groaned loudly and her grandmother laughed in return. "Have a good trip. And remember the ticktock of your clock, my darling."

She didn't need that kind of reminder. She could hear her own biological clock quite clearly. It had gotten louder since Nick had entered her life, too. And thinking of all the lonely years Yvette must have spent caused it to grow louder still.

"Please be there, Eli," Devin whispered softly. "For both of us."

Chapter Twenty-Two

The white hallways were eerily quiet, their linoleum floors shiny with polish. There were windows overlooking an inner courtyard, each one outlined in square black panes, making the clear glass in the center seem invisible beneath the onslaught of the bright, high-altitude sun.

As they got closer to the room, Yvette's steps slowed and she lagged behind Devin and Nick.

Devin stopped and turned. The long flight had taken its toll on all three of them. They'd had little sleep and long waits at horrendously busy airports. She knew that none of them looked all that chipper.

But Yvette's face was too pale. She looked as if she was going to pass out. "Are you okay?" Devin asked.

She nodded. "Fine. I have to do this at my own pace, that's all," Yvette explained. "You two go ahead."

Nick placed his hand under Devin's elbow. "Give her time."

One more corridor and one more turn, then they'd know whether Eli was here or not. Devin's heart was pounding, her hopes so high. As they rounded the corner a man emerged from a room and turned to face them.

At long last, her search was at an end.

"Eli!" Devin exclaimed quietly, mindful of where she was. She ran to her uncle and hugged him tightly. "We were so worried! I had to open your letter and... Is she all right?"

He pulled back from her embrace, nodding slowly. "She's going to be fine. This time," he added, his smile a sad one. "What are you doing here?"

Devin wanted to shake him, until she stepped back and really looked at him. Eli was exhausted, and she knew he hadn't slept for days. His gray suit was rumpled, his tie askew, white hair springing out all over. He was the picture of a mad scientist. Part of it was an image he nurtured. The rest was pure stress.

"You didn't tell anyone where you were going," Devin said crossly. "And you've been gone for more than a week."

He looked confused and surprised. "I didn't? I thought I'd left a message on that last tape for Myrtle. No, maybe I didn't," he said absently. "There was so much to do and not much time." He hunched his shoulders. "I'm sorry, Devin. It must have slipped my mind."

Since Natalie had erased the tape they'd never know if he had or not, but that wasn't important. She'd found him, safe and sound, if rather the worse for wear.

Eli cocked his head, staring past her at the man walking toward them. "Nick? What are you doing here?" Now he really looked confused. "What's going on? Did you find out who was taking my papers?"

"It's a very long story," Nick told him, shaking his hand. "And it can wait. C Group is looking for you."

Eli groaned and rubbed his face with his hands. "I forgot all about that mess." He patted the breast pocket of his suit, then looked around, puzzled. "Devin, give me a pen and piece of paper."

She pulled both out of her purse, placing the paper on it for him to use as a surface to write on before handing it to him.

He scribbled a phone number down and handed everything back to her. "Call that number and tell them I've got a solution for them." Devin was looking at him expectantly. "No, I can't tell you anything about this. Protocol."

"I'll take care of it," Devin promised.

Eli frowned. "How did you find me?"

He hadn't seen Yvette, who was now standing beside Nick, almost hiding behind him, in fact. Devin's heart went out to her; Yvette's face was filled with apprehension.

"Eli?" She said his name softly, hesitantly.

"Yvette!" Eli turned, truly stunned. Tears welled up in his blue eyes, glistening under the fluorescent lighting. "Oh, God, Yvette." He held his arms open and she walked into them, tears streaming down her face.

Devin moved back and stood watching them from the shelter of Nick's arm around her shoulders. She, too, felt on the verge of tears.

"Did we do the right thing?" Yvette asked him.

Eli held her close. "For our baby, yes, but why did we let this split us apart?"

"I don't know. I've never married, I've never loved anyone else but you," Yvette told him, her hand cupping the side of his face.

"Nor I, my love, nor I," Eli assured her. "Though Lord knows I certainly tried to find someone to take your place, no one could compare, no one came even close."

"All those wasted years," Yvette murmured. "I'm so sorry."

Her tears fell freely, mingling with Eli's as he brushed his cheek against hers. "Hush, love. It's going to be all right." Eli rocked her gently in his arms, oblivious to everything but Yvette, his first and only love. "Shh," he murmured softly. "Everything will be fine now."

Devin and Nick walked away from them, also wrapped in each other's arms as they went outside to the brilliant sunshine waiting for them.

Vast mountain peaks stood before them, lightly sprinkled with snow even in summer. The air was cool, refreshing after the summer heat of Phoenix.

"Have you been here before?" Nick asked as they strolled along a quiet street, relaxing for the first time in days.

Devin could smile easily now. As Eli had said, everything was going to be fine. "Never. Have you?"

"Nope. It seems like a nice place to vacation. Want to stay awhile?" Nick asked.

Life with Nick, sudden and impetuous. Devin stopped and looked at him soberly, her elation over finding Eli ebbing away as she faced another aspect of reality. Life *without* Nick. "Are you going to tell me about your past?"

"Jerry never could keep his mouth shut," Nick grumbled. "You know who I am. Why are you so worried about who I was?"

She took a deep breath. "Because I don't think people ever really leave their past behind, not completely."

"Let's sit down on that park bench." Once they were seated Nick still hedged. "What do you want to know?"

All the pieces added up, and she had to know the truth. "Have I fallen in love with a thief?" she blurted out.

Her directness didn't surprise him one bit. "Not exactly. Like Frank, I was an industrial spy," he answered candidly. The shocked look on her face surprised him. "You suspected as much," Nick added. "Aren't you pleased your instincts were right?"

"Yes and no." His flippant attitude was making her angry. "How can you be so casual about this?"

"Because that part of my life is over. Finished."

She was confused. He sounded so convincing, so why wasn't she elated by the last bit of news? Did knowing about his past change the way she felt about him?

"How did you get started? And what exactly did you do?"

"I told you once I was the black sheep of the family. My father and I never got along—still don't—but that's no excuse."

"No, it isn't."

Nick smiled at her reprimanding tone. "Anyway, I was working for one of the companies my family owned a sizable chunk of, and it was pointed out that if my boss had certain information belonging to another firm under the same ownership umbrella, then his business could really take off, with an enormous increase in profits."

"You couldn't resist the suggestion?" Devin asked dryly.

He raised his eyebrows. "I was young, very rebellious at the time and the thought of doing something like that was exciting to me. Turned out it was easy to get the data and doing it *was* very exciting," Nick explained. "Since the companies were all owned by the same group, everyone benefited in the end. More jobs were created, and the stockholders made more money."

Devin frowned. "But it was still stealing."

"You could look at it that way," Nick replied.

"How did you look at it?" Devin asked angrily.

Nick shrugged. "I figured I was helping everyone out. So I started looking around for ways to be of even more help. One thing led to another, my trade-school days if you will, and I became quite good at my job. I was a fast learner, and I learned from some of the best."

"Like Frank?"

"Like Frank. But Frank and I were very different in one sense—I was picky about the jobs I took. Eventually I ended up acquiring certain types of information on companies that in turn were used to expose their illegal practices to the public," Nick replied.

Devin frowned. "A modern-day version of Robin Hood?" she asked sarcastically.

"Not exactly."

How did he explain this without betraying confidences he'd sworn never to expose? There was one instance he could talk about, since the injured party certainly wasn't keeping his mouth shut, either.

"Take Jerry's case as an example," Nick continued. "He used to work for an accounting firm back east that was using some, shall we say, unusual bookkeeping techniques on their clients to rip them off. When those techniques were exposed, a scandal erupted, followed by a criminal investigation that shut the company down."

"Jerry was your accomplice?" she asked incredulously.

"Not knowingly and only that one time."

Devin tucked a stray hair behind her ear. "You used your best friend and stole private information to expose a crime, so that made what you did okay?"

Nick sighed. "No, but at the time I certainly thought so. Looking back I realize that wasn't the case, but I was enjoying what I was doing too much to see the whole picture. I was only trying to hurt those who were already taking advantage of others. Indirectly, I ended up hurting people like Jerry, but that was never my intention."

At least he was being honest. "Did Eli really hire you?"

"Not for money, no. I owe him a debt I can never repay. Eli knew someone was messing with his papers and he wanted to know who it was. Of course, it turned into a whole lot more than I bargained for, but..." He trailed off, smiling at her. "I like the way it turned out, don't you?"

She wasn't going to be deterred that easily. "Oh, yes. The favor," Devin recalled. "You said he saved your life, didn't you? Pointed out how dangerous the work was?"

Nick took a deep breath and blew it out slowly. This was tougher than he'd thought it would be. "Look, Devin, there are things I've done that I'm not proud of, but they're in the past. I *do* believe a person can leave the past behind. So does Eli. So does your *grandmother.*"

"How did you and Eli meet?" she persisted.

He leaned back against the bench and looked up at the blue sky. "It was the only time I was ever caught in the act," Nick admitted, trying not to sound proud of the fact. "How was I supposed to know Eli only slept three or four hours a night?"

"You tried to steal from Eli?"

"Not directly. I had been hired to prove this company was involved in illegal dumping of pesticides. Eli was a consultant for the company. He was visiting the owner's estate for the weekend." Nick smiled at the memory, but when he saw Devin's expression he quickly sobered. "He caught me red-handed. It was a humbling experience."

"But he didn't turn you in?"

Nick chuckled. He couldn't help it. "No, he offered me a beer and we proceeded to get rip-roaring drunk together."

"I don't believe this!"

Nick looked right into her stormy blue eyes. "It's true. Eli listened to my side of the story and pointed out that I was doing all the wrong things, but for the right reasons. Unfortunately, the law would never view it that way, especially since I was usually paid by one company to expose their competitor's wrongdoings. Put simply, Eli helped me turn my life around, and that's a pretty large debt to owe anyone."

"But you didn't leave it all behind, did you?" Devin accused. "Don't deny it. You really enjoyed our little escapade."

Nick placed his hands on top of hers. "I got a kick out of it, yes. But so did you," he pointed out.

Spots of color appeared on Devin's cheekbones. "Be that as it may, I want my life to return to normal."

"So do I." He smiled. "Or at least as normal as my life gets. Doing this bit of skulduggery made me realize how much I don't miss it, and how much I want other things, equally exciting things, not just for me, but for us."

She wanted to believe him, wanted desperately to have a future with him. "I don't know, Nick . . ."

"Devin, I'm still the same man you made love with. What I've told you doesn't make me a different person, it just changes how you perceive me."

Devin swallowed. The warmth of his hands on hers was getting to her, irrationally making her want him even more than before. Two of the most important people in her life had already accepted his past. Why couldn't she?

"You have to accept me as I am. My past is part of what made me who I am today. It can't be changed. Either you accept it, believe in me, and trust me, or it's over."

Was she foolish to follow her heart? She could hear Lucinda telling her to go for the brass ring. Should she trust her instincts? Eli's voice was in her mind, loud and clear, telling her that love was not a science, and there was precious little else you could trust.

"It's not just your past," Devin said. "You're impulsive, I'm methodical. I need some routine, you would prefer a surprise a minute. And to top it all off, I take the reality of life as it comes. You're an idealist, just like Eli."

The way she said it made it sound like an accusation, a crime of some sort. "To a certain degree, maybe I am. But there's nothing that says two people have to agree on everything to have a good relationship," Nick said. "In fact, you just said it yourself. Why do you suppose you get along so well with Eli, Devin?"

"I like his company," she returned. "He's—"

"A change of pace? A breath of fresh air? Opposites attract?" Nick smiled. "Just stop me when I get to a cliché you like. There are hundreds to describe why you like Eli. And why I fell in love with you," he added softly.

Nick *was* a lot like Eli, and the thought was both scary and exciting. Was she going to follow her heart and forget the past, for a chance at happiness? The lost years between Yvette and Eli danced through her mind. Is that what she wanted? Or was she going to admit that sometimes people could change for the better? Even herself.

Devin turned her hand over beneath his and slipped her fingers between his, grasping them tightly. "The past *is* past. Let's walk."

They strolled along the street, avoiding the park where a group of rowdy children had just shown up to play. This was an ideal spot for a vacation, the one she was supposed to be on, anyway. For once, the cautious part of her was small, hard to hear. The rest was asking, why not?

She glanced at Nick. "Will you tell me more about the jobs you did?" Devin asked.

"Nope."

Her eyes widened. "Never?"

Nick smiled. "I didn't say that, but it won't be anytime soon." Some of them he'd never admit to anyone. "Remember what Lucinda told you."

"Don't slouch?" she asked innocently.

"That, too," he said, putting his hand on the small of her back. "But I mean I'll tell you when I'm ready."

"And how long will that take?"

"Oh, fifty years."

"Fifty!" Devin stopped and put her hands on her hips. "I'm not waiting fifty years. Ten," she bargained.

"Ten?" Nick shook his head. "No way. Forty."

"Get real, Nick Lang, twenty is pushing it."

"All right, twenty-five."

"If I have to wait twenty-five years to hear all of this story, it had better be really good," Devin warned him. "Or, so help me, you'll regret it for the next twenty-five!"

Nick laughed. "There's more Wingate in you than you'd like to admit, you bargainer. I promise, on our twenty-fifth wedding anniversary, to tell you a tale you'll never forget."

"Who said anything about marriage?"

Nick swept a startled Devin into his arms. "I did."

"What are you asking me, Nick?"

"Devin, are you always going to be this difficult?"

She kissed him on the chin. "Not always. I believe a person can change, remember. I'll only be difficult for the first twenty-five years. Give or take a year."

"I'm not telling you any sooner," Nick warned.

Devin grinned and wrapped her arms around his neck. "We'll see, mystery man. We'll see."

Take 4 bestselling love stories FREE

Plus get a FREE surprise gift!

HARLEQUIN HISTORICAL CHRISTMAS STORIES · 1992 ·

Capture the magic and romance of Christmas in the 1800s with HARLEQUIN HISTORICAL CHRISTMAS STORIES 1992, a collection of three stories by celebrated historical authors. The perfect Christmas gift!

Don't miss these heartwarming stories, available in November wherever Harlequin books are sold:

**MISS MONTRACHET REQUESTS by Maura Seger
CHRISTMAS BOUNTY by Erin Yorke
A PROMISE KEPT by Bronwyn Williams**

Plus, as an added bonus, you can receive a FREE keepsake Christmas ornament. Just collect four proofs of purchase from any November or December 1992 Harlequin or Silhouette series novels, or from any Harlequin or Silhouette Christmas collection, and receive a beautiful dated brass Christmas candle ornament.

Mail this certificate along with four (4) proof-of-purchase coupons plus $1.50 postage and handling (check or money order—do not send cash), payable to Harlequin Books, to: **In the U.S.**: P.O. Box 9057, Buffalo, NY 14269-9057; **In Canada**: P.O. Box 622, Fort Erie, Ontario, L2A 5X3.

ONE PROOF OF PURCHASE

Name: _____
_____

Address: _____
_____

City: _____
State/Province: _____
Zip/Postal Code: _____

HX92POP   093 KAG